THE POISONED PAWN

ALSO BY PEGGY BLAIR

The Beggar's Opera

THE POISONED PAWN

PEGGY BLAIR

PINTAIL

PINTAIL

a member of Penguin Group (USA), a Penguin Random House Company

Published by the Penguin Group
Penguin Canada Books Inc., 90 Eglinton Avenue East, Suite 700, Toronto, Ontario, Canada M4P 2Y3
(a division of Pearson Canada Inc.)

Penguin Group (USA) Inc., 375 Hudson Street, New York, New York 10014, U.S.A.
Penguin Books Ltd, 80 Strand, London WC2R 0RL, England
Penguin Ireland, 25 St Stephen's Green, Dublin 2, Ireland (a division of Penguin Books Ltd)
Penguin Group (Australia), 250 Camberwell Road, Camberwell, Victoria 3124, Australia
(a division of Pearson Australia Group Pty Ltd)
Penguin Books India Pvt Ltd, 11 Community Centre, Panchsheel Park, New Delhi – 110 017, India
Penguin Group (NZ), 67 Apollo Drive, Rosedale, Auckland 0632, New Zealand
(a division of Pearson New Zealand Ltd)
Penguin Books (South Africa) (Pty) Ltd, 24 Sturdee Avenue, Rosebank, Johannesburg 2196, South Africa

Penguin Books Ltd, Registered Offices: 80 Strand, London WC2R 0RL, England

First published in Penguin paperback by Penguin Canada Books Inc., 2013
Published in this edition, 2014

1 2 3 4 5 6 7 8 9 10 (RRD)

Copyright © Peggy Blair, 2013

*Publisher's note: This book is a work of fiction. Names, characters, places, and incidents either
are the product of the author's imagination or are used fictitiously, and any resemblance
to actual persons living or dead, events, or locales is entirely coincidental.*

Manufactured in the U.S.A.

ISBN: 978-0-14-318976-3

Visit the Penguin US website at **www.penguin.com**

IN MEMORY OF CHIP,
WHO TAUGHT ME ALL ABOUT COURAGE, JOY,
AND UNCONDITIONAL LOVE

Before the endgame,
the gods have placed the middle game.

—SIEGBERT TARRASCH

THE POISONED PAWN

ONE

Hillary Ellis almost lost her balance as she bent down to pick up the passport she'd dropped on the tarmac. A soldier in camouflage fatigues watched her closely, cradling his machine gun. She avoided his eyes and walked quickly up the metal stairs to the airplane.

I need to stop shaking, she thought. All I have to do is get out of here and I'm safe.

"Welcome on board," the flight attendant said as she checked Hillary's boarding pass. "Your seat is by a window. In the thirteenth row. On the left-hand side." *Bad luck.*

As Hillary sat down, a short black man walking towards her row eyed the empty aisle seat. He was not much larger than a child, although he leaned on a cane. It was hard to guess his age, but there was no mistaking his white collar. *Damn.* He looked at her as if she should have expected him, as if she should know him. When she didn't respond, he removed his hat and said something in Spanish, offering her his hand.

"I'm sorry," she said, forcing a tight smile as he seated himself beside her, resting the cane against his knees, "I don't speak any

Spanish." She reached for her purse and removed a book, signalling her desire to be left alone.

"Ah, my name is not Spanish, but African," he said in perfect but accented English as he peered at the book's cover. "I am sure you will enjoy the story of Katerina, the shrew who became an obedient wife. Although more frequently, from what I've observed, the opposite occurs. But don't worry," he laughed, "I won't ask you to confess."

Hillary flinched. He's only making conversation, she thought. *Calm down.*

She flipped through *The Taming of the Shrew* without reading any of the pages. She'd be home by the early hours of Christmas Day. In the lawyer's office on Wednesday, most likely. Her Christmas gift to herself, working out the finances, changing the locks. Moving forward with her new life. *I did it. I didn't think I had the guts.*

The priest examined his seat belt, bemused. Hillary was surprised when the flight attendant didn't lecture him to do it up before the airplane sped down the runway.

Once they escaped the ground, he looked across her and out the window but kept to himself. *Thank God.* The adrenalin was wearing off, but her hands still trembled despite the two rum-and-Cokes she'd tossed back in the airport. The hard part wouldn't be guilt; she never felt guilty about anything. It would be pretending that she cared.

Her mother had coached her from childhood how to act, how to lie. "Don't trust anyone," she'd said from the moment Hillary began to toddle. "Not even me. Especially not your father."

When the bar service started, the man's eyes were closed. The stewardess looked through him to take her order. As she leaned over, Hillary caught a whiff of perfume that smelled like bitter almonds.

She handed the woman some change and asked her to make it a double. She checked the inflight movie. *Mr. & Mrs. Smith.* Two spouses secretly trying to kill each other. Startled, she turned it off.

The blue cartoon plane caterpillared its way home, inching across the overhead screen. Somewhere over Boston, she started to feel nauseous. She coughed and swallowed hard.

"Are you alright?" inquired her seatmate. He said something else she couldn't hear. Her ears buzzed. Images in the cabin swooped; waves of dizziness, a rapid, irregular pounding in her chest.

"Airsick," she said, struggling to breathe. When he produced an airsickness bag from the pouch in front of his seat, she was mortified.

"Try doing this," he said, and mimed blowing into it. "It may help."

She put the bag over her mouth and breathed in and out deeply. Maybe she *was* hyperventilating, her nerves catching up with her. If this was what Mike's panic attacks were like, she owed him an apology. *Too late now.*

She unbuckled her seat belt and staggered to the washroom at the back of the plane. She splashed water on her face and neck, examined herself in the small mirror above the metal sink. For a woman approaching forty, she still looked damn good. But her cheeks were bright pink despite the sunblock, and her eyelids were swollen.

It must be the flight, she thought. Cucumber slices will fix those. Once I'm back in Ottawa, I'll pamper myself. Buy a little black dress. I'll feel a million times better once this flight is over.

But by the time the airplane landed, she wasn't feeling anything at all.

TWO

Hector Apiro kneeled on the ground beside the body, careful to avoid the fluids pooled beside it. He lifted the woman's stained cotton dress to check the colour of her bloated torso. He turned his head to avoid the smell.

"Happy New Year, Dr. Apiro," said Detective Espinoza, squatting down to speak to the small physician. "How long do you think she's been dead?"

Fernando Espinoza had been promoted to the Havana Major Crimes Unit a day or two earlier to replace Rodriguez Sanchez.

Espinoza probably didn't expect to hit the ground running quite so quickly, thought Apiro. But the boy handled himself well. Unlike the dozen or so *policías* who flooded into the dark alley as soon as the call came in, the young detective managed to keep his stomach contents down.

Apiro made a mental note to have his technicians bring some brooms and mops along with the tarps they would need to move the body. He hoped they had some tucked away; good mops weren't easy to find.

"And to you, Detective Espinoza. I'm surprised you're not out celebrating."

"And miss the excitement? Not a chance. Besides, the parties will go on for hours."

Apiro smiled. The young man's good-natured enthusiasm was infectious. Ricardo had made a good choice. But then, Inspector Ramirez was well-known for his skill at scavenging talent as well as supplies. "From the state of decomposition, I'd guess ten days. Maybe two weeks."

The pathologist was finding it difficult to be more precise. The temperature had hovered at nearly thirty degrees Celsius for most of December. The record temperatures made it a challenge to measure the body's internal temperature accurately.

A complicating factor was the woman's race. Skin discolouration often proved helpful in ascertaining how long someone had been dead. After a few weeks of decomposition, the exposed skin of a Caucasian victim would have turned black. But this corpse was Afro-Cuban, almost ebony to begin with. Her face, arms, and legs were the same hue as the skin beneath her clothing.

Her eye colour wasn't helpful either. Within seventy-two hours of death, everyone's irises changed to brown and then black.

And so it goes, thought Apiro. Despite our differences, when it comes right down to it, we are all the same. Death is the great equalizer.

"I'm assuming she was stabbed to death?"

The surgeon looked at Espinoza and smiled kindly. It was a perfectly legitimate question, and the answer seemed obvious. But as a man of science, Apiro had learned to withhold judgment until he had all the facts.

"I don't think she committed suicide, if that helps."

The woman had an eight-inch knife sticking out of her chest

cavity, or what was left of it. The knife was intact; it was the body around it that was collapsing.

"Funny that no one saw the body, if it's been here that long."

"I wouldn't necessarily assume they didn't," Apiro said. He stood up painfully, his short legs aching, his knees sore from the concrete.

Apiro lived with achondroplasia—dwarfism. It left only his torso a normal size. His arms and legs were short, his head and hands large.

Despite his condition, Apiro had once been renowned internationally as one of Cuba's leading plastic surgeons. Cuba had some of the best in the world, but they had to be creative, given their limited resources. Performing the occasional autopsy allowed Apiro to try new methods of cutting and stitching without costly operating rooms, nursing staff, and supplies. Besides, as he often joked, plastic surgery was simpler when there was no need for anaesthetic.

He snapped off his latex gloves and placed them carefully in his medical kit for sterilization and re-use.

"The people in this area have no love for the police," he said to Espinoza. "Frankly, the only thing that surprises me is that no one took the knife."

The occupants of the Callejón sin salida, or Blind Alley, were notoriously suspicious of the Cuban National Revolutionary Police. The feeling was mutual.

Blind Alley was supposedly constructed following spirited discussions between its creator, an artist, and the Cuban gods as to their requirements. It was an unofficial temple for the worshippers of Santería gods and a leading source for the marijuana and other plants used in their secret rites. But it was also a place where the screams of men and women frequently pierced the night as the *orishas* purportedly travelled through them.

Espinoza nodded. "Should I have Dispatch contact Inspector Ramirez? It's the first homicide of the year."

"Not unless you want to be demoted back to Patrol." Apiro grinned. He made a note of the time for his report. 0056 hours, Monday, January 1, 2007. "It's his day off."

THREE

Mike Ellis paid the cab driver and lifted his suitcase over the knee-high snowdrifts. He'd been away from home for two weeks, but it felt eons longer. A Cuban jail cell gave a whole new meaning to the word *infinity*.

Hillary had left him standing on the Malecón on Christmas Eve, stunned and angry at her revelation that she was flying back to Ottawa early, that their marriage was over. She didn't know he'd been arrested the next day, accused of sexually assaulting and murdering a street child who had followed them along the famous seawall, begging for money.

There were no lights on in their Westboro townhouse. Rolled-up flyers poked through the iron railing on the front steps. He turned the key and opened the door, switched on the lights. The house smelled stale, empty.

"Hillary?"

He opened the door to the hall closet. His wife's boots were inside on the mat. But Hillary would never take a chance on wrecking her designer shoes on the slushy, salt-laden sidewalks.

Ellis ran upstairs to check the closets in the master bedroom. Dozens of pairs of shoes were lined up in neat rows: Imelda Marcos had nothing on his wife. But there were no empty clothes hangers. Was she really gone?

Ellis sure as hell hoped so.

He walked back to the kitchen and opened the fridge. Anything that was edible before they left on their so-called vacation was now coated with green mould.

There were a couple of beers and some canned juice. He pulled the caps off the bottles and emptied them down the drain.

His New Year's resolution was to stay sober. He'd found a higher power in Havana, although he couldn't describe it. But he was starting to believe in fate, after the way that so many people's lives had turned out to be linked together like some kind of cosmic chain gang.

He poured himself a glass of juice and collapsed in a chair. Without Hillary, he had a clean slate, a chance to start over. The muscle above his heart corkscrewed. He breathed in deeply, forced himself to relax.

The doorbell rang. He looked at his watch. It wasn't quite 1 A.M. The early hours of New Year's Day were a funny time for a visitor.

He opened the door to find two uniformed policemen on the stoop. The taller of the pair faced away from the door. The other stamped snow from his rubber overshoes.

Damn June, thought Ellis, noticing the thick stack of letters stuffed in the mailbox. She hadn't looked after anything.

Miles O'Malley slowly pivoted. Usually he was smiling, but not now. Ellis's heart began to bang a tattoo. There were only two times that the head of the Rideau Regional Police Force wore his dress uniform that Ellis knew of—at police graduation ceremonies and when he had to inform a family about a death. Ellis had no idea what O'Malley would wear if he was about to charge one of his detectives with murder.

"Can I come in, Michael? Martin, you wait outside for a moment, that's a good man."

The young patrolman nodded. He avoided looking at Ellis's face as he stood aside to let O'Malley through the door. "I'll sit in the car, Chief."

O'Malley entered the living room and sank into an armchair. He took his hat off and held it in his thick fingers. He ran one hand over his smooth bald head. "Ah, Michael. I'm so sorry. I have bad news. It's about Hillary."

"Hillary? What about her?" The crippling muscle at the top of Ellis's chest tightened. He hadn't had an anxiety attack for a week, but he could feel one starting. Damn it, Hillary had my pills, he thought. I'll have to get a refill from Walter.

"I don't know exactly how to tell you this. But Hillary's dead."

"She's *what?*" Ellis stood up, knocking over his glass of juice. He looked at the wet stain on the carpet in shock. The rug was a genuine Persian; his wife had expensive tastes. He was struck with a profound weariness, and a sense of foreboding. Oscar Wilde had it right: When the gods want to punish us, they answer our prayers.

"Sit down, lad. She became ill on the flight back from Havana. She was on life support until Friday morning, when she finally passed away. She didn't suffer, if that helps. She never regained consciousness."

Ellis sank back into his chair. "I can't believe it," he breathed. "Why didn't someone tell me?"

"Her parents didn't know she was in the hospital until the day she died, Michael. They thought she was in Cuba with you, having a marvellous vacation. Once they found out, they couldn't reach you; the consulate didn't know where you were staying. I wanted to come to tell you in person. I'm so sorry."

"But I phoned here; I left messages. All my mother-in-law had to do was check the answering machine and she would have known Hillary had caught an early flight. June was supposed to be looking after the place, making it look lived-in while we were away."

Ellis walked over to the old black answering machine. A red light blinked. He pushed a button and heard his own metallic voice.

"Hillary. It's Mike. I'm calling from the Parque Ciudad Hotel. I need to talk to you right away—" He hit "skip." A beep. The same voice, the same plea. And then a series of urgent messages from the General Hospital, asking him to call the critical care ward immediately.

"I know you feel like blaming someone," said O'Malley, "but sometimes things like this happen. It's no one's fault."

"You said she got sick—sick from what?"

"They're not sure yet. They're running tests. It could have been food poisoning."

"But that's insane," said Ellis. "Hillary hardly ate anything in Cuba. She peeled every piece of fruit, for Christ's sake. She wouldn't even brush her teeth with the tap water. Besides, I was with her right up until she left for the hotel to pack to come home. We ate in all the same places."

O'Malley shrugged. "Maybe something they served on the plane."

"My God. I can't believe it." Ellis shook his head as tears filled his eyes. But they weren't for his wife; they were for his partner. If Hillary hadn't seduced him, Steve Sloan would be alive. "Where is she? Where's the body?" He wanted to see for himself, to make sure.

"Ah, Michael, I'm sorry to tell you this. But the remains were cremated this morning. The coroner said they could go ahead; they'd done an autopsy. He's still waiting on some results, but it looks like the finding will be undetermined or accidental death."

"Cremated?" That was a shock. Ellis thought Hillary's parents would have insisted on an open casket. With all the Botox his wife injected, he half expected O'Malley to tell him the funeral home had exploded. We should never have got married, he thought. Steve was right.

"Take a few days off, Michael. I know how bloody hard it's been for you. And now this. Is there anything I can do to help?"

Ellis shook his head. "No, I'll be alright, Chief. I think I'm going to sit down now and get drunk. Maybe you can stay and have a drink with me. It's not quite the way I expected to celebrate the New Year." He shook his head, unable to believe it. Erased into ashes. *Till death do us part.* "You're right; it's been tough."

Ellis flashed back to the interrogation room; the stained, damp holding cell he'd shared with frightened Cubans. They'd jumped whenever they heard footsteps. Every backfire in the street had terrified him, reminding him of the very real prospect of being executed by a firing squad. He tried to control his breathing, to ease the pain at the top of his heart.

And now Hillary was dead. How was he supposed to react? He exhaled slowly, forcing the taut muscles above his heart to relax, willing himself to stay calm.

"Now, you know I'd never say no to a whisky, Michael."

Ellis went to get the bottle while O'Malley called his man in to join them. Fate, it seemed, had a sense of humour. Sobriety would have to wait.

"Detective Ellis took it a lot better than I expected, Chief," said Constable Mullins as he staggered down the driveway, two empty bottles later. "He sure got mangled up in that 'trouble with man' call, didn't he?"

O'Malley nodded. "It's hard to know what's going on in that head of his sometimes because of it. He was a handsome lad once. I can't imagine what it's like, living every day with that disfigurement. I'm sure he thinks of his best friend every time he looks in the mirror."

"Can't they do something about those scars with plastic surgery?"

"Now, that I don't know. He's still recovering, Martin. I'm worried about him. First Steve was killed and Michael so badly mutilated in the same attack. And now his own wife has passed away without him even knowing. He's a good man, but there's only so much anyone can handle before they break. Best give me the keys, man. You're starting to weave."

Mullins handed the car keys over sheepishly. He stepped around to the passenger side of the unmarked car. O'Malley folded himself into the driver's seat.

"She was gorgeous, that wife of his. I could never be anywhere near her for more than a minute or two before I had to excuse myself and find a place to settle down, if you know what I mean. Thick blonde hair, long legs, a little thin for my taste, but a lovely woman nonetheless. I'll tell you this, whatever they say in public, a lot of officers' wives will be glad she won't be flirting with their husbands at the Christmas parties anymore. My own included."

The patrolman turned his head towards Ellis's house as he pulled his car door closed. "Did you hear that?"

"Hear what, son? I don't hear anything. Too late for fireworks. It's long past midnight."

"It must be my imagination. I could have sworn I heard him laughing."

FOUR

Inspector Ricardo Ramirez rolled out of bed, groaning. He walked heavily to the kitchen and picked up the phone, scratching himself sleepily.

"This is the clerk to the Minister of the Interior," a woman said. "The minister wants to see you immediately. He is extremely busy, comrade, getting ready for the Liberation Day festivities. You should be grateful he is taking time from his busy schedule to interrupt your holiday."

Unfortunately for Ramirez, Francesca did not share his gratitude. Examining a corpse at a crime scene, even one so badly decomposed, he thought later, would have been preferable.

"I'm sorry, Francesca," he said, as his wife walked into the kitchen, her hair tousled, "but I have to meet with the Minister of the Interior. It shouldn't take long."

She raised her eyebrows. "You promised we would go to the opera today, Ricardo. Can't they leave you alone for a single day?"

"I'll get the tickets as soon as we're finished, I promise."

"You'd better hope there are still tickets left," she said, frowning. "I'll believe you once we are actually sitting in the theatre, listening to the Peachums plot to murder their son-in-law for his money."

Ramirez kissed her on the side of the mouth. "Sweetheart, I'd better get dressed and get going or I'll be late."

"Will he even notice if you're not there?" she said. "That man is such an idiot."

Ramirez dashed down the three flights of stairs to the street and started up his car. He drove quickly through Old Havana, steering the mini-car around ancient taxis, his hand kept firmly on the horn.

The small blue car sliced cleanly through crowds of hung-over, sunburned revellers who made the nearly fatal mistake of thinking the sidewalks were safe. Ramirez was amused at how quickly even non-athletic, middle-aged men leaped out of the way like Chinese acrobats as the car hurtled to its destination. But being late for a meeting with a member of the inner Cabinet was at least a disciplinary offence, if not a capital one.

The dead cigar lady slid sideways on the passenger seat. She clung to the door handle as the car skidded to a stop. Ramirez had not yet been able to get her to communicate with him. She seemed to think the large knife sticking out of her chest was all he needed to know.

In the hours since she'd materialized in the police parking lot, she'd spent most of her time looking disappointed in him. She must have been someone's mother-in-law, thought Ramirez. That look of stark disapproval, conveyed with a single raised eyebrow, took years to perfect.

Ramirez was regularly haunted by the ghosts of crime victims. His Vodun slave grandmother had warned him they would come—messengers sent by Eshu, the Cuban *orisha* in charge of the crossroads. It was her gift to Ramirez as the eldest son. Although he sometimes thought it was his curse.

Ramirez had been raised a Catholic, despite the government ban on Catholicism. His father was Catholic. But his African grandmother had believed in Santería. This had caused consternation on the part of his mother, who had enthusiastically embraced the Cuban policy of official atheism.

"The true mystery of the world is what we see, Ricky, not what we don't," his mother warned him after his beloved *mamita* died. She placed little stock in superstition, none in ghosts. "Your grandmother's illness made her believe many things that weren't true."

"But Papi believes in God, and Fidel Castro says God isn't real either," the confused boy protested.

"Talk to your father," she said. But his father had no satisfactory answer.

Ricky was only nine when his grandmother passed away. Before she died, she made him promise to keep her ghosts a secret. Young Ramirez liked the idea of secrets, of ghosts. It was exciting, like a sunken pirate ship or a giant squid that washed up on the beach.

His *mamita* correctly predicted that he would become a police officer when he grew up. The visions began to appear as soon as Ramirez started investigating homicides.

At first, he thought they were hallucinations, caused by the same rare dementia that claimed his *mamita*'s life. But Hector Apiro ruled that out after he found an old autopsy report that established she'd died of natural causes.

Hyperthyroidism was the illness Apiro thought might account for the occasional trembling in Ramirez's fingers and legs and the times he was out of breath.

After ruminating about it, Ramirez wasn't entirely convinced that Apiro was right. After all, Apiro had attempted a diagnosis without full patient disclosure. Ramirez had not told Apiro, or his own wife, for that matter, that he saw ghosts. He wasn't sure how they would react, not to mention his mother. Apiro had also mentioned that some other illnesses, like tumours and strokes, could cause hallucinations.

Until Ramirez could see a specialist, which might take months, he'd decided it was best to treat the ghosts as if they were real.

After all, his grandmother's final words were a warning: "Do nothing, Ricky, to anger the gods."

FIVE

Inspector Ramirez parked his car and walked briskly down the cracked concrete path to the government offices at the Plaza de la Revolución. The dead woman trailed behind.

The landmark building that housed the Ministry of the Interior was decorated with a huge outline of Che Guevara's head and the words *Hasta la victoria siempre.* Che had used the phrase to end his last letter to Fidel Castro. But like everything else in Cuba, it was nuanced. Without punctuation, it could mean either "We will always fight until victorious" or "Wait for me until I come home."

The old woman tagged along as Ramirez entered the building. He strode past a long row of black-and-white photographs hanging on the wall. She stopped in front of one of them and scrutinized it closely. Ramirez glanced at the image as he nodded to the minister's clerk, who was seated behind a scratched wooden desk.

Raúl Castro had been photographed with a priest and two prisoners in the Sierra Maestra mountains in the thick of the revolution. Fidel Castro's younger brother wore camouflage pants and a khaki hat. The prisoners were counter-revolutionaries, supporters of Fulgencio Batista, on their way to the firing squad, if they had survived that long.

"*La China roja,*" Raúl Castro's men had called him. It was a play on words—"Red China." But because of the female article, China could also mean "Chinese woman" or "painted china." This resulted in much gossip and speculation about the clothes Raúl wore in private.

"The minister will see you now," the clerk said, to Ramirez's surprise. She waved him straight through to the minister's office for the second time in less than a week.

He opened the heavy door, allowing the dead cigar lady to precede him. The old woman coyly held her fan to her face and fluttered her lashes. For a moment, the years slipped away, and Ramirez glimpsed the passionate young woman she once was.

The minister sat behind a massive mahogany desk. He tapped a cigar on its smooth surface. His desk was almost the same size as Ramirez's car.

"Happy Liberation Day, Minister."

The politician nodded impatiently. "Your travel authorization to Ottawa has been approved," he said. He seemed distracted. "You will leave Wednesday. Two days should be enough. The travel costs will come from your department's budget."

The minister placed a *tarjeta blanca*, an exit permit, on the desk's polished top. "As you know, the Canadians have arrested Rey Callendes. We want him brought home."

Home. It was a strange word, thought Ramirez, to use in relation to a foreign national. He lowered himself into one of two soft brown leather armchairs. He glanced at the signature on the permit. The minister's scrawl was readily identifiable by the looped *y* that circled beneath his surname.

This was a complete departure from the rules. Special travel authorizations, even the urgent ones, usually took months. Normally, in these circumstances, a letter of invitation would be required from the Canadian government, as well as a declaration that it would pay all costs.

Travel documents were supposed to be legalized at the Consultoría Jurídica Internacional. And one could expect to spend an entire day queuing up at a Bank of Credit and Commerce branch to divest oneself of three years' wages to pay for them.

Which was why so few Cubans travelled. *Salida ilegal del país* was considered treason. Thousands of political prisoners served time because they had tried to leave Cuba without the proper paperwork.

"That's good news," Ramirez said, his heart sinking. He could only imagine how angry Francesca would be when she found out he was leaving the island without her. "Do you have any further details about the charges?"

"The Canadian authorities have informed us that his laptop was full of rather indelicate photographs. Small boys. It's believed some were Cuban. There's concern his arrest will cause quite an international scandal once word gets out."

"I can imagine," Ramirez nodded. A Catholic priest caught travelling with child pornography *would* draw attention.

"About this business with Detective Sanchez," said the minister, waving his hand dismissively. "His funeral will be held on Thursday. Full military honours."

Ramirez felt a wave of regret that he would not be able to attend, even if the military honours were a sham. "As his superior officer, I would have liked to be there."

"There are more important matters for you to deal with in Ottawa. Here," the minister picked up a second document and tossed it to Ramirez. "The Canadian lawyer, Celia Jones. Have her attest this while you are in Ottawa. You can assure her, if she is reluctant to do so, that we don't plan to use it in court."

"If that's the case, may I ask why we need a sworn document?"

The minister snorted. "Your job is to carry out orders, not to question them."

"I'm sure she'll ask."

"Tell her there's a bigger picture."

Ramirez nodded slowly. He wondered if anyone would paint it for him. The dead cigar lady, he noticed, had removed the fabric flower from her white bandana and held it loosely in her fingers.

The politician gestured, waving his cigar. "I want the contents of that attestation reflected in your final report to the Attorney General about Sanchez's death. And I want to see that report before you file it."

"I see," said Ramirez, starting to understand what was expected of him.

He glanced at the ghost. She began a slow circuit around the room, holding her flower in both hands. A woman with a generous rear end, she waddled behind the minister as he paced back and forth in front of the cracked window overlooking the square.

The politician finally sat down, again tapping his Montecristo on the surface of the desk. The cigar lady pulled out her own hand-rolled cigar. On the point of *machismo*, she won handily; hers was twice the length of his.

Ramirez scanned through the pages of the attestation. It had been prepared by Luis Perez, according to the page at the back of the document. And as was so often the case with the corrupt prosecutor, the document was full of lies.

It stated that Detective Rodriguez Sanchez died on December 29, 2006, in a Viñales boarding school while accompanied by Celia Jones, a Canadian lawyer. It said that Sanchez lost his life bravely and courageously when he fell through a rotten floor while investigating crimes against children committed by representatives of the Catholic Church.

It was translated into English well enough, although Ramirez hoped the sentence that said Sanchez had been extremely well "licked" by his colleagues was simply a typing mistake.

It was true that Sanchez died in Viñales. The floors in the boarding school were certainly rotten enough to kill someone, as in so many Cuban buildings, even those not abandoned for years. It was also true that when it was open, its students were routinely abused by Catholic priests.

What the affidavit failed to mention was that, two decades earlier, Sanchez was one of them. Rodriguez Sanchez died on the steps of the school, not inside. He blew out his brains with his service revolver as Celia Jones looked on, horrified.

Sanchez committed suicide only minutes before Ramirez arrived on the scene. The inspector was too late for the rescue he'd hoped to effect. Not of Jones, Sanchez's hostage, but of his protegé. Ramirez was still trying to cope with Sanchez's death and the fact that he had known so little about his best detective, a superb investigator and a man Ramirez had considered his friend.

"Do you want this statement notarized too?" Ramirez asked.

"Of course," the minister said indignantly. "It is a legal document. It has to be genuine."

Ramirez managed not to laugh. *Genuine* evidently meant something other than true to politicians.

The minister lit his cigar and drew on it deeply several times. The cigar lady stood behind his large chair, her flower once again pinned to her bandana. She looked over his shoulder at Ramirez, fanning herself in the heat. She pointed to the attestation.

Ramirez nodded. He folded the papers and slipped them into his jacket pocket.

Securing the return of Padre Callendes to Cuba in only three days would be difficult. Cuba lacked a formal extradition treaty with Canada, and with most countries, for that matter. Even foreign judgments from civil courts were unenforceable. But persuading a Canadian lawyer to swear a false affidavit would be next to impossible.

Still, as the minister himself had emphasized, these were not requests but orders from the highest levels. Ramirez would have to think through the practical problems involved in carrying them out. But it seemed to him that he had advanced up the political food chain several levels. He was no longer a lowly vegetable but more of a sheep.

The minister exhaled, sending a cloud of fragrant smoke overhead. He looked relieved. A conspiracy of sorts existed between them now, even if its object was known only to the politician. But Ramirez was sure he would eventually discern what it was. As Hector Apiro once observed about conspiracies, it takes more than one bird to flock.

"Do we understand each other, Ramirez?" the minister asked, standing up. It wasn't really a question; the meeting was over. The politician had smoking to do.

"Perfectly," Ramirez lied. He reluctantly pushed himself up from the comfortable chair.

He checked his watch. There was still time to get tickets to the opera. He hoped those, and the promise of Canadian soap, might placate his wife.

But first he had to find Apiro and get his advice on what to do next.

"Oh, Inspector Ramirez? I almost forgot," said the minister, drawing on his cigar. He smiled unexpectedly, which made Ramirez uneasy. "Happy New Year."

SIX

Inspector Ramirez looked out the window in Hector Apiro's thirteenth-floor office in the medical tower, watching a young patrolman slouch against a lamppost on the sidewalk below. Apiro had gone down the hall to get water for coffee. It was the one treat the pathologist allowed himself, and he was always happy to share: fresh beans from the *bolsa negra*, the black market. Rationed coffee was cut with chickpea flour as neatly and efficiently as if the government bureaucrats responsible had been coached by Mexican drug dealers.

The old woman had managed to squeeze her rather large rear end into Apiro's small swivel chair. She waited impatiently for Ramirez to finish his business with Apiro and start investigating her murder.

If this apparition was real, thought Ramirez, Eshu had certainly lived up to his reputation as a prankster. All his other emissaries had been extremely polite. They willingly disappeared whenever Ramirez needed time alone. They enjoyed riding in his car and wandering around his family's tiny apartment. They offered whatever silent assistance they could, along with the occasional mute, but gentle, criticism. They never spoke, only gestured.

But this one made it clear that she wasn't impressed with his inability to decipher her clues. In fact, she gave Ramirez the impression she considered him somewhat clueless.

Apiro opened the door, carrying a kettle in his large hands. He appeared downcast.

"I'm sorry, Ricardo. No coffee today. The water isn't running. What little trickled from the tap was dark brown. I'll have to postpone the autopsy I'd planned for this afternoon. Luckily, our refrigeration units are working. Did anyone tell you about the woman's body that was discovered near Blind Alley this morning? She was elderly, perhaps seventy or eighty."

The old woman listened intently as Apiro described the crime scene. "What's interesting is that under her bandana, her head was completely bald. I don't think it's from cancer; we have barely any chemotherapy these days, what with supplies being so short. I think she shaved it. Very odd. If I can do the autopsy tomorrow morning, will you be able to join me?"

"I think so. After that, Espinoza will have to handle that file. It looks as if I'll be going to Canada sooner than I expected." Ramirez described in detail his conversation with the minister. "He wants to read my report before it goes to the Attorney General. He's even given me a script to follow." He pulled out the attestation from his pocket and handed it to the pathologist.

Apiro lit his pipe and nodded thoughtfully as he read through the document. He shook his match to extinguish it.

"Interesting. It's odd for someone with the minister's work ethic to be this engaged in a file, isn't it? And why not let the Canadians deal with Rey Callendes? Why do you think he wants him brought back to Cuba?"

Ramirez shook his head. They were all good questions, for which he had no real answers. "Some of the children in

Callendes's photographs were Cuban. There could be a connection to Sanchez he wants covered up."

"Perhaps he is concerned about the effect it would have on tourism if word got out that a Cuban detective was involved in a child sex-abuse ring. Although I don't know how that could happen. Something like that would never be reported in *Granma* or on television for fear of scaring off tourists."

"I agree, it's very strange."

"By the way, Ricardo, I found out some information today about that little girl, the one Señora Jones wants to adopt. The child's name is Beatriz Aranas. She's three years old. Unfortunately, she has serious health problems. She contracted rheumatic fever following a strep infection last year. She should have received antibiotics as a preventive measure afterwards, but too often there weren't any. The last infection damaged her heart; that's why she's in a wheelchair. She needs surgery, perhaps even a transplant if her condition deteriorates further. But these days, such procedures are problematic because of the shortages."

Ramirez sighed. "Señora Jones will be devastated. And if that's the case, I really don't know how I'll be able to persuade her to sign this attestation. That was the only thing I could think of that might work—helping to arrange the adoption."

Apiro smiled. "I'm only surprised you haven't asked me to call Francesca and falsely attest that you are at the Gran Teatro right now, waiting in the *cola* for tickets."

Ramirez looked at his watch and jumped to his feet. "I totally forgot. I'd better get over there before it's too late."

He glanced at the ghost. She tapped her wrist and frowned.

Ramirez breathed a little easier once he slipped the pair of tickets into his pocket. He walked back to his car, still troubled by the minister's orders.

Apiro was right. There was something important going on behind the scenes. Once Ramirez knew what it was, the rather unequal relationship he had with his superior was likely to change dramatically. Of course, he still had to deal with his *real* superior.

He drove home slowly, shifting uncomfortably in his seat. Beside him, the old lady held her flower out like a posy. Ramirez understood the form of appeasement she was suggesting, but he had no money left for bribes.

The afternoon breeze ruffled the crocheted curtains. Outside, birds sang arias, hidden in the leaves of fragrant magnolia trees. The devastated buildings across the street were bathed in golden light.

It was humid and sticky inside their apartment, and getting hotter every minute.

"I *knew* this would happen, Ricardo. You always work late, and you never come home for dinner. And now you're leaving the country?"

The use of *always* and *never* was a particularly bad sign. It meant Francesca was not going to raise a specific complaint that Ramirez might respond to, but rather a collection of grievances she'd stored up over time.

"Christmas Day was supposed to be your day off, too," she said. "But I had to entertain your relatives alone. Every night last week you came home late and were out of here by dawn. You toss and turn in your sleep, but you won't tell me what's going on. Sometimes I think you are having an affair."

"I would never do that, Francesca," said Ramirez. "You know there is no other woman for me."

"Not with a woman, Ricardo. With Hector Apiro."

Ramirez barely stifled a laugh. He walked into the kitchen cautiously and put his arms around his wife's sturdy body. "Now, Francesca, you know how silly that is." It was a poor choice of words, he realized, as soon as they escaped his mouth.

"You think I'm silly?" Francesca snapped, pushing him away.

"Of course not," Ramirez said, attempting to recover quickly. "But Hector no longer works so many nights himself. He has a girlfriend now. She was a patient of his long ago. She was close to that little boy, Arturo Montenegro, the child murdered on Christmas Eve. She came forward as a witness. That's how she found out Hector was still in Havana. They seem happy together. I think we should invite them for dinner now that we have the new coupon book."

Even the lure of gossip was not enough to distract his wife.

"If Hector Apiro is not working nights anymore, then why are you? Don't try to change the subject, Ricardo. I know something is going on."

Ramirez sighed. Francesca was right. He *was* working long hours, exceptionally so. And she would be furious if she knew how many of the murder victims whose deaths he investigated had followed him home.

His most recent case sat on a wooden chair in the corner of their tiny living room. The old woman held her long, thick cigar loosely in her stained fingers, bored. Legs crossed, swinging one of her feet, she watched the back-and-forth of their marital conflict as if she'd heard it all before.

"Francesca, *cariño*, maybe you should look at this from a different perspective," said Ramirez. "The ministry will pay me to spend two days in a country where there are shops. Think of all the things I can buy that we can't get here."

He thought she would like the idea of him shopping for her. His mistake, as it turned out. The old woman held her cigar like a gun and pointed it at his groin, cocking the trigger.

"Paid for with *what*, Ricardo? The twenty-five pesos you get as salary each month? Sometimes I think you are the only policeman in the entire Cuban police force who doesn't take money from the *extranjeros* before sending them home."

Ramirez frowned. As the senior officer in charge of the Havana Major Crimes Unit, he felt he needed to set an example. Someday, beyond any doubt, Fidel Castro would be gone for good.

Despite popular belief, the old man was not supernatural; he couldn't live forever. Although he might just come back, thought Ramirez, as he watched the cigar lady throw down her fabric flower and grind it into the floor.

Once Castro died, billions of American dollars would surge into the capital. If Ramirez began to take the relatively small sums offered by tourists now in exchange for throwing out their charges, how would he possibly resist the major bribes then?

Religion causes even good men to commit evil deeds, his Yoruba grandmother had cautioned. But money, he'd discovered, was its own religion.

"Would you have me put a price on my integrity?"

"This from a man who steals rum from the exhibit room?"

Ramirez winced. Of course he took things from the exhibit room. He confined himself to scavenging items that were no longer needed as evidence but necessary to the day-to-day functioning of his unit: rum, batteries, film.

The batteries and film were needed for crime-scene photographs. The rum, because they needed a strong drink sometimes, after the terrible things they saw. Perhaps a little more rum these days to help quiet the trembling in his hands. But he had never accepted a bribe.

Francesca wasn't finished. She had one more blow to strike before the referee called the fight. Hardly fair, thought Ramirez. I am already pinned to the ground.

"We have two small children to worry about. And your parents are elderly. They depend on us more and more. You come home from this meeting with nice talk of Canada. Of soap and shampoos, of toys we can't afford. But while you are at work, I am the one standing in the queue with a ration book, watching the smug wives of young *policías* walk by with bags stuffed full of steak and chicken from the black market."

She knew how to throw a punch.

The old cigar lady used one hand to hold up the other in victory. Ramirez smiled uncomfortably.

By the time the performance began, Francesca's anger had retreated. She slipped her warm fingers into his—a kind of truce. The battle wasn't over, but for the moment she would hold her fire.

Yes, we argue, thought Ramirez, but so does every couple. The fighting is not important. It's how we make up that matters. At least we don't try to kill each other.

"If I remember correctly," Francesca whispered as the curtains parted, "the first singer who played Polly Peachum ran away with her married lover in real life. You should be careful I don't find one myself, what with you working late so often."

"You already *have* a married lover," said Ramirez.

SEVEN

Clare Adams opened Miles O'Malley's office door a sliver, just enough to put her head through. "There's a woman here to see you, Chief."

"Who is it?" O'Malley crinkled his forehead. "I don't have an appointment in my schedule. I'm meeting the mayor in half an hour to talk about the free needle exchange and how the hell we're going to manage the public outcry about it. 'Not in my backyard.' Bloody people. Whose backyard should it be in?"

Adams lowered her voice to a whisper. "Her name is June Kelly. She's quite insistent. I asked her what it was about, but she won't tell me. She says she needs to talk to you, and that she has to go right to the top or they'll cover it up."

"Who are 'they'?"

"Not sure. But I think you should talk to her." She slowly mouthed the words "or she'll never leave."

"Great. The first conspiracy of 2007. Is she a wing nut?"

His assistant smiled. "She seems coherent enough. But emotional. And very angry."

O'Malley followed Adams into the reception area. A small woman in her late sixties or early seventies sat beside an even older man with a kindly face who appeared terribly embarrassed. Probably her husband, O'Malley guessed from the wedding ring and his look of long suffering. She'd been crying, eyes puffy and black tracks of makeup down her cheeks. She seemed vaguely familiar. And Clare was right, the woman was almost rigid with anger.

"Mrs. Kelly? What can I do for you? Please, come in." O'Malley motioned to the husband to join her, but he shook his head.

"I'll wait here, thanks," the man said, rolling his eyes. His expression made it clear he'd heard quite enough of his wife's tirade.

"That man murdered my daughter," the woman said loudly as she got up to follow O'Malley. "And none of you people are doing a goddamn thing about it. Walter, you need to go plug the meter. Wait in the car for me. If you don't, these bastards will give us a ticket."

Her husband got up wearily and made his way to the elevators.

As O'Malley moved to shut the door, he turned to his secretary, raising his eyebrows. It was a prearranged look to let Clare know she should call him in a few minutes and pretend he had an emergency to deal with.

"Murder's a pretty serious allegation," he said, offering Mrs. Kelly a chair. "Perhaps you can tell me what you're talking about."

"Mike Ellis is what I'm talking about."

O'Malley sat down. That's why he recognized her: from the service. Michael's mother-in-law.

"I'm terribly sorry for your loss, Mrs. Kelly. I met your daughter several times at social events. She was a lovely woman. What makes you think her husband had anything to do with her death?"

"I don't know how he did it, but he did it alright. My daughter had an affair. He found out about it. She was terrified he was going to kill her. She found things on his computer. Links to websites about how to slip poison into someone's food without them knowing."

The police chief leaned back in his chair. "They were having marital problems?"

"Did you hear what I just said? He planned to kill her. I'd call that having marital problems."

O'Malley wasn't surprised to hear that Hillary Ellis might have had an affair. Police work was wretchedly hard at the best of times. Policemen worked long hours, saw terrible things, drank far too much. The divorce rate was sky-high, significantly higher than the fifty percent failure rate for civilians. And with shift work, affairs were endemic.

Michael Ellis had almost been destroyed by the accident. If his wife had found comfort in the arms of another man, O'Malley could hardly be critical. Yet Michael had never raised an eyebrow when other men ogled his gorgeous wife. He didn't seem to care in the least what she wore or how much she flaunted her sexuality. O'Malley didn't believe he would harm her; he simply wasn't the jealous type.

"You've had a terrible shock. But I can assure you, your daughter's death was nothing more than a tragic accident."

"You listen to me, you bloody fool. That information on his computer proves he was trying to find a way to do it. I'm not going to let you cover this up."

O'Malley narrowed his eyes. "What are you suggesting, exactly?"

"I don't know *how* he did it. Just that he did. Look at these." The angry woman waved a roll of papers in the air. "Hillary gave them to Walter before she left. In case anything happened to her. I'm telling you, she was scared to death of that man."

"Please listen to me, Mrs. Kelly. It was impossible for Michael to kill your daughter. He was out of the country when she died."

"You look at these. And try to say that to me with a straight face." She threw the papers on his desk.

O'Malley picked them up and skimmed through them. She was right, but for the wrong reasons. He forced himself not to smile. The first page had Google search results for the keywords *poison*, *food*, and *Cuba*.

The first hit was "Find the best deals for poisons in food in Cuba!" From there, it only got worse. The woman might as well have tinfoil on her head.

"You say these came from his computer?"

"You check his laptop. Even if he tried to erase those links, they'll be on it somewhere." Spittle flew from her mouth. "He goddamn well killed her. And believe me, if you won't do anything about this, I will."

O'Malley tried not to show his relief when his telephone finally rang.

EIGHT

Inspector Ramirez was filling out the paperwork for his trip when the scratched black phone on his desk trilled.

"The Canadian lawyer, Señora Jones, is on the line. She would like to speak to you," said the switchboard operator.

"Thank you, Sophia. Aren't you supposed to be working Dispatch tonight?"

"I took yesterday off to watch the parade. I agreed to work switchboard all week to make up for it."

The first day of January was Liberation Day, the anniversary of the Cuban Revolution. It was forty-eight years since Fidel Castro toppled Batista's dictatorship and imposed his own. It had been a classic bait-and-switch, thought Ramirez, who admired Castro's ingenuity.

"Ah, yes, the commemoration of the revolution. I missed the parade, unfortunately," said Ramirez, although he wasn't at all disappointed. Just one of Fidel Castro's speeches could seem as if it lasted for weeks.

But Castro was still recovering from an undisclosed illness. His brother, Raúl, was the acting president. This had changed the usual dynamics. When imagining a future without Fidel Castro, Cubans alternated between hope and fear.

"Were there the typical speeches?"

"Of course," said Sophia. "But much shorter with El Comandante in the hospital. Raúl only spoke for three or four hours. I hear you are going to Canada soon, Inspector." She sounded wistful. "I hope someday I can leave the island, too. To see what it's like to live in a country that has cows and chickens. Sometimes I think I would kill for a pencil."

Ramirez chuckled. "I'm sure that day will come, Sophia. Not when you will kill someone for—or even with—a pencil, but when we will be able to travel more easily. Things are changing quickly. The fact that I'm going to Canada is proof of that. Don't be envious. A week ago, I expected to enjoy the first days of the New Year drinking *añejo*. Now it looks as if I will spend it in a country whose citizens come here to get away from their harsh winters. I'm starting to wonder just which *orisha* I have offended."

Sophia chuckled. "Did you throw out a bucket of water on New Year's Eve?"

"Of course," Ramirez said. "But we had to pull ours from the ocean. We had no running water."

The Cuban custom was to wash away bad luck by throwing water out the window at the stroke of midnight. Maybe that's why Cubans are so unlucky, thought Ramirez. We seldom have clean water to throw away.

"Enjoy your trip," Sophia said, as she transferred the incoming call. "Be sure to come back. Not everyone does."

"*Hola*, Señora Jones," said Ramirez warmly. "I was planning to call you. I should be arriving in Ottawa around 11 P.M. tomorrow night, but my visit will be brief. I have to fly back Friday evening."

"I wanted to call you as soon as I heard. One of our detectives has been assigned to take you around to your meetings with the RCMP. His name is Charlie Pike. He's aboriginal."

"An Aborigine? From Australia?" asked Ramirez, puzzled.

"No, sorry, not Aborigine. Indian. I guess 'First Nations' is the politically correct term these days."

So Ramirez would be working with an indigenous police detective. He had not known there was such a thing. There were no indigenous people left in Cuba; the Tainos were extinct.

"I thought perhaps Señor Ellis would be working on this case. As I recall, he's in your Sex Crimes Unit, isn't he? Is that not the unit dealing with the arrest of Rey Callendes?"

"Oh, I thought you knew. But of course, how could you? Mike's on bereavement leave. His wife died while he was in Cuba." Jones hesitated. "She took ill on the plane. Everyone's shocked. She was only thirty-nine."

"Died of what?" Ramirez glanced at the two small black audiotapes sitting on his desk.

"The chief medical examiner is waiting for lab results to find out for sure, but they seem to think it was food poisoning. All I've heard is that she had really high blood pressure and deep-pink skin. She was in a coma from the moment she stepped off the plane."

The image of a zombie—the undead dead—lurching down the airplane steps crossed Ramirez's mind. But he doubted that was what Señora Jones meant.

"Poor Mike," she continued. "He didn't even know she'd been sick until he got back to Canada. By then, she'd already been cremated."

"Even without knowing the cause of death?"

"The coroner's office did an autopsy. There was nothing to suggest foul play. They don't keep a body long if they don't have to."

"Señor Ellis must be stunned." And maybe even relieved, thought Ramirez. Death was much less expensive than divorce in a country like Canada, from what Ramirez understood. In Cuba, people simply separated, with regrets that things didn't work out. With so little property to fight over, a few pesos to a notary and it was done. But Ramirez had heard stories of how vicious North American lawyers could be about such matters.

"Honestly? I don't think it's hit him yet," said Jones. "Anyway, it's not Mike's unit that's handling the Callendes matter but the RCMP. They're the ones who arrested him at the airport. We're working with them because we have overlapping jurisdiction."

Ramirez picked up one of the black cassette tapes and rolled it in his fingers.

Ordinarily, given the circumstances and timing of Hillary Ellis's sudden death, Ramirez would be suspicious. But Ellis had a strong alibi. Ramirez and Sanchez had personally investigated his whereabouts for the hours leading up to Arturo Montenegro's death, from the time the couple argued on the Malecón to the wife's early departure to Canada.

Still, that would be impressive, thought Ramirez. If Ellis had found a way to murder his spouse from another country, he was a genius. He decided to mention it to Apiro, who was good at puzzles.

Ramirez glanced at the cigar lady, raising his eyebrows. She shrugged her shoulders. As he watched, the old woman removed the flower from her bandana. She plucked at the petals as if playing the children's game his American mother had taught his sister when they were small. *He loves me, he loves me not.*

"Tell me, will I be able to shop during my brief visit? Francesca has perfume and chocolates on her list, but I think she would settle for soap. Getting soap here requires one to line up for hours at a *bodega*."

"Absolutely. Where will you be staying?"

"Somewhere downtown. It sounds like a French castle." Ramirez shuffled through the papers on his desk, looking for the reservation.

"You must mean the Chateau Laurier. It's a great old hotel. It's supposed to be haunted by the ghost of its founder. He died on the *Titanic* a week or so before it opened. Some people swear there's a dead child there, too." She chuckled. "I hope you're not afraid of ghosts."

"Not at all," said Ramirez. "But our government would never let them stay at a tourist hotel."

Jones laughed. "You'll be right across the street from the Rideau Centre. It has every type of retail you can imagine: restaurants, clothing, shoe stores."

"Excellent," said Ramirez, pleased. If he brought home *tacos*, women's shoes, all would be forgiven.

"By the way, Alex and I have three tickets to the opera on Thursday night at the National Arts Centre. It's *Pagliacci*. Would you care to join us? We can go out to dinner first. Celebrate your visit to Canada."

"How kind of you." Opera was Ramirez's passion. It was the original basis of his friendship with Apiro, since he had proven wholly incompetent at chess. And *Pagliacci* was one of his favourites, an opera about a play within a play. Canio, acting out his role as an actor in the internal play, killed his real wife and lover in his jealousy over their off-stage affair.

"Yes, of course I'd love to come. My wife and I went to see *The Beggar's Opera* at the Gran Teatro yesterday. Do you know it?"

"I love it," Jones said. "I saw the one where Macheath died at the end instead of being let out of jail."

"Ah, yes. It's one of those operas where the ending can change.

I had not heard of that particular version," said Ramirez. "But the theatre owner and the writer of the original opera were Gay and Rich, which I found amusing."

Ramirez glanced at the spectre. With the burned end of her cigar, she pointed to the knife buried in her chest and then impatiently at his watch. She's lost her life, but not her personality, thought Ramirez. His Vodun grandmother had always said it was easier to change a person's future than their personality.

"The one we saw was terrific," said Jones. "All the main female characters were really men. And the audience was supposed to call out warnings like, 'Watch out, he's behind you!' 'Don't drink it!'"

The dead woman threw the flower at his feet and applauded madly. It's as if she's watching a performance, thought Ramirez. What is she trying to tell me?

"I will look forward to it. And please pass on my condolences to Señor Ellis if you see him. I can't imagine how I would manage if something happened to my Francesca."

Ramirez looked again at the small black tape in his hand. When Ellis confessed to Ramirez, Ellis had no idea Hector Apiro was standing on the other side of the mirrored glass in the interview room holding a tape recorder. Ramirez slipped the tape into his inside jacket pocket. He still wasn't sure how he was going to carry out his assignment. But if Canada was anything like Cuba, it couldn't hurt to have a little leverage.

"Before we say goodbye, Señora Jones," said Ramirez, "I have some news for you about the child in the orphanage. I'm afraid it is not good."

A hesitation on the other end of the line. "Your government won't let her go?"

Ramirez described the child's medical issues.

"But that's outrageous," Jones said, shocked. "She's dying because she can't get antibiotics?"

"I agree," said Ramirez, "but there is nothing we can do about it. It's because of the trade embargo. As you know, we are very short of supplies, including medicine."

"Couldn't Alex and I bring her to Canada for surgery and adopt her here?"

"I'm afraid adoptions these days can be quite political. Fidel Castro has personally intervened to prevent any child from leaving Cuba since the 1960s, ever since Operation Peter Pan. The Catholic Church persuaded Cubans to send thousands of children to the United States for a better life, but many were abused."

"Is it a matter of paying someone money?"

"It's not that simple," said Ramirez.

Jones sighed. "Now that I know all of this, I want that little girl in Canada more than ever."

"I had not thought you would still wish to proceed, Señora Jones, once you found out how sick she is."

"I probably forgot to tell you this, Inspector, but Alex is a cardiologist. That child deserves a chance with a family that will love her."

"Let me speak to Dr. Apiro. He may be able to make the case for a medical transfer. Perhaps we can negotiate things from there. But you must understand, this won't be easy."

Almost as daunting as persuading a foreign lawyer to swear a false affidavit, thought Ramirez, as he hung up the phone. Although his odds of success might have dramatically improved. The child's illness could bring him a step closer to securing the lawyer's assistance.

He looked at the apparition. She held her cigar like a scalpel and drew an X across her chest.

NINE

Charlie Pike looked through his third-floor window. The back alley was dark and secluded this early in the day. It was littered with used condoms and dull needles that glittered dimly, frozen in the hard ice until spring thaw.

The old man didn't know Pike was watching. But an elderly man who shot up in an alley behind a police station was definitely past caring. The old man was careful to tighten his tourniquet just so. He wanted to make sure the vein he chose was a good one.

You'll have fewer and fewer to choose from, once they collapse, thought Pike. You'll start using your toes, the backs of your legs. When you start injecting in your neck, you won't have much time left. Maybe then I'll find out your name.

The junkie plunged in the needle. Pike watched his expression change, saw the pain melt from the old man's face as the drug took hold.

A hooker weaved unsteadily into the alley; she slipped a little on the ice. But the old man didn't notice. He was essentially *gone* now. Still physically there, but mentally far away.

In a few minutes, when the rush wore off, the dull weight of heroin would carry him back to earth, his euphoria gone. He would be heavy with exhaustion, lethargy.

The woman rifled through the man's pockets for money that wasn't there. She pulled out a new syringe in its plastic package and tottered back to the street triumphantly.

She was rock bottom too, Pike figured. Stealing another junkie's fixings so she could escape for a few minutes from the emptiness and isolation of living in a mostly white world.

Pike shook his head. The bulletin board in the Rideau Regional Police Homicide Unit was full of posters of missing Anishnabe women. They had hitchhiked from their remote reserves to the city. They couldn't wait one more day, one more hour, to have something *more*.

The hooker was still alive. That made her one of the lucky ones. She just didn't know it.

He could arrest her for theft, but the City of Ottawa was about to start a program to give clean needles to addicts anyway. And the old man would forgive her; he had no interest in white man's justice.

In a few minutes, Detective Charlie Pike would walk downstairs to make sure the old man was okay. He'd stop at the canteen to buy him soup, or coffee, as he had done every day that week and the one before. He'd give him some money, make sure the old man had enough blankets to keep his legs warm.

It was doubtful the old man was hungry, or that he noticed the cold much anymore. Smack did that. It killed your appetite first. Then your soul.

But Pike's father had been Ojibway. Anishnabe. And Charlie Pike had been raised to make sure that elders were fed first.

The old man had initially refused to accept Pike's food. Instead, he'd carefully placed the hot soup on the frozen ground, an offering to the *manitous*. He had the translucent look of those with little time left. He wasn't as old as Pike had thought when he first saw him at a distance. Maybe late sixties.

"I have nothing to give you back," he said to Pike softly. "If I accept this, I will owe you."

Pike nodded. To the Anishnabe, accepting a gift brought with it a corresponding obligation. The old man was right to be cautious.

"Then how about if you tell me a story, *mishomis*?" The word meant "grandfather." Pike used it as a term of respect.

And so the old man told Charlie Pike about Nanabush, or Nanabozho, as he called him. About the legend of how the first spring began.

The old man held the hot container of soup in both hands, blowing through his missing teeth to cool the surface before he took small sips. There were jail tattoos on his fingers.

He spoke quietly. Pike strained to hear the soft words of his own, unused language.

"Nanabozho was the oldest boy of four brothers. Chipiapoos was the next. After him came Wabosbo and Chakekenapok. Nanabozho was responsible for living things, Chipiapoos for the dead. Chakekenapok was supposed to look after winter. But when Chakekenapok was born, their mother died. Nanabozho blamed Chakekenapok. He chased him and tore him into pieces. Where his body fell, the drops of blood turned into smooth rocks.

"After Chakekenapok died, Nanabozho ordered Chipiapoos not to leave the lodge. But Chipiapoos was a little boy; he wanted to play. He ran outside to slide on the frozen lake and fell through the ice. Nanabozho searched everywhere until he realized Chipiapoos was dead. He was angry and bitter that the *manitous* took his little brother. He shaved off all his hair to show his grief. And every day after that was winter."

"And then what happened, *mishomis*?"

The old man breathed lightly. He shook his head. "I am sorry. I am too tired to keep talking. I get weak after I put this poison in my arm. But it helps with the pain. That and telling these old stories. The soup went down good, *miigwetch*. I will tell you next time I see you, if you still want to hear it." He pulled himself up, gathering his blankets. "It was good to speak in my language. *Giminadan gagiginonshiwan*."

Pike nodded. "*Gigawabamin menawah*." See you again.

Pike looked out his office window every day after that, looking for the old man. Their routine was now well-established.

After he shot up, the old man would tell Pike a story in exchange for coffee, soup, or a sandwich. As the old man came to trust him, he gave Pike a little more information. Pike felt sometimes as if he was ice-fishing on a frozen lake. Letting out the line slowly, gradually. Waiting for the fish to come to him.

"I'm dying," the old man said during one of their visits. There was no sadness in his voice. He presented it as a fact. "I don't have much time left. I have hepatitis." From drugs or from the water on his reserve, Pike wondered. But he didn't pry.

They sat together in the cold on a bench, on the thick, faded blankets the old man had collected. He refused to go to a shelter.

"I want to hear the wind blow at night and the birds sing in the morning. I want to see the sun when she comes up. I grew up in the woods, you know, before they took me away to that school. The forest, up till then, that was my church."

Pike liked the old man, his humour, his gentleness. "If you feel well enough today, maybe you can tell me the rest of the story about spring."

The old man nodded and pulled his woollen blankets around him. His breath rose like puffs of smoke.

"Many moons passed with only winter. The *manitous* were afraid Nanabozho's grief would destroy him and everything else. They decided to hold a feast to honour him. They filled a pipe with tobacco and gave Nanabozho a beautiful otter-skin bag. Nanabozho's pain and loneliness began to ease when he saw these things, and realized how much they cared. As the cold in his heart melted, *ziigwan*, spring, finally came."

"What is your name, grandfather?" asked Pike. "Is there someone I can call for you? Do you have any family?"

"I have no name," the old man said. He looked away, his eyes tearing up. "They took me from my family. And then they took away my name."

TEN

"How very interesting, Ricardo," Hector Apiro exclaimed. He was standing on his stepladder, leaning over the old cigar lady's remains. There was no sign of the spectre in the autopsy room, but then Ramirez's ghosts tended to avoid the morgue. Perhaps they felt that being killed once was enough.

"I've only seen North American Indians in movies. They are always portrayed as large half-naked men carrying tiny axes and wearing face paint and feathers. They grunt instead of speaking and are usually the last of a dying breed. Their horses jump on their hind legs quite frequently. And they whinny a lot."

"I hope you mean it's the horses that whinny," Ramirez chuckled.

Apiro laughed as he struggled to pull the knife from the woman's chest. He had a staccato laugh that always reminded Ramirez of a night gull. It was impossible for Ramirez to hear the small man cackle without starting to laugh too. The knife popped as it came out. It made the sound of a toilet plunger. It was a large knife, Ramirez noted, the type used by fishermen for gutting fish.

"Hmmm," said Apiro. "That was deeply embedded in the rib cage, almost all the way to the spine."

"Someone must have been very angry at her."

Apiro shook his large head. "I'm not sure. Usually, when that's the case, we find multiple stab wounds."

"I have a feeling she might have been difficult to get along with."

"Did you know her?" asked Apiro, surprised.

Not when she was alive, thought Ramirez. Although I'm certainly getting to know her now. "Well, she has that kind of face, don't you think?"

"Now, Ricardo, you must be careful about stereotypes. Some people can appear as sweet as sugar cane and yet be vicious. Like one of those little dogs on the street that wags its tail when you offer it food and then bites you on the hand. Appearances can be deceiving. Ask any of the patients whose noses I've shortened or whose breasts I've enlarged."

Ramirez nodded. If anyone knew how misleading appearances could be, it was Hector Apiro.

Apiro had been placed in an orphanage at the age of four by parents he believed were ashamed of his deformities. He was old enough then to know he had parents, just not who they were. He was a highly intelligent little boy, often hurt by the bullying of other children. He made up for it by excelling at his studies.

His misshapenness was the reason Apiro had decided to become a plastic surgeon. He took great pride in making others look more normal, since he could do so little for himself. He enjoyed operating on the dead. Occasionally, he was known to alter their flaws, improving what he referred to as their "final appearance."

Ramirez was frequently awed by Apiro's brilliance. The small doctor had mastered many disciplines besides medicine and chess. He was an avid historian and philosopher, and spoke several languages. Ramirez enjoyed the banter they carried on in the morgue, despite the difficult crimes they investigated together. Or perhaps because of them.

Apiro stepped down from the stepladder holding the knife delicately in his gloved fingers. He reached for a plastic bottle of Luminol and sprayed the handle with a single sweep. "Hold your breath, Ricardo. I don't have any face masks at the moment. This substance can be toxic."

Apiro placed the knife under an ultraviolet lamp. The handle glowed iridescent blue for a moment.

"Ah, here we go. See? A small smudge. Luminol is wonderful at picking up blood residue. Perhaps we will be lucky and find DNA from the person who killed her. Even luckier if I have enough supplies to find out."

Since October, the American trade embargo had been enforced more rigorously. The United States government wanted to take advantage of Fidel Castro's failing health. But bullying makes us stubborn, thought Ramirez. It's like World War II, when Churchill called British citizens to arms by urging them to collect rubber bands. So, too, we Cubans. Except we save everything.

"Interesting that Canada has an indigenous population," Apiro said as he clambered back up his stepladder. "That's impressive. Here, of course, it was quite different." He shook his large head sadly. "Thousands of Taino villagers welcomed the conquistadores with gifts of tobacco and fish. Imagine their confusion, their disbelief, when they were butchered, their chiefs burned alive. All of this was a violation of international law, of course. The Spaniards were not supposed to conquer any 'discovered' people willing to trade with them. But then, as now, the Pope could invent any law he wished. There are only a few traces of the Tainos left, a word here and there, although I find Taino

DNA in the blood of *mestizos* sometimes. Not much to show for what was once a generous and civilized society. It's another reason I am such a devout atheist. Well, that," Apiro smiled, "and my Jesuit upbringing."

I should check the *bodegas*, Ramirez thought. *Jaba* was a Taino word for a bag made of woven palm fronds. Cubans called their shopping bags *jabas*. Under the Plan Jaba, the elderly were permitted to jump the queue when getting rations. The old woman was the type to push her way to the front of the *cola*. Someone would have noticed.

"Why *are* you an atheist, Hector?" he asked.

"I've always found the Catholic God to be a paradox." Apiro paused. He turned to look at Ramirez, holding his scalpel thoughtfully. "Vengeful and punitive; turning women into salt for simply looking backwards. And yet seemingly incapable of taking any steps to stop evil. A timely and well-placed bullet in Hitler's skull would have saved millions. Prayers did nothing. Words are rarely stronger than swords or bullets, however much they may hurt."

"I agree with you that some men are so inherently evil that the only reasonable thing to do is to remove them from society," Ramirez said. "But even Voltaire said if there was no God, it would be necessary to invent one."

"And I believe we did," Apiro grinned. "But then, Voltaire also said that a clever saying proves nothing."

Ramirez chuckled. "So what are your thoughts about this woman's murder, Hector? It seems straightforward this time, no?" The inspector gestured toward the knife, which still rested on the counter. The blue iridescence had disappeared from its handle like magic.

"Ah, now, Ricardo, one would naturally assume that a fish knife plunged into someone's heart would cause their death. But look here," Apiro pointed his gloved finger at the woman's chest. "There is almost no blood around the wound. Or on her clothing. She was stabbed, yes, but that's not what killed her."

"Then what did?" asked Ramirez, puzzled.

"I am not sure yet, but I can tell you this. By the time that knife was hammered into her chest, she was already dead."

ELEVEN

"By the way," said Inspector Ramirez. "I spoke to Señora Jones this morning. Michael Ellis's wife died last week. She became ill on the flight back to Canada. The Canadian medical authorities think it may have been food poisoning. What do you think?"

"Hmmm," said Apiro. He lit his pipe. "The timing is a little suspicious, isn't it?" He lowered his large head and puffed until the embers in the bowl of his pipe glowed red.

Ramirez was grateful that the refrigeration unit that stored the bodies in the morgue was working again. It had been out of service for more than a week. The smell of decaying flesh permeated the space. Cigar smoke, like pipe smoke, helped to mask it. The petroleum jelly product they once put under their noses to block the smell of decomposition was no longer available.

He reached for a cigar in his pocket and cupped his hand around Apiro's match, drawing deeply until it lit.

They sat comfortably together in the haze, smoking. Apiro was seated on the second rung of his wooden stepladder. Ramirez sat beside him on a round wooden stool. This arrangement allowed them to discuss matters face-to-face despite the difference in their size. Ramirez often thought these moments in the morgue, even with dead bodies resting in the drawers and on the gurneys, were among his happiest.

For one thing, there were no distractions—his ghosts always stayed on the other side of the metal doors. And for another, he always felt completely at ease with Apiro, to whom abnormalities were normal, to whom life itself was the anomaly. Maybe Francesca was right. Maybe he *was* having an affair with Hector Apiro.

"Well, you know what they say, Ricardo. Once one eliminates the impossible, whatever is left, however unlikely, is usually the truth. Do you know anything about her symptoms?"

"High blood pressure, deep-pink skin. She fell into a coma on the airplane."

"I suppose it could be food poisoning," said the surgeon. "There have been issues with flight kitchens before. Insufficient disinfection; food not cooked long enough. Although that is more often associated with rather unpleasant gastrointestinal disorders. But there are some very dangerous chemicals that turn up occasionally in the food chain that can turn skin that colour. Cyanide, for example." Apiro drew on his pipe. "Do you remember the early 1990s, when tens of thousands of Cubans suddenly went blind? They stumbled around the streets of Havana like something from a horror movie."

"I remember it well. I was a young police officer at the time, working foot patrol. It was complete chaos. The *houngans* claimed they were zombies."

Thirty-four thousand Cubans were afflicted. There was near panic in the city until the epidemic passed. Most recovered, although some never regained their sight.

"I had forgotten all about that, Ricardo," Apiro chuckled, shaking his head. "The voodoo doctors spout such nonsense. The foreign epidemiologists thought it was a virus. But no tourists became sick, which made that unlikely. Personally, I always suspected cyanide."

Ramirez formed a circle with his lips as he exhaled. His smoke ring floated to the stained ceiling and hung below the flickering fluorescent lights. An entire day without a power outage. Water running again. Maybe it would be a Happy New Year after all.

"Cyanide? What from?"

"Bootleg rum, probably. I said as much to Castro. He attended all the medical briefings. If our folate levels are normal, most people can handle a little cyanide without serious physical harm. But we've been affected by rationing. The fact that tobacco often contains traces of cyanide could well have pushed the victims' overall exposure to toxic levels. To his credit, Castro assured me he would act."

"Those extra beans in our rations were probably your fault, then," said Ramirez. "I'm not sure if I should thank you. Do you think Señor Ellis could have somehow poisoned his wife's food before she left Havana?"

"Perhaps," Apiro nodded, puffing on his pipe, "but I don't know how. It's virtually impossible to obtain that form of cyanide here."

Ramirez nodded slowly. "Come to think of it, the sniffing dogs at the airport picked up nothing in his baggage when he arrived here. Would they have detected it?"

"Of course, if they were trained to," Apiro said. "Their noses are thousands of times more sensitive than our own. The beagle there is the best of the bunch. A remarkable animal, really. Highly cost-effective. He works for even less than we do."

Ramirez laughed. His own salary was a little more than Apiro's. But the beagle worked for scraps.

TWELVE

Celia Jones sat at her desk, buried behind stacks of paper. Theoretically, she was on vacation for another few days; in reality, the holiday was over.

She had hoped that preparing the tedious paperwork to account for her trip to Cuba would take her mind off little Beatriz's illness. But itemizing her expenses for the Rideau Regional Police Force's accounting department was proving torturous.

There were two official currencies in Cuba. The tourist peso, the CUC, was the one foreigners were required to use. It was illegal for Cubans to have even one in their possession. The CUC was worth fifteen to twenty times as much as the domestic peso, but the rate fluctuated all the time.

Despite the laws against it, she'd paid for some things in Havana with domestic pesos and others with CUCs. Only the Parque Ciudad Hotel had provided her with receipts. She'd be tied up for months trying to get reimbursed. A Cuban dictatorship had nothing on Ottawa bureaucrats.

An email from O'Malley pinged in her inbox. "Stop by when you have a moment. Miles."

"You are rescuing me from accounting hell," she typed back, and hit "send."

She stood up and stretched. She walked down the hall, said hello to Clare, and poked her head through O'Malley's open door.

The police chief sat behind a large desk, chewing on a pencil. He'd quit smoking now that it was illegal in public buildings. He claimed it was a selfish pleasure that never satisfied him anyway.

"What's up?"

"I had the dearly departed's mother here first thing this morning. Practically frothing at the mouth. She swore at me so much, I thought she might have Tourette's. She wants us to lay murder charges." O'Malley leaned back in his chair and folded his big hands behind his neck, grinning. "I was almost in fear for my own life."

"Yeah, right." O'Malley was as big as Paul Bunyan. Good looking, afraid of no one, thought Jones. A *guapo*, they would say in Cuba. "And just which dearly departed was that?"

"Hillary Ellis. June Kelly is her mother. She says Michael murdered her daughter. She gave me these." He pointed to a sheaf of papers. "Apparently they came from his computer. Take a look for yourself."

Jones flipped through the pages. A guide to do-it-yourself poisoning. She burst out laughing.

"Buy a poison-dart frog on the internet and throw it at someone? Collect snake venom? I love this one: make your own 'posin out of caster beens.' Personally, I wouldn't take advice on how to get away with murder from someone who can't spell. I don't mean to be rude, but is this woman nuts? She can't expect you to take this kind of nonsense seriously."

"She was quite rabid," said O'Malley. "She told me she wanted to see Michael fry as she slammed the door behind her. I didn't have the heart to tell her we don't have capital punishment anymore. And that we never did have the electric chair."

"Is she going to come after you now, if you ignore her allegations?"

Celia Jones's job as the police department's lawyer involved risk management. She was supposed to protect the Rideau Regional Police Force from lawsuits and bad press. And, wherever possible, from crazy old women.

"I may need to watch my food for a while," O'Malley said, chuckling. "But seriously, it's a sad situation. I assured her that we would keep her informed of whatever conclusions the Chief Medical Examiner's Office reaches. If Ralph Hollands finds anything suspicious, I said we'll follow up with her then."

"I doubt there's anything *to* find, Miles. Hillary got sick on a flight. I don't see how Mike could have had anything to do with it."

"I agree. But best if we keep on top of this. Look, Celia, can I leave it up to you to deal with Ralph? He may need help liaising with the Cuban authorities. I don't think anyone in his office speaks Spanish. Mrs. Kelly is the type to go running to the media. You know what they're like. They'll publish just about any juicy allegation, truthful or not. And she's full of them."

"You mean full of *it*. In other words, you want me to deal with her so that you don't have to."

"You see? There's that fine legal mind of yours at work." O'Malley grinned. He looked at his appointment book and scribbled down a number on a pad. He tore off a page and handed it to Jones. "Here. They own a drugstore. She said it's best to call her there; the home number's unlisted."

"For this, you owe me," Jones said. "I don't suppose you have any pull with Accounting, do you?"

THIRTEEN

Inspector Ramirez removed his jacket and unbuttoned the collar of his cotton shirt. With the wind finally calm, it was a scorching-hot day. Even the cooler rooms of the beautiful multi-turreted building that served as police headquarters were hot and humid behind the thick stone walls.

A green gecko hung upside down by the cracked window, breathing lightly. Ramirez ignored the small intruder and sat behind his desk.

The Minister of the Interior had instructed Ramirez to deduct the cost of his airfare from the Major Crime Unit's already meagre annual budget. Ramirez would need to complete a mountain of documents to explain the reason he was transferring funds out of the country or risk being investigated by Cuban Intelligence for fraud.

That would be embarrassing, Ramirez thought. I would have to bribe them to drop the investigation. That's when stealing money from the exhibit room *would* be a necessity.

A tall Afro-Cuban man knocked on Ramirez's open door. "Inspector Ramirez? Do you have a moment?"

The man wore a light coloured shirt and a black suit that had seen better days. It was stained with ingrained dirt on the pant legs and jacket cuffs. But Ramirez could hardly criticize him for that. All Cubans had problems keeping their good clothes clean, with dry cleaners few and far between and the continual shortage of laundry soap. Some used diesel, which worked well but smelled, and there was always the danger of exploding into flames if someone nearby lit up a cigar. Dressing well was a risky business.

"Yes?" Ramirez looked behind the stranger. He had no police escort, which meant he had to be a plainclothes policeman from another division.

"My name is Juan Tranquilino Latapier. I have been sent here from El Gabriel," the man confirmed. "I understand you are investigating the death of an old woman who was stabbed with a fish knife?"

"News travels fast," said Ramirez. "Yes, the body was found early yesterday." He was surprised a detective from a small village outside Havana had heard of the murder.

The tall man smiled, revealing perfect white teeth. "I have a similar file, although mine involves two children. Both were stabbed to death, but in one case the knife was left behind in the body. I understand that was the same with your victim. I am only in Havana for a few hours, but I thought perhaps we could assist each other. Share information."

"Of course, Juan. Please, sit down. Tell me more about your investigation."

Latapier sat across from the inspector on one of the two badly worn upholstered chairs. "The two children were murdered about a year ago. The first was a little girl named Zoila. You may have heard of this. It caused quite a stir locally."

"Zoila?" Ramirez cast his mind back. The name was vaguely familiar. "I think I read about it, probably in a police report."

"She was barely four years old when her body was found. She

was disemboweled in her own backyard, the heart cut from her chest."

"That's disgusting," said Ramirez, thinking of his little daughter, Estella. "What kind of monster would do such a thing?"

"Well, that's the problem; I don't know for sure. The locals believed that *brujos* took her body parts as amulets and used her blood in their cures. But only a few weeks later, a second child was killed, a ten-year-old. She was mutilated the same way, only this time a fish knife was left behind, stuck in her heart. The second death happened while the suspects in Zoila's murder were in jail. They were convicted of Zoila's murder. Their appeal is being argued this week."

"I see." Ramirez thought for a moment. "And when you heard of this woman's murder, you wondered if a mistake had been made in the convictions. Because of the knife."

Juan Latapier nodded. "Exactly. The suspects had strong alibis, although the judges disbelieved them. I believe the two deaths are connected, and that the bodies were mutilated to cast blame on the *brujos*. I want to be sure, in my own mind, that these men are guilty before they are executed."

He's principled, thought Ramirez. Which was almost as unusual in the Cuban National Revolutionary Police Force as someone leaving behind a perfectly good knife at a crime scene.

"Interesting. We don't yet know who our victim was," said Ramirez. "I was planning to have one of my men go through missing persons reports. We've had Patrol asking questions door-to-door, but with no results. She was found in an alley near the Callejón sin salida. Because of this, I'm not completely sure how rigorous the inquiries have been. Blind Alley makes some of our officers nervous."

Latapier nodded. "I have never been there, but I have heard it is a place where the spirits gather."

Ramirez glanced at his watch. Juan Latapier's visit was a welcome excuse to ignore his paperwork and do some real police work before he left for Canada the next day.

"Look, I have a car with a full tank of petrol. Why don't we drive over there and see what we can find out?"

Latapier spread his arms wide. He smiled and bowed slightly. "That's why I'm here."

"Excellent," said Ramirez, reaching for his jacket. "But don't be surprised if they refuse to talk to us."

"They won't talk to me," Latapier nodded. "But they may talk to you."

"Excuse me for asking, Juan, but how long have you worked in El Gabriel?" Ramirez put his arms through the sleeves of his jacket. "I usually stop in your station whenever I go by. I don't recall seeing you."

"I've been there for years, but I'm almost always in court."

"I apologize, then. You must be older than you appear."

Latapier laughed. "I used to be heavier, too."

Juan Latapier folded himself into Ramirez's small car. "There was almost no blood on our victim's clothing," Ramirez explained. "Our pathologist says she was already dead when she was stabbed."

"What was she wearing?"

Ramirez used his side-view mirror to check the corpse in the back seat. His rear-view mirror was missing, and it had proven impossible to find a replacement. The old woman waved at him and waggled her fingers.

"A long white dress with ruffles. No sleeves. And a white bandana with a big white fabric flower on it. She looks like a cigar lady." He smiled at her reflection. "Too old to be a bride."

The elderly cigar ladies were famous in Havana. They wore fancy clothing and flowers and carried giant cigars. They were always happy to let tourists take their photographs in exchange for a few pesos.

"Our pathologist says she could have been seventy or eighty; it's hard to say. You know how badly the cigar ladies age. There was something strange, though," said Ramirez, steering his small car down the Avenida del Puerto. "Her head was shaved bald."

"Hmmm," said Latapier. "White is the colour worn by initiates into Santería. They shave their heads so that the *orishas* can enter their bodies more easily."

"An *ahijado?*"

It hadn't occurred to Ramirez, but Latapier could be right. Being initiated required a full week of praying, divining the future with shells, and animal sacrifices.

The most devout believers dressed in white for three months while they dedicated themselves to a particular *orisha*. They acted like antennas whenever their god wished to communicate with mortals. A shaved head was supposed to provide better reception.

Before it merged with Catholicism to become Santería, the Yoruba religion had hundreds of gods. Only a few dozen remained. Even most baptized Cubans wore bead bracelets or necklaces reflecting which one they followed.

Ramirez glanced again at the old lady reflected in his side mirror. She wore three strands of beads around her neck—red, black, and white. Eshu's colours, thought Ramirez. She was brave. Few wore them, for fear of accidentally invoking him. If you stamped your feet three times, it was said he would come. But given Eshu's role as the intermediary between the living and the dead, this could have unpredictable results.

It made Ramirez wonder if the angry old woman had stamped her feet once too often.

FOURTEEN

As she walked back to her office, Celia Jones thought about Hillary Ellis's sudden death. June Kelly was right about one thing: Mike and his wife had some serious marital problems.

Jones had read all the psychiatric and medical reports in Mike's file. She'd relied on one of them to prove his innocence in Cuba: a fertility test that established his blood type.

Mike had been on disability leave from the Rideau Regional Police for months. In June 2006, when he was still in Patrol, he and his partner, Steve Sloan, were dispatched to a "trouble with man" call in a Lowertown walk-up. The two constables were standing at the top of the stairs when the suspect opened his door and slashed Mike in the face. In the scuffle, Sloan's gun discharged, wounding Sloan. He bled to death before the ambulance got there. Despite his serious injuries, Mike shot and killed the suspect. The first policeman on the scene found Mike crying in a pool of blood, cradling Sloan's head in his lap.

Mike was cleared to return to work in November by the departmental shrink, Richard Mann. Post-traumatic stress disorder, the psychiatrist said. No way of knowing if Mike would ever fully recover, but diazepam was supposed to control his panic attacks.

O'Malley promoted Mike to detective and put him in a section where he wasn't likely to deal with armed men. Into a desk job, essentially, in the Child Abuse and Sex Crimes Unit. He'd just started there when he and Hillary decided they needed a vacation.

There were passages in Dr. Mann's report that worried Jones the more she thought about them.

For one thing, Mike was infertile. And yet the Cuban police had found a package of birth control pills in their search of the Havana hotel room where the couple stayed. But according to Dr. Mann's notes, Hillary Ellis had just found out she was pregnant when Mike was wounded. She miscarried the following week.

Whoever got Hillary pregnant, then, it wasn't Mike. That was motive.

There was another red flag, too. A week before they left for Havana, Mike asked Jones to witness their signatures on an amendment to his departmental insurance policy. In addition to the standard million-dollar life insurance coverage, they added a million more. Each was named as the other's primary beneficiary, with Hillary's parents the residuary beneficiaries. Meaning if one of them died, the other got it all.

A little less than three weeks later, Hillary was dead.

Sherlock Holmes once stated that the most repellent man he'd ever known had given money to charity, but the most fetching woman he'd ever met had poisoned three small children for their insurance proceeds.

Mike Ellis was hardly fetching anymore. Not since the "accident," as O'Malley always referred to it. An accident that left Sloan dead and Mike almost unrecognizable. But Mike stood to gain two million dollars in insurance benefits from his unfaithful wife's death. *Tax-free*. It made Jones wonder just how charitable he really was.

FIFTEEN

A stray dog lay curled on the sidewalk, panting in the heat. Inspector Ramirez and Juan Latapier stepped around it; so did the cigar lady.

She accompanied the two detectives until they reached the piled stones and twisted metal that formed the pillars at the entrance to Blind Alley, then halted like a stubborn mule. It made Ramirez feel uneasy that even a ghost didn't want to pass through Blind Alley's gates.

She waved goodbye as they stepped into another world.

The buildings that ran the length of the alley were covered with African murals painted from leftover paint supplies. Frenzied designs, as if the hands of the artist were possessed. A full-size Chango doll balanced on a beam. At least, Ramirez hoped it was a doll.

African death masks glared at them, trapped in the gaps left by missing bricks in crumbling walls. Huge coloured obelisks towered beside palm trees. Colourful shrines were littered with gifts to the different *orishas*: Obatala, the god of peace; Babalu Aye, the god of illnesses; Chango; Oya; Yemayá; Oggun.

Chango was the god of machetes, hammers, and shovels.

Oshun, the goddess of lust and love, was the promiscuous younger sister of Yemayá, mother of fishes. Oggun was responsible for swords, guns, and crucifixes.

Blind Alley was once called Smuggler's Alley in honour of its founder, a man who, like Oggun, had brought weapons into Cuba. But it had been transformed by the *orishas* and their human conduits into a centre for Afro-Cuban drumming and dancing, trances and possession.

The alley held the sacred drums that summoned the gods. To the believers of Santería, it was a portal, a gateway to the other side.

The *babalaos* claimed that the police were kept away by sacrifices they made to Oshosi, the god of traps and spell-casters. Oshosi was also known as Saint Norbert, a Catholic canonized for restoring sight to a blind woman; hence the name Blind Alley.

But most police considered Oshosi their own *orisha*, since he was also the god of courts and prisons. It made for a certain ambiguity that left Ramirez wondering which side Oshosi would favour if he and Latapier ran into problems.

"You say your police are afraid to come here?" asked Latapier, smiling. "That's funny. I feel right at home."

"My men try to stay away from Blind Alley," said Ramirez. "They say arresting people is one thing, engaging in the supernatural another. Personally, I worry more about the *babalaos* than I do about spirits. I'm never quite sure where they get their blood sacrifices. There may be a shortage of animals because of rationing. But there's never a shortage of police."

Ramirez and Latapier joined a crowd of people gathered around a young black woman who danced frantically on the cobblestones as drummers pounded the sacred drums. Her feet looked swollen, but she seemed oblivious to the pain. Her bald head was covered with paint splatters. Her sweat formed coloured trails as it ran down her cheeks.

The sound of the conga drums built in volume and intensity even in the few minutes that Ramirez and Latapier were there. Women chanted in Yoruba; they swayed and clapped to the beat. The young woman began to scream, whirling and spinning in her white dress as a *babalao* watched. The hairs on Ramirez's arms stood on end, despite the heat.

"It seems unusual, to have an initiation during the week," said Latapier quietly. "I thought the *nangale*, the purification ceremony, was conducted on Sundays."

"Maybe everything is skewed because of the holidays."

They skirted the crowd to get to an art gallery built so deep underground it was almost completely buried. The stone stairs curved as if bent by the hands of giants.

Once inside, it was damp and cool. Ramirez took a deep breath, gratefully filling his lungs. The shrieking above them was muted by the thick walls. Even so the drums filled the space like a pulse, as if the earth had a heartbeat.

Ramirez looked around. The gallery smelled like a *botánica*, a shop that supplied herbs for Santería rituals. Dozens of paintings hung on its walls. An Afro-Cuban man piled books into stacks for sale, seemingly oblivious to the ceremonies taking place above ground.

"Excuse me, we need your help," Ramirez said to the man and showed him his badge. "My name is Inspector Ramirez." He turned to introduce Latapier, but the detective had walked away and was examining a painting on the wall.

"Of course," the man said. "My name is Carlos Neruda. What can I do for you?"

"The body of a woman was found not far from here early on New Year's Day. An elderly woman. Afro-Cuban. She was

dressed completely in white. I'm hoping you might know who
she was."

"Why would you think that has something to do with me?"
Neruda asked, looking nervously around the gallery.

"We assume she came from around here. And that she may
have been an initiate."

"We, meaning who?" said the man.

"The Major Crimes Unit. I'm the inspector in charge of the
section that deals with homicides. And this woman's death was
no accident, believe me."

"How did she die?"

"She was stabbed through the heart."

Ramirez gave him only part of the truth. The exact cause of
death was still unknown, but in a police investigation, it was
always useful to hold something back that only the killer could
know. He made no mention of the fish knife. "The murder may
be linked to that of two children. In one case, the victim's heart
was cut right out of her body."

Carlos Neruda visibly flinched. "We practice Santería here.
Not *brujería*."

The noises above suddenly stopped. The silence was almost
more startling than the drumming and screams had been.

"No one has accused you of witchcraft," said Ramirez.

"You seek answers in the wrong place. A *bruja* would never be
accepted into our initiations. We do not believe in black magic."

The dark man's eyes flicked to a painting on the wall, the one
Latapier was scrutinizing.

"Look here," Latapier said to Ramirez, calling him over.

The inspector joined him. The painting was formed from
splashes and dribbles of white, black, and red paint. The paint
looked as if it had been thrown wildly on the canvas. And yet the
image was immediately recognizable once one's eyes adjusted to

the artist's technique. As Ramirez examined it, a woman's body emerged, almost as clear as a photograph.

The portrait had incredible energy. An elderly black woman was garbed in white, her head flung back. Her body was twisted and contorted as she danced in front of the drums. There was no doubt in Ramirez's mind: it was the woman who waited outside the gates.

Ramirez pointed to the painting. "Was this woman initiated into Santería here, in Blind Alley?" he asked the gallery owner.

The man shifted his weight from foot to foot. He avoided Ramirez's eyes. "I have sworn an oath to the gods to keep our ceremonies secret."

"The name of the artist, Señor Neruda. Or I will arrest you for obstruction. I would not wish to see you in a situation where you had to rely on the gods to protect you in jail."

His bluff had the desired effect.

Latapier and Ramirez walked back up the narrow stone steps. The drummers were gone. There was no sign of the initiate. The singers had melted away into the crowd. *Turistas* sat at the outside bar, holding watery, overpriced drinks as they were hustled for money and soap by *jineteros*.

"This is good, Juan," said Ramirez. "We have our first solid lead." They had the artist's name: Luis Martez. And Martez's address.

"She was just an old woman, Inspector Ramirez. I didn't know her," Luis Martez said. He lived about fifteen minutes from the Callejón, on the top floor of a building that was falling down. The one-room studio was full of stacked canvasses, a small metal bed, a television, a wash basin, but little else. None of his other canvasses displayed the same frenetic strokes used in the painting in the gallery.

"When did you paint that portrait of her?"

"She was at a *rhumba* in Blind Alley in December. Around three weeks ago. She danced with fury, as if she were decades younger. She was screaming the whole time that Oya had taken over her body. I wanted to see if I could paint a woman who claimed to be possessed. It was as if Oya grabbed the brushes from my hand. I found myself throwing paint at the canvas, wildly, almost out of control. The face of the old woman formed on the canvas almost by itself, then her body. Let me tell you, it was a powerful experience."

Ramirez raised his eyebrows. "You said she 'claimed' she was possessed. You didn't believe her?"

"I paint; I try not to judge. I admit, at first I wasn't sure she was really possessed or making it up. But when she finished dancing, I couldn't help but notice there were *veves* on the stones beneath her feet."

The Santería believed that after possessing a human body, the *orishas* left symbolic paintings behind. *Veves* were portents of the future, tokens of thanks to the drummers for their skills. Ramirez was skeptical, having stopped more than one *babalao* at night with a small jar of paint concealed beneath his clothing.

"It looked like a heart with a knife through it. It could have been a blob of red paint. I may have interpreted it artistically, fair enough. But then, the gods are not renowned for their artistic talents, are they? It's difficult to manage a brush using someone else's hands."

"Did you know her name?"

"I heard someone in the crowd call out to Mamita Angela. That's all I know. The painting is a good one, don't you think? I thought it captured the spirit of the old woman perfectly. But I couldn't keep it in the apartment."

"Because?" asked Ramirez.

The artist shrugged. "In case I had captured Oya as well."

Ramirez's cell phone rang as they walked back to his car. It was Detective Espinoza.

"Listen, Inspector, I made some calls. One of the policemen who works on the Malecón investigated an old woman a few weeks ago. She fits the description of our victim. He received a complaint that she might be engaged in animal sacrifice; she was trying to find a live chicken. The police officer who responded couldn't find any evidence to support a charge of animal cruelty."

That surprised Ramirez. Animal cruelty could mean anything in this country. Eating pork without a ration card was sufficient for an arrest. "And the woman's name, Fernando?"

"Angela Aranas. I have an address for you, too."

Ramirez wrote it down. It wasn't far from where they were.

"Excellent work. We'll check it out before we head back to the station. I have a visiting detective with me, from the station in El Gabriel." He clicked off his phone. "Luis Martez was right," he said to Latapier. "Her name *was* Angela. Her last name was Aranas."

"That's funny," said Latapier. "My wife and I have picked out that name, Angela, if we have a girl. The baby's due in a few months. And Aranas is my wife's family name as well, so my daughter will keep it. My wife is Basque."

"Well, it's a lovely name, Angela," said Ramirez. "Congratulations. Your first?"

"Yes," the dark man smiled. "My wife is finding it difficult, what with all the food cravings. They're so strong, her mother is convinced we will have a son."

"I can imagine," Ramirez grinned. "I think we all have food cravings. I go to sleep some nights dreaming of chickens."

Ramirez's stomach growled. He realized he hadn't eaten all

day. "We can stop at a vendor's on the way back. Maybe grab a *tortas de lechón*. Although these days, a pork sandwich is all squeal, no pig."

"I should get back to El Gabriel soon. But I appreciate the offer. I'm just not that hungry."

"You must be the only Cuban who isn't," Ramirez smiled. "Do you have time to check out this address with me?"

"I'm happy to, Inspector. But then I really do have to leave."

Ramirez nodded. He started up his car, feeling beads of sweat trickle down the back of his shirt. He envied Latapier, who seemed unaffected by the heat.

"Perhaps the killer believed the old woman cursed him and murdered her to stop his bad luck," Ramirez mused aloud. "He may have believed she was engaged in such matters, if that was the rumour around here. Particularly if the police believed it themselves."

"You don't believe in witchcraft, Inspector?"

"No," said Ramirez. He thought the *houngans* were charlatans. "You?"

"I used to. The problem in a small place like El Gabriel is that many still do. And sometimes what people fear is more important to them than the truth. After Zoila's murder, even innocent activities by the *santeros*, like dancing, took on sinister connotations. Before long, everyone, including the judges, reacted to their superstitions instead of looking at the facts."

"Facts don't lie," Ramirez said.

He tried to think back to what his grandmother had told him about *brujería*.

"The *brujos*, they make dolls, little man. They put a person's hair in them, or a piece of their clothing, parts of their fingernails. Maybe a tooth. They turn into bats or birds, sometimes cats. They can put poison in someone's food or hide charms in their room and no one knows what they do, no one sees them. You be careful if there's a cat in the bedroom, Ricky. You watch out. And don't you never kill a bat, you. You kill something without knowing what you do, you end up destroying not just that but yourself. Bad things, they come around."

"I studied *brujería* when I took criminology at the University of Havana," said Ramirez. "There was a textbook we had to read. By Fernando Ortiz, the famous academic. He said the *brujos* weren't dangerous at all, that it became part of a race struggle between Africans and other Cubans."

"Fernando Ortiz? I didn't know he was a professor. He's been in the courtroom every day, listening to our arguments, making notes. He told me during a recess that the judges were biased, that the prosecution had exaggerated the evidence against the *brujos*."

"Ortiz? It must be someone else. Fernando Ortiz has been dead for decades. Castro read his book when he was a law student; that's why we have laws against racism. But it's an interesting point you raise. Someone may well have staked that old woman through the heart if they thought she was involved in black magic."

Although if she was, thought Ramirez, that was a dangerous thing to do.

"It could have been a *curandero* who did this," said Latapier.

A *curandero* was a witch-hunter, supposedly able to remove a curse for a price.

Yes, it could have been a *curandero*, thought Ramirez. One who offered to use his supernatural powers to rid someone of a curse and then concluded that plunging a fish knife through someone's heart was a more efficient way of removing the problem. But that wouldn't explain the deaths of the two little girls.

"What is the name of the man who was convicted of Zoila's murder, Juan? The man whose appeal will be heard this week?"

"Domingo Bocourt was the principal suspect. He was charged

with two others. What bothers me is that the only information implicating him and his friends came from the local mayor. He started to blame Bocourt before the police investigation was even completed. That makes me suspicious. I think he knows who killed these girls and is lying to protect them."

Ramirez was impressed. It was easy to convict the guilty. Convicting the innocent was far more difficult.

The door to the old woman's apartment creaked open as soon as they knocked on it. The frame had rotted through. Dozens of cloth dolls stared at the two detectives. They were stacked on the narrow bed, the wooden chairs, the small kitchen table.

Angela Aranas had collected ceramic saints and statues of Yemayá, the black Virgin Mary; they were scattered everywhere. Seashells littered the dusty plank floor.

A large black doll resembling Chango slumped in a corner. It had multiple strands of red and white beads around its neck.

"See here? Shells. She either believed in divination," said Latapier, pointing to the floor, "or someone else predicted her future."

"It would have been a very short session," said Ramirez.

Latapier sat down on one of the wooden chairs.

"Do you believe in Santería, Inspector?"

"As much as I believe in any religion. Why do you ask?"

"A true believer would never leave Chango lying on the floor. The Santería believe that Chango will kill you if you disrespect him."

Ramirez doubted that Chango had the time to take out his rage over such minor infractions. But then again, petty crime was the lifeblood of the Cuban justice system.

"Then maybe Chango killed her," said Ramirez.

He walked over to the table and picked up one of the dolls.

It was small and handmade, with a smiling, happy face and carefully stitched clothes. The others were the same, crafted from scraps of fabric. Only the Chango doll sported the angry face of the warrior.

"These aren't voodoo dolls," said Ramirez. "They're toys. Perhaps she intended to donate them to a school. Or to a government daycare."

"Or perhaps," Latapier said, entering the kitchen area, "she was planning to send them to an orphanage. Look." He pointed to a piece of brown paper tacked to the wall.

It was a drawing of children playing in a yard. A little girl smiled from a wheelchair. Another leaned on crutches. At the bottom, an inscription: "El orfanato, Viñales." A child's drawing, the caption added by an adult.

"You could be right," Ramirez said. He walked back into the living space, far too small to be considered a separate room, and looked more closely at the shells lying on the floor. "A Santería initiate would never treat objects like this with such disrespect."

Latapier thought for a minute. "Suppose Señora Aranas wasn't involved in Santería, then. What if someone killed her and tried to make it appear that she was? Shaved her head and dressed her in white clothes after she was dead. They could have thrown the Chango doll and the shells into her apartment. That would explain the lack of blood on her clothing and the general disarray here."

"But why would someone want to make us think she was involved in the black arts?"

"To lead the investigation down a false trail. That has to be it," Latapier said, frowning. "Why else stab a knife into someone who's already dead? They must have done that to hide the true cause of death. Does your pathologist know what killed the victim?"

"No," said Ramirez. "But he's working on it. I agree with you, Juan, that things may not be all they appear. I'm leaving the country tomorrow for a few days. I'll assign this file to one of my detectives, Fernando Espinoza. He can start questioning her neighbours, and see if the orphanage in Viñales has any more information. Where can he reach you if he finds out anything related to your file?"

"I could be difficult to find, what with court, but I have to come back to Havana on Saturday morning to pick up a relative."

"Good. I'll be back by then. Why don't you track me down then."

Ramirez called the switchboard and asked to be patched through to Detective Espinoza.

"We're at Señora Aranas's address, Fernando. Have a patrol car bring you over. You'll need to secure the scene until Dr. Apiro's team arrives. Bring something to nail the door shut when they're done. And some yellow tape, if you can find any."

They waited in Ramirez's car, the doors open to ease the stifling heat, until a patrol car pulled up in front of the building, discharging the young detective. Ramirez got out to give him instructions. Then he drove the El Gabriel detective back to headquarters and said goodbye.

He looked at his watch. It was almost 7 P.M. No wonder he was hungry.

As he drove home, Ramirez wondered if his instincts were right. Could a child's drawing hold the key to three brutal murders?

SIXTEEN

Mike Ellis jumped when the alarm rang. He pulled a pillow over his head and groaned. He pounded the top of the clock radio to make it stop, but the noise continued. He finally realized it was someone persistently ringing the front doorbell.

What the hell? He looked at the time. Almost noon. Drunk, he'd slept in again.

So much for his plans to join Alcoholics Anonymous. He hadn't been sober since O'Malley showed up on his doorstep. He thought about ignoring his visitor, but whoever it was wasn't going away.

Ellis staggered to his feet and wrapped a bath towel around his waist. He opened the front door a few inches, trying to keep the frigid air outside. He blinked back the bright glare from an overnight snowfall.

A woman with a stiff helmet of blonde hair stood on his front step, a man behind her. She stepped forward, firmly pressing the palm of her hand against the door to keep him from slamming it in her face.

"Yes?" he asked, irritated. It was too fucking cold to have

Jehovah's Witnesses at the door. He thought about dropping the towel, wondered if that would make them go away.

"Detective Ellis? I have a few questions for you. My name is Jennifer White. Can I come in, please? It's freezing out here."

Ellis looked up and down the street. There was a white media van parked in front of his house. Several cars idled nearby. A man lifted a large camera onto his shoulder and began filming. Car doors quickly opened and shut.

"Look, there he is."

A gaggle of reporters jumped over the glittering snowbanks, calling out questions.

"Detective Ellis, how did you do it?"

"What do you have to say about your mother-in-law's accusations?"

"Why did you poison your wife?"

"Any comment on today's story?"

"Oh my God, look at his face."

Ellis grabbed the rolled-up newspaper on the front step and slammed the door, hard. He pulled the living room drapes tightly closed.

The light on his answering machine blinked with at least a dozen messages. He hadn't even heard the phone ring, he'd been so drunk. He skipped through them. Requests for interviews. CBC. CTV. Global.

The story was in the City News section. "Distraught Mother Claims Daughter Poisoned by Detective Husband." At first he thought it said "Defective Husband." He had to read the story a few times before the full import of the allegations hit him.

Shit, shit, shit.

There was a picture of him and Hillary on their wedding day. Hillary in white, model-thin, barely recovered from her anorexia. Mike smiling, pretending to be happy, his face the way it was before the shooting.

Damn June. He skimmed through the story, trying to focus, desperately trying to sober up. He stumbled into the kitchen and downed a glass of tap water and a couple of Aspirins.

His telephone rang again. He let the answering machine pick up and was about to disconnect the line when he heard who it was.

Ellis snatched up the phone. "I have a bunch of reporters standing on my doorstep, Celia. And a television van parked across the street. Do you know what the hell is going on?"

"Oh, shit, Mike. I was calling to give you a heads-up. Your mother-in-law was here yesterday making crazy allegations. We had no idea she'd go running to the press. O'Malley was in my office a few minutes ago. He's absolutely furious they'd report this bullshit. Those were his exact words."

"I never laid a hand on Hillary," said Ellis. Which was almost completely true.

"I know. Listen, O'Malley's going to send a patrol car over to keep the media away from your door. We can't make them go away altogether—freedom of the press and all that. But leave this to us to deal with, okay? And stay calm. O'Malley doesn't believe a word of it. Even the story in the paper is sympathetic to you, if you read it carefully. The reporter describes June as completely overwrought. They're treading a fine line between reporting and defamation, and they know it. But at least they didn't put the story on the front page. That means they probably don't believe it themselves."

"Then why report this crap at all?" said Ellis. He threw the paper in the garbage bin.

"That's what news is like these days, Mike. Anything to sell papers. They'll print a retraction eventually, I'm sure. It just won't be on the front page."

"A fat lot of good that will do."

"I agree. But there's nothing we can do: the story's out. Mike, why is your mother-in-law doing this to you?"

"I don't know," Ellis said. He thought of the joke about the guy who made a Freudian slip at a dinner with his in-laws. Instead of saying "pass the salt," he said, "you've ruined my fucking life."

Ellis sighed. "Stressed out, I guess. They've had a hard couple of years. A new Superstore opened just down the road from their drugstore. It has a pharmacy. That took away a lot of their business. They're in their seventies, and they're about to lose everything. And June's always been a bit of a drama queen. Hillary told me a few things about her childhood. If it wasn't for Walter, I don't know what she would have done. A super nice guy, but you know the type. Browbeaten. Mild-mannered. Wouldn't hurt a fly."

Hillary described her mother, on the other hand, as a woman who once stood on the gravel driveway and threw rocks at her young daughter's back when she tried to walk away from an argument.

"Oh, you're charming enough," she told Hillary repeatedly, forcing her to sit in the kitchen while she ranted, "but no one will ever really love you. With your looks, men will just use you and throw you away. That's what men are like. Even your father will say one thing and do something else. Men lie all the time, understand? All of them. And you're just like your father. Two peas in a pod."

Hillary was eleven years old.

"I used to plot ways to kill her," Hillary had confided in her husband. "I even thought of using rat poison. They always kept glass bottles full of it below the kitchen sink. But I was smart enough to know I'd get caught. I left home when I was fifteen. I wasn't going to let my mother destroy the rest of my life, too."

Ellis had felt sorry for his wife; so conflicted with guilt. Children were supposed to love their parents, but how was a daughter supposed to react when her own mother hated her?

He'd never really understood the reconciliation that took place a month or two before they left for Cuba. But with her daughter dead, June Kelly had apparently decided to hate him instead. What did the psychologists call it—transference?

"Well, she was over here, haranguing O'Malley," said Jones. "He thinks it's because she can't accept what happened without wanting to blame someone. But you weren't even in the country, for God's sake. Trust me, the media won't follow this for long. There's always other news to grab their attention. I was with you in Cuba, remember? Everything's going to be okay. I know you didn't do anything wrong."

But Mike Ellis heard something in her voice. Celia Jones wasn't quite as sure as she wanted to sound.

SEVENTEEN

The abrupt sound of the telephone diverted Charlie Pike's attention from the old man shooting up in the alley. He picked up the receiver. Miles O'Malley's voice boomed on the end of the line. Pike sat up a little straighter.

"Charlie, my boy. We have a bit of a situation," O'Malley said, never one to waste words.

O'Malley still spoke with a heavy Irish accent, although he had been in Canada for over thirty years. He started as a foot soldier, as he described it, in the tough streets of Winnipeg back in the days when all cops walked a beat. O'Malley fought his way up the ranks at a time when the Irish were considered stupid, illiterate, and drunk. We've always had that in common, thought Pike. Pike's scarred knuckles, like O'Malley's, showed just how hard it was to break certain stereotypes.

Pike could almost see O'Malley frowning, his big black eyebrows knitted together, rubbing his fingers over his smooth scalp. O'Malley had shaved his head bald, long before it was popular, to see how people would respond. He decided to keep it that way when they kept staring. It made him feel vulnerable, he said. Gave him nothing to hide behind. And for some reason, O'Malley thought that was good.

Pike waited for the chief to explain the reason behind his call. He looked out the window. The old man was curled into a fetal position, oblivious to the cold. Soon, he would begin coming down. The shakes would start, the nausea, confusion. Then the overwhelming urge to do it again.

"Have you read today's paper? There's a story about Michael Ellis."

"Yeah, I saw it." Pike had the Ottawa daily folded on his desk. He didn't believe the allegations for a moment. By the end of the piece, even the reporter seemed to recognize that June Kelly was a troublemaker. The story was full of disclaimers, half-truths. But the newspaper had printed the story anyway. Mike would have a lot of sympathy in the department. That reporter better hope she didn't run any red lights.

"Poor man was trapped inside his house all this morning by the bloody media. I've sent a patrol car over to keep the reporters a good distance away. This is the last thing he needs while he's trying to cope with his wife's death. That lad has been a shit magnet for months."

"Do you want me to get him out of there?"

Tobacco, booze: Charlie Pike had been raised by some of the best smugglers in the world. Except as far as Pike was concerned, they weren't breaking any laws. When it came to First Nations, the federal and provincial governments were like two fleas fighting over who owned the dog.

"No, Charlie," O'Malley laughed. "But I want to keep an eye on things. We have that Cuban policeman arriving in Ottawa tonight. I'd like you to meet him at the airport and make sure he doesn't get ambushed by the press. They'll be wanting to ask him about the Callendes charges. We want to make sure the good inspector doesn't accidentally say something to feed the sharks."

O'Malley explained the charges Ellis had faced in Cuba. Of all his detectives, he knew Pike could be counted on to be discreet. "Poor Michael. He's been to hell and back."

"How would the reporters ever know he was in a Cuban jail?"

The old man outside rolled on his back and spread his arms on the ground like a snow angel. Pike moved away from the window. The old man was entitled to some privacy as he fell back to earth.

"They won't. But they'll be after Ramirez when he arrives, because of that priest, and it might slip out if they ask him why he's here. I want to be on the safe side. Michael may be on compassionate leave, but he's still one of my men. If the press finds out he was accused of murdering a Cuban child, this will be the top story in every newspaper and television station across the country. It won't matter that he was never charged. His life will be destroyed."

O'Malley was still politically incorrect enough to refer to his officers as men even though at least thirty percent of them were women. But O'Malley was essentially indifferent to race and gender. He often joked he couldn't discriminate even if he wanted to, because everything he saw was grey; he was literally colour-blind.

The media didn't see things quite the same way. Charlie Pike's first encounter with them was in 2003, when he was promoted from Patrol to Drug Squad. He was one of the first aboriginal detectives in all of Canada. It was something he occasionally felt proud of, despite his general ambivalence towards most Canadian institutions.

O'Malley had recommended against giving the interview. "I won't tell you what to do, lad, but those bloody people rarely have good news on their minds."

But Pike believed he could be a role model for First Nations youth, who felt alienated from the police and were all too frequently harassed by them. It was one of the two reasons he'd joined the force. The other was O'Malley.

He sat in the downtown television studio in his new suit and freshly cut hair, hoping to make a good impression. The host started by welcoming him to the morning show and then asking him how he felt about working on the Drug Squad when so many drug users were aboriginal.

"It's so widespread, Detective Pike. Are our aboriginal people predisposed to alcoholism and drug abuse?" the big-haired woman asked, managing to combine racism and paternalism in a single sentence.

"Are you suggesting I'm an alcoholic?" Pike said quietly.

He hadn't touched alcohol in years. He felt his chest tighten, the way it did in the woods when he sighted a moose. I'm not one of your aboriginal people, he thought. You don't own me.

"No, of course not *you*, Detective," the woman said. She leaned back, folding her arms, a smile plastered on her face. This interview wasn't going quite as she'd planned. "But don't your people typically have trouble with drugs and alcohol?"

"My people used to have trouble *getting* alcohol," Pike answered. "It was against your laws, for a long time, for my people to have a drink in their own homes without being arrested. Just thinking about having a beer was enough to put an Indian in jail."

O'Malley said that at first he roared with laughter as he watched the woman squirm. But he'd laughed only briefly. And after that, when Pike continued speaking, he cried.

"But, yes, there are quite a few aboriginal people who struggle with addictions. Not surprising, when you know how many of them were little children when they were dragged away from their families and put in residential schools hundreds of miles away from everything they knew.

"I've heard the elders' stories, the few times they'll talk about it. How they were beaten with pitchforks and fan belts and coat hangers if they tried to speak their own language, or visit with their brothers and sisters, or because they wanted to play. The religious people in charge of those schools thought it was okay to rape and beat little children, so long as no one found out. So, yes, I guess some of us do have problems with drugs and alcohol. I think of that every time I see an Anishnabe woman selling herself on a corner for a few dollars so she can get enough drugs to forget what happened to her. Someone came up with the idea of residential schools as a way to 'civilize' us. They wanted to take the Indian right out of us. But it wasn't one of *my* people."

The woman blanched.

Pike had nothing more to say. That was a long speech for him, despite his mother's Mohawk heritage. He wiped the television makeup off his face with the back of his jacket sleeve and walked out of the studio.

After that, Pike had nothing to do with reporters. Except to make sure they stayed out of his way.

"Sure, Chief. Does he speak English?"

"Fluently. You'll have to identify yourself to him, though. He won't be expecting you."

Or anyone remotely like me, thought Charlie Pike as he hung up. But then, neither would the reporters.

Pike pulled his mouth into something close to a smile. If they bothered him this time, he had his gun.

He looked out the window at the old man again and walked downstairs to buy some soup.

EIGHTEEN

A morning spent on paperwork; the afternoon lost to meetings. Inspector Ramirez looked at his watch. He had only a few hours before his flight. He hoped to find a warm coat in the airport lost-and-found, or, more accurately, the stolen-and-expropriated. His bag was packed with his few belongings, but he still needed supplies.

He walked down the hallway and nodded to the pretty clerk who sat at a desk outside the exhibit room. Rita Martinez was a young woman who favoured short skirts and low necklines.

He let himself into the exhibit room and pulled the heavy door tightly closed. The storage room was lined with rows of battered metal shelves, each piled high with numbered boxes. Since so many ordinary activities had been criminalized, the dusty containers held all manner of exhibits, from stuffed toys to machine guns. But like the garbage dump at the city's edge, the room's contents had been well picked over. Members of the Cuban National Revolutionary Police Force were highly skilled at recycling.

He kept digging until he found the box he wanted, one with the exhibits from the Michael Ellis investigation. He removed a plastic envelope full of Polaroid photographs and put it in his jacket pocket. He also retrieved a digital camera that belonged to a foreigner who had snapped a picture of Señor Ellis with Arturo Montenegro before the little boy was murdered.

Candice Olefson lived in Ottawa; Ramirez planned to return it. Given the dire shortage of cameras, he had briefly considered keeping it, but there was no point. He had no memory cards and they weren't easy to find. Besides, Celia Jones had promised Olefson the camera would be given back to her.

He returned the box to the shelf and signed the appropriate forms to indicate these items were in his possession.

He could not fail to notice, as he rifled through adjacent exhibit boxes, how many held empty plastic envelopes that should have contained money. Euros, German marks, Chinese yen, British pounds, Canadian dollars, all gone.

He was looking for one box in particular. It contained exhibits from an illegal rum smuggling operation that he and Sanchez had put a stop to. An investigation that continued to provide Ramirez, not to mention the Minister of the Interior, with a reliable source of well-aged rum. Of the twenty-four crates initially seized, only six remained.

Ramirez finally found the file he was looking for. He retrieved a plastic envelope that contained American dollars. The currency was worthless in Cuba: illegal to use, possess, or exchange. That was the only reason the money was still in the exhibit room and not in some *policía*'s pocket. But in Canada, the bills could be of value. If Ramirez didn't help himself to them, someone else would, as soon as Castro legalized the currency again. He opened the envelope and rubbed the crisp, green bills between his fingers.

"Give me a ten dollars bill green american," Castro wrote to President Franklin D. Roosevelt when he was fourteen years old. "I have not seen a ten dollars bill green american and I would like to have one of them. Thank you very much. Your friend, Fidel Castro."

When the currency had been legal in Cuba, ten American dollars was the difference between children who had milk to strengthen their bones and those who didn't. In Ramirez's family, only Estella was entitled to milk rations. When she turned seven, she'd be too old.

Ramirez's monthly salary of twenty-five pesos, generous by Cuban standards, was barely enough to cover his family's basic needs. And Francesca was right, his parents were getting older.

His mother was Cuban by marriage only. Once his father died, she might not receive any government support. It worried Ramirez. He needed a raise but knew that getting one was as unlikely as Castro calling a democratic election.

Ramirez looked at the American bills, imagining what he could buy with them in Canada. He ran his fingers over the face of the dead president. The dead cigar lady watched him intently from the shadows.

"What do you think?" he whispered. "Did you ever want something for someone else so badly that you were willing to risk your own future?"

She pointed to her throat and shrugged.

"Look," said Ramirez, frustrated at their inability to communicate. "We take other things from the exhibit room already. Like rum. And money buys rum. What's the difference?"

Flawed reasoning, Apiro would say. Faulty logic. Like the child who kills his parents and claims to be an orphan. Or the murderer who argues that he didn't kill, it was his gun.

He waited for the old woman to wag a finger at him, to silently scold him for even considering it. Instead, she looked at him the way his mother used to when he was a small boy weighing the risks of misbehaviour.

"Yes, I know there may be consequences," he acknowledged. "But surely moderation can be taken to extremes."

Ramirez pocketed the money. He slipped the clear plastic envelope back in the file and returned the box to its original location. It wasn't a large amount, but he felt like Judas; he'd sold his principles for a few pieces of silver.

He let himself and the dead woman back into the corridor and re-entered the usual late-afternoon bustle of the police station. He walked by the luscious Rita Martinez again without even noticing her new breasts.

No one had seen him slide down the ethical cliff except a ghost who might not be real. But Ramirez had crossed a moral line, and he knew it. The inspector and his apparition walked sadly into the light.

NINETEEN

Officer Fernando Espinoza—no, wait, that was *Detective* Espinoza now—was on his first week in the Major Crimes Unit. Espinoza was hardly able to believe his good fortune. Just by doing his job on foot patrol and helping to identify a murdered child, he had received a big promotion. And here he was, barely twenty-one years old, already a detective. Working at a much better-paying position—almost fifteen pesos a month.

As he walked to the front door of police headquarters, he saw Apiro deep in conversation with a woman on the sidewalk. And not just any woman. She was almost six feet in her high heels. Thick, streaked-blonde hair, a low-cut blue top, tight skirt. Her voice was husky, as deep and rich as molasses.

Was she Cuban or foreign? Espinoza wasn't sure.

"*Hola*, Dr. Apiro," he called. "Excuse me for bothering you, but I wondered if I might have a minute of your time."

"Of course, Detective. Maria, this is Detective Fernando Espinoza. He was recently promoted to Major Crimes. Detective Espinoza, this is Maria Vasquez."

Maria, Espinoza guessed, despite her name, was no virgin.

Besides, the surname Vasquez came from the Basque country, and everyone knew that Basque women were feminists.

Espinoza stood on the balls of his feet, trying to look a little taller. He liked strong women.

"I'll leave you two men alone to talk business," said Maria.

Espinoza was quite surprised when she leaned down and kissed the pathologist on the cheek before she walked languidly away. He wondered if she was the doctor's cousin, or maybe a neighbour.

"Forgive me for interrupting your conversation, Dr. Apiro," Espinoza said. "I wondered—do you have any idea yet what killed that old woman in the alley? I will be handling the investigation in Inspector Ramirez's absence."

"No, not yet," said Apiro, as he pulled his thoughts from one woman to another. "It looks as if she died of a heart attack, but the damage from the knife wound and the degree of decomposition are making it difficult to know what might have caused it. I'm still running tests."

"I know how busy you are," said Espinoza. Both men watched Maria's hips swivel as she moved fluidly away from them through the crowds of tourists. "Forgive me for asking, but is Maria married? She's very beautiful."

"That she is." Apiro shook his head, smiling wistfully. "And no, she's not."

Apiro didn't volunteer any other information about his mysterious friend, and Espinoza didn't ask. But as he opened the heavy front door to the police station, allowing the pathologist to enter before him, Espinoza wondered why the little doctor sounded so sad.

Detective Espinoza sat on a wooden swivel chair in his new office. Well, not quite an office, but the desk Inspector Ramirez had assigned to him for his first murder investigation.

It was better than the corner of the Malecón for which he had previously been responsible. There, he had been required to stand in his cheap black shoes on the hard, cracked concrete throughout his entire shift. At least in Major Crimes he could sit down.

"Stabbed through the heart *after* she was dead? Do you think she was a zombie?" Espinoza had asked Ramirez.

Espinoza believed in zombies. In fact, many Cubans believed that Fidel Castro, hovering between life and death for almost a year since his botched surgery, had become one.

"I don't know what she was," Ramirez laughed. "I only know that someone killed her. But try to find out if she had any family, Fernando, will you? That may help us track down her killer."

It was late at night, but Espinoza sat at his desk, idly flipping through the stack of papers. He was working his way through hundreds of missing persons reports. He hoped to impress Ramirez when the inspector returned from Canada by telling him he had found the victim's relatives. And maybe her killer as well.

The manager of the building where Señora Aranas had lived had been of little assistance. She had a son, he said. But he hadn't seen the man in years.

As he thumbed through the pages, Espinoza held back a yawn. So many people had gone missing from such a small island. But then, with all the people trying to escape on rafts made of rubber tires, it was hard to keep track of the Cuban population. It would be almost more productive to have missing tire reports.

A young woman walked past his desk. He watched her turn the corner towards the exhibit room, admiring her legs. She was very pretty, and around Espinoza's age. Civilian clothes, her dress cut just low enough to catch his interest. She must be a clerk, he thought. A *mangito*, that one. Those breasts, *carumba*. He let out a low whistle and hissed in appreciation. The detectives sitting at their desks beside him grinned.

When she came back towards his desk, Espinoza called out, "Hey, *linda*," using the slang for "beautiful." "I'm off at midnight. You want to have a drink somewhere?"

"With you?"

"You see someone else here?" He held his arms out, palms up, and looked around as if he were the only officer working late.

She shrugged, but a smile tugged the corner of her mouth. "I'm working night shift, *consorte*. And when I get off work, I have other plans. You think I don't have a boyfriend waiting?"

I have plans for you too, thought Espinoza, eyeing her appreciatively. A *cuarto* somewhere, if he was lucky enough to find an empty room in one of the few hotels that Cubans could rent. A little *hoja* later on, if she felt like fooling around. If not tonight, well, maybe soon. But no sex at his apartment: he still lived with his parents. And probably would for years, despite the big pay increase.

"Maybe so, sweetheart," he smiled. "But you won't have any more boyfriends after you go out with me, I promise. Come on, one drink. You don't want to spend the rest of your life wondering what you missed, do you?"

Neither of them could legally enter a Havana nightclub, not even Espinoza, unless he was on duty. Those were for the *turistas*, who flooded the streets at night looking for echoes of Hemingway. But a nice bottle of rum and the cool breeze along the Malecón had started more than a few romances on a hot Havana night.

"Join the *cola*," she said, teasing. "I'll think about it." She tossed her thick brown hair, and he knew right then that he liked her.

"Hey, you," he said as she walked away, swaying her hips. "I don't even know your name."

"Rita," she said. "Rita Martinez, Detective Espinoza."

She already knew who he was. This is very good, thought Espinoza, leaning back in his chair. Very, very good.

"*Cuidate*, Rita Martinez." You take care. "I'll see you later."

TWENTY

Ricardo Ramirez was colder than he believed possible. The pilot had apologized; there was a problem connecting the passenger boarding bridge to the terminal building of the Ottawa International Airport. Passengers needed to step outside to walk the short distance from the plane.

Ramirez stumbled forward across the tarmac on cramped geisha feet. He grasped the front of his black wool overcoat, trying to keep it closed where it lacked buttons. But this cold knew no boundaries. In just a few minutes, he was shivering uncontrollably. He had been unable to find gloves, and his fingers stung.

Ramirez could actually feel the frozen soles of his light leather shoes slapping the ground. His first impression of North America was one of acute discomfort.

Minus twenty-five degrees Celsius, the pilot had said. Fifty degrees' difference between Ottawa and Havana. Nothing could have prepared Ramirez for that.

The bitter cold slapped his face like the back of a hand. It was crisp, clean, invisible. But menacing, like the ocean. Air and water. He had never thought of them as similar in kind. He had not realized, until this minute, that air could be deadly too.

Ramirez blew on his rapidly swelling fingers. Somehow, he managed to pull open the heavy glass door to the terminal building. Following the other passengers, he limped up the stairs and down carpeted hallways, past large murals of tulips and the Canadian Parliament Buildings.

He identified himself at the foreign arrivals section as a Cuban police officer, in Ottawa to assist with an investigation.

In the warmth of the terminal, his fingers and feet began to thaw with a thousand tiny pinpricks. He stamped his feet, trying to get his circulation flowing. He was surprised at how much his extremities hurt, as if stung by angry bees. He hoped his limbs would soon start working properly again. It was as if his body had been appropriated by an *orisha* at a *tambour*; it had the clumsy, lurching movements of the possessed. *Padrons*, Cubans called them derisively. Those who danced badly.

Ramirez was surprised when the Customs officer, not much more than a teenager, asked only how long he would be in the country. At home, it took hours to go through Customs, to have every bag checked for illegal substances, for weapons, for propaganda. Here, he was cleared in minutes.

The Customs officer flipped through the pages of Ramirez's passport and thumped on one of them with a rubber stamp. "Have a nice visit," he said, handing it back with a broad smile. "Welcome to Canada. Have a good New Year."

"*Gracias*," said Ramirez, surprised to be so quickly determined non-threatening. "And to you."

Ramirez looked for exit signs as he walked down a wide carpeted corridor rimmed with stores and car rental agencies. He passed an elderly security guard dressed in the same white shirt, dark pants, and navy-blue tie as the others. His shoulder flash read "Commissionaire."

Not really any security at all, thought Ramirez. The man was in his sixties at least and had no gun. Not a single machine gun in evidence, no sniffing dogs. Ramirez could take this whole airport hostage, if he wanted to. Break this old man's neck like a twig.

In exchange for what? he wondered. What would he ask for? How much money would he get for a Canadian airport?

Members of the Front de libération du Québec had demanded flights to Cuba after they murdered a Canadian labour minister. That had always amused Ramirez, that political prisoners from Canada thought for some reason his country would treat them better than their own. The dissidents in Cuban jails would *kill* to get to Canada.

The elderly commissionaire smiled at Ramirez, oblivious to his near-death experience. He pointed to the escalators.

Ramirez arranged his frozen face into what he hoped passed as a smile and took the stairs. An extraordinary waterfall ran down the entire wall from the second floor to the main level of the terminal. A giant flat-screen television on the adjacent wall flashed weather updates, news, and advertising in two languages: English and French.

He had not seen real news in years, only community programming. Most of it was stories about the Communist Party, beekeeping, and nutritional advice.

He was mesmerized by the continuous line of script that ran across the bottom of the screen, updating news by the second. A magical board rotated advertisements beside it, marketing banks, lawyers, real estate.

So this is Canada, he thought, looking around. Canadians were responsible for many of the crimes the Major Crimes Unit investigated. Not because of anything they did themselves, but because they were so easily victimized. He was starting to understand why.

The newness of everything was as shocking as the cold. It was a far cry from the worn-down, crumbling city that Havana had become in its decades of isolation from the trading world. A row of clean and shiny taxis waited outside the floor-to-ceiling glass windows. He wondered how expensive they were and whether a driver would accept his American dollars.

Ramirez was almost at the exit when a tall woman with an enormous head of hair approached him tentatively. "Inspector Ramirez?"

"Yes?"

He was surprised that she knew who he was. It hadn't occurred to him that Canada had its own *cederistas*, citizen spies. The KGB had come up with the concept of the Committees for the Defence of the Revolution, but Castro had perfected it.

"You *look* like a Cuban police officer, if you don't mind me saying so. I'm Jennifer White. Would you be able to answer a few questions about the charges against Father Rey Callendes, please? I have a cameraman outside. Is it true that children in your country were also sexually abused by this priest?"

A reporter, then. Most reporters in Cuba were in jail. Those that weren't would never dare ask a Cuban detective about an investigation. Ramirez wasn't sure how to respond, but guessed that less was more. "I am sorry, Señora, I missed your name."

"Jennifer White, Inspector." She rooted through her purse and handed him a business card.

He looked around cautiously as he slid it into the pocket of the wool coat. No one was paying the least attention to their discussion. In Havana, a reporter would instantly have been under the eyes of a dozen policemen. There would have been a foot race to see who would apprehend her first.

"Señora White, I am in town for only a few days." He smiled at her, trying to charm her. "At this point, all I can tell you is that I am very cold."

"Of course," the woman said, writing furiously in a notebook. "So, you don't actually deny that the charges involve the sexual abuse of children in Cuba, then?"

"I'm sorry?"

"We understand that some of the photographs on the laptop that was seized were of Cuban children. Is that correct?"

Ramirez hesitated. "I'm afraid I can't really comment on an investigation."

"Well, thank you, Inspector Ramirez, for confirming that there is one under way."

As she sped away through the revolving glass doors, Ramirez heard her say into a cell phone, "There's our headline story, Victor. Get a long shot of his head."

Ramirez walked slowly towards the revolving doors, confused as to what had transpired, and wary. A long shot to the head? He kept his eyes open for a rifle.

He was startled when a rough-looking man with tattoos and a long ponytail blocked his way. A gun, not a rifle, poked through the opening in the man's jacket. Ramirez's heart jumped. He had not brought his own firearm, uncertain if it would be returned to him if seized by Canadian airport security. Guns were hard to find in Cuba; if he lost the one issued to him, there were no coupons to replace it.

"Excuse me," Ramirez said, and tried to walk around the stranger. He had no knife, no means of protecting himself. Only his useless, frozen hands.

The man stepped in front of him again. Ramirez looked around for a policeman but saw no one who could assist him. My God, he thought frantically. I am about to be robbed in a foreign country that has no armed security. In Cuba, there were *fianas* on every corner. Here, not a single one. Only old men with clip-on ties and plastic pens.

"Rick Ramirez? My name is Charlie Pike. Chief O'Malley asked me to give you a ride."

TWENTY-ONE

"Detective Pike. Of course. A pleasure to meet you," Ramirez said, as he tried to get his heartbeat down to normal. For some reason, he had thought Charlie Pike would be wearing a feathered headdress and carrying a small hatchet. Silly ideas that Hector Apiro had planted in his head.

Still, Detective Pike looked more like a prisoner than a police detective, with ink-blue tattoos on the backs of his fingers. He wasn't wearing a suit, only jeans and running shoes, a light jacket, no hat or gloves. Unlike Ramirez, he wasn't shivering at all.

Ramirez started to walk towards the glass revolving doors. Detective Pike blocked him once more. Ramirez realized that Pike was trying to prevent the cluster of men with television cameras on the sidewalk outside from shooting his *picture*. He breathed out, relieved. So irrational, he thought. But I am new to this country. It will take me a while before I understand how things work.

"Not that way," said Pike. "There are reporters out there, waiting for you. They aren't allowed to bring their cameras inside the airport for security reasons, unless they have airport approval. I made sure they didn't get it. We'll take the skywalk to the parking lot. My truck is parked up there. Is that all the baggage you have?"

"Yes." Ramirez had only the single carry-on bag, packed with his few warm things. Mostly borrowed—some, like the coat, pilfered. He had worn his heaviest suit jacket under the coat but already knew it would not be enough. He owned no suitcase and couldn't borrow one; no one he knew possessed one either.

They walked up a flight of stairs to the second level of the terminal. It was filled with shops. One was named Virgin, which startled Ramirez, until he realized it sold books and CDs, not women. Another was stocked with enough perfumes and body lotions to make Francesca swoon.

A shop called Relay held even more goods: candies, chips, soda pop, and bottled water. At least thirty different newspapers were stacked in neat rows on white metal shelves.

"Do you mind? I so rarely see foreign newspapers."

Ramirez stopped to look at the names of the papers, greedy for outside information. He scanned the headlines. An ice storm in Nebraska. Two female Komodo dragons had laid fertile eggs without a male. An Elvis sighting. A baby with two heads.

"I expected there would be more international news," the inspector remarked, disappointed. "About politics and economic matters."

"Those are just the tabloids," Pike frowned. "They make things up to be sensational. All the papers do these days. Don't worry, this is Ottawa. You'll get more than enough news while you're here. Probably too much."

Ramirez inclined his head towards the newsstand. "Do people actually read such stories here?"

Pike nodded. "You'd be surprised. And this is nothing compared to what's on the internet. Most of it's pornography; the rest is garbage."

"Ah, yes, of course, the internet." Ramirez followed the long-haired detective towards the signs for the parkade. "In Cuba, it is available only to tourists, although some of my staff have access for investigative purposes."

All computer searches were kept under surveillance by Cuban Intelligence as well as the Major Crimes Unit. That had been Sanchez's assignment, monitoring the internet, looking for *jineteras* with web pages and child pornography.

They walked past a store with maple-sugar candy; a display of bright art painted on canvas. Another store sold purses, brief-cases, scarves, and ties. Ramirez already felt overwhelmed. He wondered how Canadians could pick out what to wear each day with so many choices. In Cuba, most stores had only a rack or two of wares; the other shelves were empty. Even in Havana, the *bodegas* generally had only one brand of canned goods. If they had anything to sell at all.

A blast of freezing air assaulted them as automatic doors opened to the parkade. Charlie Pike led Ramirez to a red pickup truck with giant tires. Ramirez had never seen tires so large except on military trucks and tanks.

"You know what the Ojibway say, Inspector. No tires are too big for an Indian."

Ramirez laughed. He hoped it was meant as a joke and was relieved when Pike chuckled.

There were large piles of a grey substance pushed to the sides of the parking lot. It took a moment before Ramirez recognized it as snow.

"You can expect the media to be all over you about the Callendes matter," he cautioned, as he pointed something at the passenger door. The truck's horn sounded and its lights flashed, startling Ramirez. He realized Pike had some kind of electronic key. It was a new truck, American. Ramirez hadn't seen one in decades. Pike loaded Ramirez's bag into the back seat.

"There was a reporter waiting for me at the bottom of the stairs in the arrivals section," said Ramirez. He pulled out the business card and looked at it more closely. "A woman. Jennifer White."

"What did you tell her?"

"The truth," said Ramirez. "I told her I was cold."

TWENTY-TWO

Fernando Espinoza walked into the men's washroom. It was only minutes before midnight. He admired his reflection in the mirror, slicked down his hair with water. He imagined dancing with Rita Martinez. Touching that firm body, kissing those full lips.

He unbuttoned the top button of his shirt. He leaned into the rusty mirror, checking his teeth, adjusting his shirt collar.

Yes, Fernando, you are a fine-looking man, he thought.

And that Rita Martinez. *Esta heba estaba para comérsela con ropa y todo.* She was hot enough to eat with her clothes on.

Espinoza was washing his hands in the cracked sink when a woman screamed.

He ran out of the toilet, reaching for his gun. He and several police officers scrambled towards the stairwell. Others huddled in a circle at the top of the stairs. He caught a glimpse of a man on the floor wrestling with a woman.

"What is it? What's going on?"

Then he realized the *policía* wasn't trying to subdue the woman at all.

Rita Martinez lay on the floor, gasping for breath like a fish flopping inside a boat. He shoved the gun back in his shoulder holster. "Is something stuck in her throat?"

He pushed his way through. As he leaned over Rita, her panicked eyes fixed on his. The edges of those full lips around the red lipstick were already blue from lack of oxygen.

"She can't breathe," a large Afro-Cuban woman from the cafeteria said frantically. "Oh my God, someone do something. I don't know what happened. I brought up some coffee an hour ago and she seemed fine. And then, when I came back to get the empty mugs, she started to stagger, and then she fell down, right there on the floor."

"Rita, you're going to be fine. Is she choking?" Espinoza asked the man kneeling beside her.

"Her mouth and throat are clear, no obstructions."

"Maybe it's an insect bite," said one of the detectives. "An allergic reaction."

"Rita," Espinoza said, "look at me." He squatted and took her hand. He held her wrist between his index finger and thumb. He took her pulse as he watched the second hand tick by on his watch. Over two hundred beats a minute. "Can you speak to me?"

She shook her head and gripped his hand tightly. Her eyes rolled back in her head as she convulsed. Her hand went limp in his fingers. The rapid pulse under his fingertips suddenly stopped. She was no longer breathing.

"Call a doctor," Espinoza said firmly. "Get Dr. Apiro here, *now*."

TWENTY-THREE

Just after Christmas, Maria Vasquez had agreed to move into Hector Apiro's cramped flat. But when she saw it, for the first time in almost a decade, she expressed second thoughts.

"I can't live here, Hector," she exclaimed. "Look, your bed is much too small for both of us. And I am far too old now to sleep on the couch in your spare room the way I did before."

"What do you mean?" Apiro asked, crestfallen. "Have you changed your mind?"

He tried to conceal the overwhelming sense of loss that crept through him. The broken heart that Maria had so recently repaired began to rip apart like torn fabric.

"Don't be silly," said Maria, patting his arm. "You won't be able to get rid of me that easily. It simply means we have to wait until we can find a proper bed. After all, it has to be at least queen-size." She laughed. "Living with someone isn't all about making love, you know. It's about sleeping together, too."

Apiro breathed a sigh of relief. But he didn't know. He had never made love to a woman before Maria. And he had never shared a bed with anyone in his entire life. Not even at the orphanage.

"Where will we find one?" Beds are expensive, thought Apiro, and difficult to acquire. How can I possibly afford one on my salary?

"Leave that to me, lover," she winked. "Remember my favourite saying: Life is a struggle, but eventually you find shoes that fit."

Apiro had to admit that when it came to finding a suitable bed, a Cuban prostitute had significantly better resources than he did.

Apiro and Maria sat at the tiny wooden table between Apiro's kitchen and living space, the chessboard between them, the window open. The grey smoke from Maria's first attempt at cooking rice was almost gone. Their eyes only watered occasionally.

Apiro had started to teach Maria chess when she was fifteen, when she first stayed with him during her treatment. They resumed their lessons as if only a few hours, rather than nine years, separated them.

"I want to show you the moves in a famous match between Martin Ortueta and José Sanz Aguado that took place in Madrid in the 1930s," said Apiro. "Petrosian told me he devoted his entire life to chess after he was shown this series of moves. He was only ten years old."

Tigran Petrosian was the Soviet Armenian grandmaster. He taught Apiro chess when Apiro was studying reconstructive surgery in Moscow. Petrosian had emphasized the need to wait for one's opponent to make a mistake and then pounce quickly.

Apiro arranged the pieces until he was satisfied. "What do you think, Maria?"

Maria wrinkled her forehead as she concentrated on the sequence. "It's simple," she said, "but brilliant."

Apiro smiled. He was pleased that Maria so easily grasped the strategy behind the moves. She had an agile mind. Like many brilliant men, Apiro had spent much of his life struggling to fit in, but being with her was effortless.

Perhaps, Apiro thought, it is because she is so beautiful that she wants to be with me. Knowing it's not her appearance that's important but that I accept her for what she is. And in return, she accepts me.

"Sometimes chess can be that simple," said Apiro. "But remember the Kotov syndrome. Under pressure, a player can make extremely unwise decisions. The Poisoned Pawn variation is a good example. A player places a pawn where it can be easily captured. If the other player takes the bait, his own men are exposed to attack. But the ploy is risky, because it can reveal both sides' weaknesses."

"I love chess. It's so much like life."

Apiro nodded. "It brings out the best but also the worst in us, because there is nowhere to hide behind one's choices. The author Vladimir Nabokov created one of my favourite characters, a brilliant chess player named Luzhin who began to confuse reality with chess. But few chess games are ever perfect. One can replay one's moves over and over again in one's mind until it becomes self-destructive. Luzhin eventually committed suicide. Perhaps this urge towards endless self-examination is why H.G. Wells called the passion for chess the least satisfying of men's desires."

"I think I prefer Boris Spassky's thoughts when it comes to understanding men's passions," said Maria. "Particularly when you know how much such matters interest me." She grinned wickedly, her eyes sparkling. "When he was asked if he preferred sex or chess, he answered that it depended on his position."

Apiro almost fell off the faded couch, laughing. And then someone pounded on the door.

TWENTY-FOUR

"She's not getting any air. Get me a knife. A sharp one." Fernando Espinoza was going to try mouth-to-mouth resuscitation, and if that didn't work, he'd cut open Rita Martinez's trachea. Like half the taxi drivers in Havana, he'd spent a year in medical school before he realized there were other occupations that paid better.

"Dr. Apiro will be here in a few minutes," a detective called out. "Patrol is bringing him; they're on the way. So are the paramedics."

Espinoza turned to the police officer who had checked Rita's throat. "We need to do compressions. Fifteen for every two breaths. We have to breathe for her until they get here."

Espinoza tilted back Rita Martinez's head and checked with his finger to make sure her airway was clear. Then he put his lips over hers. Her ample chest rose and fell as the two men administered CPR.

Another man produced a knife. "It's okay," said Espinoza. "The air is going in; it's not a blockage. Maybe she had a heart attack." He lowered his mouth again on the count of fifteen.

Sirens shrieked in the distance.

"Stand back, please," said Apiro, materializing through the crowd. "Everyone, please, move aside. Let me see the patient." The crowd moved aside. "You're doing CPR? Good. Keep it up while I check her vital signs."

Apiro might be short, but he had an unmistakable air of competence. His stethoscope was already out, ear tips inserted. He kneeled on the other side of Rita Martinez, speaking soothingly to her. A man who knew his business.

As soon as Espinoza removed his mouth from Rita's, Apiro checked her pulse and pulled back her eyelids. He looked at the palms of her hands. The small doctor gently parted her lips and examined her gums. "Please," he implored the people standing over them. "If you can give us a little room. She needs air."

The crowd moved back.

Apiro wrapped a blood-pressure cuff around Rita's arm and squeezed the black bulb. As he let it deflate, he frowned.

"What's wrong with her?" Espinoza asked between breaths. "I know this woman. We were going for a drink after work."

"I'm afraid she won't be joining you." Apiro turned to the man doing the compressions. "Are you getting tired?" The man nodded wearily. "Here, let me take over for a while. And what about you, Detective Espinoza? Will you be able to continue a while longer?"

"Yes," Espinoza said, and put his mouth to Rita's again. He was worried: she was getting worse.

The sirens stopped. Although it was mere seconds, it seemed to Espinoza that hours passed before he heard the heavy thump of footsteps running from the elevator. This is not at all what I expected to happen tonight, he thought. Hang on, Rita, he urged silently. They're almost here.

Two paramedics with a collapsible stretcher ran towards them.

Apiro stopped pushing. "Someone else take over, please, so I can brief them."

A detective dropped to his knees and made the sign of the cross. He began pushing on the woman's chest. "Not quite so hard," Apiro said. "We don't want any broken ribs."

The pathologist stood up. The paramedics towered over him. "She needs oxygen," Espinoza heard Apiro say quietly to one of them. "Do you have any?"

"Enough to get her to the hospital, doctor," the shorter of the two responded, as he placed an oxygen mask over the young woman's mouth. The two paramedics moved efficiently together, readying the patient for transport. They looked like a good team—partners that worked together often, able to anticipate each other's moves.

"Her lungs have filled with fluid," said Apiro. "I can hear them crackling under the stethoscope. She has petechial hemorrhaging in her gums and eyes. Tell the emergency doctors to administer intravenous fluids and activated charcoal. They need to keep her as quiet as possible, monitor her fluid and electrolytes, and do an urgent toxicology screen. And administer calcium chloride parenterally if she displays hypocalcemia. Tell them to order gas chromatography. I'll be there as quickly as I can. Put my name down as the attending physician."

"What is it, doctor?" the taller paramedic asked as they slipped the woman onto the stretcher. "She seems young for cardiac arrest. Bee sting?"

Espinoza stood back and wiped his mouth. Red lipstick stained the back of his hand.

"No," said Apiro, shaking his large head. He looked perplexed. "I think she's been poisoned."

TWENTY-FIVE

The hotel phone rang. For a moment, Inspector Ramirez wasn't sure where he was. The blue light of the digital clock on the bedside table flickered not quite five in the morning. The phone rang again. He untangled himself from the sheets.

He fumbled around in the dark for the light switch. Finally, he managed to find the telephone and pick it up. It was Hector Apiro. He sounded exhausted.

"I'm sorry to wake you, my friend. How are things in Canada? You know I wouldn't call if it wasn't important. I didn't want to wait and perhaps miss you altogether."

"Imagine a country as cold as the inside of your freezer, Hector. I feel like one of your cadavers."

Apiro laughed, but Ramirez could hear the tension in his voice.

"I hope the people are warmer."

"Yes, they are. But I know you're not calling me at this time of day to inquire about the weather."

"No …" Apiro hesitated. "I am afraid I have bad news, Ricardo."

"What is it?" Ramirez asked anxiously. "My family? Is there something wrong?"

"No, they're fine. But Rita Martinez collapsed last night at headquarters. I have been at the hospital for hours, working with the emergency physicians. Trying to keep her alive. I'm sorry to say we were unsuccessful. She's dead."

Rita Martinez was a young woman. She liked to go to the clubs with foreigners whenever she could get in. Ramirez admired her spirit, and her sense of humour. He was shocked. "Whatever from?"

"Pulmonary edema. Essentially, she suffocated as fluids built up in her lungs. If we had better life-support equipment, she might have survived a little longer, but I doubt she would have lived. The hospital is running tests. I should have some results by early afternoon; they can take eight or nine hours. But some will take longer. Maybe days."

"And what is the significance of this, Hector?" Ramirez tried to make his tired brain work more efficiently, given the urgency in Apiro's voice.

"Her symptoms were similar to those of Señora Ellis. And she was poisoned, Ricardo, I'm sure of it. If two unrelated women have died from the same toxin, there could be something seriously wrong with our food or water supply. I need to know whether this death is connected. If you can find a way to obtain copies of the laboratory reports from Señora Ellis's autopsy, that will help us here enormously."

"I'll do what I can," said Ramirez, rubbing his eyes. "I'm not quite sure who to contact. Maybe Celia Jones can help. I will be seeing her first thing in the morning." He glanced at the clock. "In a few hours. But I'm afraid it may be impossible to get you everything you need. Señora Ellis's body was cremated."

"*Coño*," exclaimed Apiro. It was one of the few times Ramirez had heard him swear. "Who would do such a thing under those circumstances? Unbelievable. Well, try to get whatever you can, Ricardo. I will be here for hours, if not in the morgue, in my laboratory. And my fax machine, for the moment, has enough toner to receive at least a few pages. After that, I'll have to make other arrangements."

When he hung up, Ramirez was worried. He wanted to call his wife, to warn her to be careful, to exercise caution when cooking.

He looked at the digital clock. It was not quite 5:30 A.M. His wife was probably deeply asleep. At least he hoped she was, and that she'd only been joking about finding a lover.

He decided to wait until seven, when she would be making the children breakfast. It took him a few minutes to figure out how to set the alarm. Then he fell asleep but slept fitfully.

When the alarm rang, Ramirez opened one eye slowly, then the other, and leaned over to turn it off. Sometimes the dead cigar lady stood beside his bed in the morning, silently urging him to get to work. But he'd seen no sign of her since he left Cuba. Perhaps she was confined to the island, like almost everyone else.

He stared at the high ceiling, the ornate gilded crown moulding. Confused, he wasn't sure where he was for a moment. Then he remembered Apiro's call.

He hastily dialed his home number, following the instructions for making long-distance calls on a card by the phone. He sighed with relief when Francesca answered. The telephone lines in their part of Havana didn't always work; the service was often out.

"I wanted to let you know I arrived safely. I hope I didn't wake you?"

"Ricky!" she exclaimed. "Edel, Estella, it's your father," she called out. "Come! He is calling us all the way from Canada. No, of course not. I couldn't sleep well last night anyway, with you away, and the heat. And the children are restless without you. I can't wait until Saturday when they get their toys."

The *libreta*, or rations book, had coupons that let children have three new toys a year. They could buy them on January 6. Día de Reyes. The day the Magi brought gifts to the baby Jesus.

"Tell me what it's like. Is Canada what you expected?"

"I'm not sure what I expected," said Ramirez. "It's unbelievably cold. I can see someone from my hotel window right now, walking a small dog on a leash, with little shoes and a jacket. Not the person, the dog."

"Oh, that sounds so funny. Until you think about it. Then it's rather sad."

"I have, if you can believe this, a refrigerator in my hotel room stuffed full of food and drinks."

"You must be teasing. Does it work?"

"The *frigo*? It even has chocolate bars in it. I am going to bring them home for the children."

"And for me too, I hope," she said. "My goodness, I haven't tasted chocolate in years."

At one time, ration books had contained coupons for chocolate after Castro's personal doctor prescribed it to him to treat an injury. But these days, chocolate was as hard to find as cell phones. Because of this, Cubans nicknamed cell phones *chocolates*.

"Here, say hello to your father." He heard the phone being passed to a small hand, and his daughter's voice.

"Papi, when are you coming home? I miss you." She was only five, and had the lisp of missing teeth.

"I miss you too, sweetheart. I'll be home soon, I promise. And I will bring something special for you."

"Edel is here, Daddy. Will you bring something special for him too?"

"Yes, of course, sweetheart."

"Do you want to talk to him now?"

"In a minute, love. Kisses." His little girl made smacking noises in reply. "Estella, make sure you give lots of those to Edel and Mama. Make Edel squirm. Make sure to kiss him until he runs away."

"I will," she said in her little voice. His heart broke when she gave up the phone.

"Hello, Papi," said Edel. He was a shy boy, an athlete. One who enjoyed baseball and soccer and played both well. But he was uncomfortable expressing emotions.

Of his two children, Ramirez was closer to his son. He already missed the warm evenings with Edel in the park across the street from their apartment, kicking around the soccer ball he found for him for Christmas. His daughter he adored, but it was his son he longed to touch. To ruffle his hair, to see him wriggle with delight.

"What is it like in Canada, Daddy?"

"Well, I have a television in my room. There is an entire channel devoted to sports. Maybe more; I haven't had time to check all of them."

Not to mention the XXX movies, as they were advertised on a cardboard display sitting on top of the television set. Ramirez had flipped through a few minutes of free previews when he arrived but found the adult movies clumsy, with wretched music.

"Really?" his son asked. "I would love to see that."

"You are good enough, Edel, that some day, when people watch sports on television, they will be watching you." He knew his son's face had creased into a smile, felt the boy's joy at the idea of a future as a professional athlete.

"Do you really think so?"

"Of course I do. Now, make sure to practice kicking your soccer ball while I am away. And don't forget, you are the man of the house now. One of my most important jobs is making sure that everyone has enough hugs. That job is yours until I return home on Friday night. Agreed?"

"Yes, Papi. Come home soon." Ramirez heard the phone being passed to his wife.

"You know, I was thinking that you were right. When you come back, we should have Hector and his new girlfriend over for dinner. Let them be the first company we invite through the door."

Cubans believed that the first visitor in the New Year would set the tone for the year ahead. That would make for an interesting twelve months, thought Ramirez. A *jinetera* and a genius. So long as they ate nothing that killed them.

"Francesca, please listen to me. There is another reason I called. I want you to be very careful about what you and the children eat until I get home. There may be something in the food that's dangerous. See if you can buy some bottled water for cooking. *Por izquierda.*" Through the left hand, on the black market. "Borrow money from my parents if you have to. This could be serious."

"Oh my," Francesca said, worried. "It will be difficult to find bottled water. Perhaps we can stretch Estella's milk a little while longer. What do you mean, serious? What kind of food should we avoid? You're frightening me."

Ramirez realized the impossibility of what he was asking. He had no idea what was responsible for the deaths. And his family had to eat something.

"A woman at headquarters died a few hours ago. A Canadian tourist has died as well. The deaths look similar. Hector thinks it could be a virulent type of food poisoning. I don't know what to tell you. Just wash everything well. And make sure you cook everything at high temperatures."

"How awful," Francesca said. "What if something happens while you're gone? Oh, Ricky, I couldn't bear it."

"I will be home soon, Francesca. I promise. I miss you."

"I miss you, too. I'm sorry I was angry before. You know how much I love you."

"You were right; we need more money. I'll think of something when I get home."

TWENTY-SIX

The Chateau Laurier reminded Ramirez of Havana the way it was before the revolution. Gilt ceilings and plush upholstery. Luxurious bedding, plump pillows. Ostentatious, but tasteful, wealth.

The only hotels that resembled it in Havana were the Hotel Nacional and some in Old Havana that had been restored with foreign money. All the others had crumbled into dust.

Ramirez showered. He wondered if the tap water was safe for brushing his teeth. Several bottles of sparkling *agua* sat on top of the mini-bar. He opened one, wincing at the price. Another week's wages.

He shaved, dressed, and ordered room service.

The waiter rapped on the door. He put the round silver tray and its domed cover on a desk, then waited patiently. Ramirez looked at the tab and realized gratuities were expected. He put an additional amount on the bill and charged it to his room. He'd spent a small fortune already, almost his departmental budget for the entire month.

The waiter gone, Ramirez removed the cover from the serving tray to reveal an omelette. He hadn't tasted eggs in years.

Before Christmas, Sanchez had intercepted a Cubanet report on his laptop. He read it out loud to the members of the Major Crimes Unit. They all laughed at the purple prose. "The scarcity of eggs feels like the parting of a loved one who abandons the house to emigrate."

Ramirez remembered the old joke: Which came first, the chicken or the egg? The embargo.

He cleaned every morsel from his plate and looked at the clock. He had to get moving. He pulled on his socks and his thin leather shoes.

He took the elevator downstairs and walked past a row of meeting rooms. Outside the rooms, all the way down the long hallway, banquet tables were extravagantly laden with fruit and breads, muffins. His nose quivered like that of the airport beagle. He was almost giddy with the smells of cooked sausage, ham, and bacon. Black-suited waiters carried silver teapots and replenished shining coffee urns. There was enough food in that corridor alone to feed his family and his neighbours for months. So much food that people seemed indifferent to it, as if the knowledge that they could have as much as they wanted removed their need for it. They stood around casually holding coffee cups instead of piling their plates full.

Ramirez watched servers do the unthinkable: scrape leftovers into the garbage. It was all he could do to restrain himself from running over to grab their hands, to plead with them to stop the waste. But it also made him think about Apiro's frightening news. Something had killed two women. Could it be spoiled food? Recycled leftovers? With all the power outages, refrigeration in Havana was never completely safe.

Ramirez walked past a gallery shop filled with art and sculptures with price tags so high at first he thought he had misread them. Then he entered the high-ceilinged lobby. He walked around a comfortable-looking sofa and upholstered wing chairs. He cast his eyes about, but there was no sign of the dead cigar lady. But then, with her thin white dress, she wasn't dressed for extreme cold.

A doorman with a long overcoat and a beige hat set the revolving glass door in motion, much as doormen would at home.

Outside, the similarities ended. Ramirez's breath formed a trail as it left his body. It was extraordinary to see it float on the air, like kerosene on a still ocean.

Ramirez waited on the marble steps watching pedestrians inch carefully along the icy sidewalks. It was just after 9 A.M. He stood, freezing in his light clothes for a good twenty minutes. He stamped his feet to keep warm.

Detective Charlie Pike finally pulled up in front. A cloud of exhaust hung in the air behind the big red truck like a giant plume of feathers.

Ramirez fumbled to open the door, his fingers white and frozen. Once buckled up inside, he slipped his hands into his pockets to try to warm them.

"Good morning, Rick. Chief O'Malley wants to meet you, so I'll take you to the station first. Then we'll go see the horsemen."

"The horsemen?"

"The RCMP. The Royal Canadian Mounted Police. We call them Mounties sometimes, too. But they don't wear red coats anymore, except in ceremonies, if that's what you were expecting."

Ramirez shivered. When he lived in Russia, the cars, mostly Ladas, had no heaters. But here, even with a fan pumping hot air full-blast, the inside of the truck was cold. The windshield was covered with ice crystals. Only a small portion of it was clear enough to see through.

Ramirez wondered how Charlie Pike could drive without gloves; how he could navigate with only a few square inches of glass free of ice.

"Don't worry," Pike said. "The truck will warm up soon. The defrost is on. At least it's running today; I had the block heater plugged in overnight."

Ramirez wasn't sure what any of that meant. But he was starting to understand that Canadians had their own vocabulary for cold weather, and for the equipment to battle it.

"By the way, Detective Pike, I meant to ask. Is the tap water here safe to drink?"

In his own home, the water was sometimes brown, the supply of chlorine to treat it erratic. Francesca would have to search the black market and pay dearly for what she could find.

"Call me Charlie. In Ottawa? Yeah, it's fine. But it's not like that everywhere. Quite a few people died a while back in a town called Walkerton when E. coli showed up in their drinking water. A few months later they found the same bug in Six Nations. That's the reserve my mom came from."

"In a country as wealthy as Canada?"

"There are First Nations all over Canada who don't have clean water. Some haven't had running water for decades. People use bottled water for everything."

"We often don't have running water in Cuba. Or electricity, for that matter. But Cuba is a Third World country."

"A lot of our reserves might as well be."

TWENTY-SEVEN

Hector Apiro had worked through the entire night on Rita Martinez's autopsy. He was exhausted, but managed to keep awake by thinking about Maria Vasquez and the way she had so unexpectedly returned to his life. *Ma vida*, he thought. My life. My everything.

Maria had changed the way Apiro saw himself. He was no longer the small child left behind at the orphanage, confused and wide-eyed, as the big car pulled away, or the misshapen, ugly dwarf that others stared at. Because in her eyes, he was a man.

Having her at his side was more than he had dreamed possible. But it also meant that for the first time in his life he had something to lose.

If Maria ate something that killed her, I would be devastated, thought Apiro. I would become a rogue dwarf, like the one in the court of Peter the Great.

The idea made him smile sadly to himself. Tsar Peter had collected dwarves. When his niece married, he held a parallel wedding for a dwarf couple from his court. Their marriage ended tragically when the small bride died during childbirth. Her husband's extreme grief and rage at his loss caused his death from a broken heart. It resulted in an imperial edict by the astonished tsar against any more dwarf marriages.

But what a funeral Peter arranged for the angry, foulmouthed dwarf he was so fond of. There was nothing remotely small about it, except the guests. Seventy-two dwarves assembled in the Winter Palace together with the smallest priest that could be found in St. Petersburg. They took the little man's body to Iamskaia in a hearse pulled by miniature ponies, accompanied by large guards.

Yes, that would be me, thought Apiro. I would rage about Maria's death until Fidel Castro sent giant guards to bury me. The only difference is he wouldn't wait until I was dead.

Focus. Apiro tried to shake off his fatigue. Scalpel in hand, he clambered back up his stepladder to the third rung, getting as close as possible to Rita Martinez's body.

He held back a yawn, knowing his tired brain was pulling oxygen into its cells, trying to keep his mind awake, alert. *Pay attention.*

He leaned over the too-young body. Almost instinctively, he checked for signs of plastic surgery. He noticed that Martinez had recently had her breasts enlarged with saline implants, which he removed. A fine job, with almost invisible scars. Expensive. A credit to her plastic surgeon.

Apiro wondered how she had paid for the surgery. A police clerk made around eight pesos a month, maybe a little more. Perhaps, like Maria and so many other Cuban women, Rita Martinez had worked as a *jinetera*, renting her company—and her body—to *extranjeros*.

It made him think of the surgery he'd performed on Rubén Montenegro and the firestorm of violence and abuse that Rey Callendes had ignited.

According to what Sanchez had told Celia Jones when he held her hostage, Sanchez was only eight years old when he was first raped at the boarding school in Viñales. Sanchez was only fourteen himself when he attacked and raped Rubén Montenegro, another student, and almost killed the child.

Of course, Apiro had no idea then who Rubén's attacker was. An emergency physician at the children's hospital in those days, he had painstakingly repaired Rubén's injuries, and when the child recovered, the authorities returned him to the school and sent his assailant elsewhere for re-education.

But Sanchez was an adult when he became involved with Nasim Rubinder, the man who had murdered Rubén's little brother, Arturo, and then callously thrown his small body in the ocean.

During the investigation into Arturo's death, Apiro discovered that Rey Callendes and the school principal, James O'Brien, had told Arturo's parents that their older son, Rubén, died in the mountains. They said he'd run away when he was fifteen and that his body was never found.

But Rubén didn't vanish in the mountains, thought Apiro. He disappeared here, in Havana, a few months after he turned sixteen, after he asked me for my help.

Why on earth had the two priests lied? Apiro shook his head, too tired to make sense of it.

The small doctor worked methodically. He removed Rita Martinez's lungs. The right one weighed one thousand grams and the left one nine hundred and fifty. Both had dark red pleural surfaces. The cut surfaces, as he had suspected, showed edema and congestion. No evidence of tumour or thromboembolism. There was nothing to suggest bronchial asthma. Not an allergic reaction, then. He stopped, removed his gloves, and clambered down the stepladder to make a note of this for his report.

He planned to examine gastric washings for heavy metal

poisoning. Besides common drugs and poisons, Apiro would check for selenium. It was sometimes found in toxic levels in corn grown in carbonaceous shale. But he knew it would be days before he would have complete results.

He climbed up the stepladder again, pulling his gloves on. He took out Rita's kidneys, the body's filters, for testing. He collected parts of the dura, brain, and cerebellum, a portion of the liver and pancreas, and a small amount of bone marrow. He retrieved segments from the large and small intestines and a portion of the spleen. In each case, he made sure to get additional tissue samples as well as blood. Samples sometimes went missing in the hospital due to the shortage of labels.

Apiro shook his head. He dropped the gloves in a container for sterilization and re-use and folded up his stepladder. There was so little time.

He had to find the toxin before someone else died.

TWENTY-EIGHT

Charlie Pike dropped Inspector Ramirez off in front of the Rideau Regional Police station.

"I park at the back. I don't want you walking through the snow with those shoes of yours: you'll freeze up like a Popsicle. I'll see you in there later, Rick. You can phone Celia from reception. She'll sign you in. Get someone to give me a call when you're done with Chief O'Malley and we'll drive over to see the Mounties."

Ramirez rang Señora Jones's extension from the front desk.

Once again, he was asked to register and produce his identification. He paced around the small lobby of the police station, looking at pictures of dead police officers on the walls. One of them was Constable Stephen Sloan. He was a handsome young man, clear-eyed, with even features. Ramirez shook his head. Sloan's death was tragic for everyone involved.

Behind him, Ramirez heard a voice he recognized. He spun around.

"Inspector Ramirez," Celia Jones exclaimed. She walked over and shook his hand.

"*¿Que bola?*" said Ramirez, smiling. How are you?

"Welcome to Canada. It's good to see you again. Chief

O'Malley is waiting for you upstairs. Here," Jones said to him, grinning, as they walked to the elevator. She handed him a plastic bag. Inside, there was something that looked like a giant red condom made out of wool. "CANADA" was spelled on it in white letters. "This is for you."

Ramirez gave her a quizzical look, not exactly sure what to do with it.

"It's a toque," Jones said. "A hat. I have a parka for you in the car that you can use while you're in Ottawa, too. As well as some warm mitts. Alex is about the same size as you. We were pretty sure you wouldn't have any. I'm working on finding you some boots."

"That's very kind of you."

Ramirez tried it on, wondering what exactly a parka and mitts were. The knitted hat fit comfortably over his ears, but he felt clumsy wearing it.

"A toke?" he asked. "Is that how you pronounce it?" It would make a particularly effective contraceptive, he thought. A hat like this would deter almost any Cuban woman who saw him wearing it from ever wanting sex again.

"No, *toque*. T-O-Q-U-E. The quintessential garment for the Canadian winter. Maybe that and long johns, depending on how far north you are. You know, I think the original word is Spanish. We all wear them here. We pretty much have to."

"Ah, *toque*. It has other meanings which are more familiar to me," said Ramirez. "For example, it can be used to refer to the *tambour* ceremony in which the Santería gods assume human shapes."

"You'll have to tell me all about that. It sounds fascinating. Maybe at dinner tonight?"

"Of course. Before I forget, what are long johns, Señora Jones?" Ramirez wondered if his English, of which he'd always been so proud, would be adequate in Canada.

"You are here for two days, Inspector? My God, you have *so* much to learn."

As they rode up in the elevator, Ramirez told Celia Jones about Rita Martinez's death. He explained Hector Apiro's concerns. "He needs to find out what killed Señora Ellis, in case others in my country are at risk too."

"O'Malley says they don't know yet, and I don't think all the test results are back. I'll see what I can do," Jones said doubtfully. "But I don't know if the Chief Medical Examiner's Office will share that information with me. Or even with the Cuban medical authorities, for that matter. Canada has crazy privacy laws. We usually can't get that kind of information without a warrant."

They walked down a long hallway until they came to a middle-aged woman sitting behind a desk, typing on a desktop computer with the largest screen Ramirez had ever seen. The technology in Canada was overwhelming. Tiny cell phones, large flat-screen televisions, and gigantic cars. In Canada, it seemed, size mattered.

"Inspector Ramirez, this is Clare Adams. Clare is the brains behind O'Malley. He's really just a puppet. She's the smart one."

Adams smiled. "A pleasure, Inspector. He's expecting you."

They walked to an office at the end of the corridor. The police chief's door was open.

"You go ahead, Inspector Ramirez," said Jones. "I'll go make some calls and see what I can find out for you. If there's anything important, I'll call Clare and ask her to put me through right away."

A massive bald man with a thick neck and heavy black eyebrows sat behind an equally large desk. When O'Malley stood up, Ramirez saw how big he really was—easily six inches taller than himself and at least two hundred pounds of hard muscle. A man who would have seemed dangerously intimidating if not for the crinkling laugh lines around his eyes.

"How are you, Inspector?" O'Malley said. He walked briskly over to Ramirez.

He took his visitor by the upper arm with one big hand, pumping Ramirez's hand with the other. A firm, fully engaged handshake. Ramirez liked him instantly.

"Miles O'Malley. Welcome to Canada. I understand it's a short stay, but we're glad to have you with us."

Ramirez fingered the small black cassette tape in his pocket. He wasn't sure how long the police chief would feel that way.

"Yes, I will be returning to Cuba on Friday. I am happy to be here, to do whatever I can to help."

"Would you like a coffee? Nothing like what you're used to, I imagine. But it should warm you up. Thirty-three below with the wind chill yesterday. Christ, that's about where it starts to be the same in Fahrenheit. Bloody cold, as you've no doubt discovered. But it's getting warmer today. We're expecting a storm."

"*Gracias*. Yes, I'm afraid the cold here is something one has to experience personally to fully comprehend."

Thirty-three degrees below zero. Ramirez was surprised his heart hadn't stopped.

A few minutes later, Clare brought in two paper cups full of coffee. Despite the heat of the brew, Ramirez was almost sorry he'd accepted. The coffee tasted as if it had been left in a tin can overnight. He cradled his cup in his hands and wondered if it would be rude to hold it against his chilled ears.

"It's unusual, isn't it, for a Cuban to be allowed to leave Cuba so quickly?" asked O'Malley.

"Very," Ramirez said. "But my government is concerned about the allegations that children were sexually abused in our boarding schools."

"Those goddamn residential schools," said O'Malley. "We had

them in Ireland too, you know. Although no one wanted to talk about it for decades. Schools where the kiddies were worked to death during the day and sexually abused all night long. There's an inquiry under way in Dublin right now. I think when it's all out in the open, the Catholic Church will fall down like dominoes. There were thousands of abuse victims at the Indian residential schools here, too. Likely hundreds more in the non-native schools. I'm guessing it happened everywhere in the world those bloody priests were sent."

Ramirez wondered if O'Malley had been abused, given his outrage. But it was hard to imagine anyone harming O'Malley, even as a child. There was nothing of the victim about him.

A phone rang on the police chief's desk.

"Damn it," O'Malley said. "I hate it when people take calls when they're in meetings. I don't have one of those bloody BlackBerrys for that very reason. Can't stand it when people use them to send messages to each other across the table instead of talking face-to-face. But Clare wouldn't interrupt us if it wasn't important. Please excuse me for a minute."

He picked up the receiver in one of his huge hands. Ramirez heard the metallic buzz of a woman's voice. The police chief frowned.

"When?" O'Malley asked, making a note on a pad on his desk, the yellow pen almost disappearing in his thick fingers. "When will that decision be made?" Then, a few moments later, "Let me know, will you, Celia? Give me a heads-up. Thanks."

He hung up the phone. "Well, Inspector, maybe it's a good thing you're here after all."

Ramirez waited.

"As you may have gathered, that was Celia Jones. Another Canadian tourist died in Havana about an hour ago. Same symptoms as Hillary Ellis and that woman from your station.

That makes three dead women in less than a week. The Chief Medical Examiner's Office says the Public Health Agency is getting very concerned. Our Foreign Affairs Department is planning to issue a travel advisory."

"Warning people not to come to my country?"

O'Malley nodded. "If those deaths are related, they don't really have a choice."

"When would they do that?" Ramirez asked, worried. Thousands of tourists would cancel their winter holidays. Maybe hundreds of thousands. It would devastate the Cuban economy. Castro would be furious.

"They told Celia it could take twenty-four hours to get the paperwork through. Maybe a little longer, because some of the staff are still on holidays. And by the way, speaking of paperwork, she said to tell you she can't get your pathologist the medical results he requested unless the family consents. There are objections from the next-of-kin, apparently."

The next-of-kin, thought Ramirez. That would be Michael Ellis. And the only reason he would possibly refuse to agree to the release of medical reports was if he feared that something incriminating might be found in them. But what? The dead women had nothing in common except Havana. Or did they?

O'Malley rubbed his thick fingers over his smooth scalp. "Did Celia tell you what was going on with Michael? His mother-in-law's been making some pretty crazy accusations to the media. She thinks he killed his wife."

Ramirez nodded without commenting. He wasn't quite so convinced that the allegations were crazy.

"Well, at least this will get this story out of the press. This proves it. Michael had nothing to do with his wife's death."

Three deaths, thought Ramirez. We have a flock.

TWENTY-NINE

Another corpse lay stretched out on a hospital gurney. Like Rita Martinez, her lips were blue, her skin deep pink. Sunburn? Apiro wondered. Or the effects of a poison?

"She collapsed across the street from the Parque Ciudad," the taller of the two paramedics explained to Apiro.

"Unconscious within minutes," the stocky one nodded. "We did what we could. Oxygen, fluids. It was faster this time. But then, it was hotter today. Witnesses said she staggered down the sidewalk like a zombie before she fell. We tried to revive her, but we lost the pulse. Dr. Ortega pronounced her dead at Emergency. We thought you should know about it. It looks so much like the other one."

The paramedic was observant, thought Apiro. Heat elevated the heartbeat. The circulatory system moved more quickly. A toxin would be absorbed faster.

"I appreciate you contacting me," said Apiro. "This could be extremely important."

The hospital administrator, Marguerita Stanza, had hovered anxiously beside them when Apiro arrived.

"The Canadian authorities want this woman's body returned

immediately, Dr. Apiro," she said firmly. "The insurance company
has a private plane waiting at the airport. Dr. Ortega has already
signed for the release of the remains. This woman's death is not
our responsibility. It has nothing to do with us."

"But I need samples," Apiro protested. He explained why.

"My God," Stanza said, shocked. "Then take what you need.
We can delay them for perhaps an hour, no more. After that, the
phones will start ringing. Assuming they're working, of course."

Even the paramedics had appeared tense as they wheeled the
gurney into an empty room and waited outside the door. Of
course they are, thought Apiro. They know we are all in danger
until I can find out what's going on.

O'Malley excused himself; he had a meeting to attend. As Ramirez
waited for Charlie Pike to retrieve him, he asked Clare Adams if
he could borrow a telephone to make a long-distance call.

"Of course," she said. "You can use the chief's office."

She took the inspector inside and excused herself, leaving him
in private. Ramirez phoned the Havana police switchboard and
asked to be transferred to the morgue.

"He's not there," said Sophia. "Dr. Apiro is at the Manuel
Fajardo Hospital. Shall I page him there and have him call you?"

"*Gracias.*" Ramirez gave her the number on the phone on
O'Malley's desk. While he waited, he read an old magazine from
December 2005. Even one year out of date, it had information in
it that was new to him. The death of John Paul II he knew of, and
the trial of Saddam Hussein, but not the bombs in the London
Underground that exploded during the G8 summit.

Everyone in Cuba, though, had heard about Hurricane
Katrina and the devastation in New Orleans. Castro had offered
to send a thousand doctors to the United States to help with its
aftermath but never received a response.

A few minutes later, Clare poked her head in the door. "There's a call for you on line two, Inspector. Just push down the red button that's flashing."

Apiro sounded dead on his feet. He apologized, explaining he hadn't slept for almost thirty hours.

"I've just heard the news, Hector. Another death?"

"Yes, I'm at the hospital now. And you are not the only one to track me down. I have just had an extremely uncomfortable discussion with the Minister of the Interior about all of this. He is not enjoying the New Year so far, I can tell you that."

"I can imagine. Tell me what you know about the third victim."

"Her name was Nicole Caron. She was another Canadian woman, travelling alone. She lapsed into a coma on the sidewalk in front of the Parque Ciudad Hotel. Unlike the others, she died on the spot. The Canadian authorities insist on conducting the autopsy themselves. Something to do with her travel insurance. The remains are already on their way to the airport. I was able to take some blood and tissue samples. I had less than an hour to work on her. I was lucky to get that."

"That's unfortunate." If anyone could have discovered the cause of the woman's death, thought Ramirez, it was Apiro.

"The minister has practically ordered me to sever any link between the two Canadian cases. He is extremely worried about the travel advisory the Canadians are threatening to impose. So, I understand, is the acting president."

"I don't blame them. It could close down the entire tourist industry in Havana."

"I don't doubt it, Ricardo, but I don't have the means to do what they want. Hillary Ellis died on Canadian soil, so I have no test results from her autopsy. As for Señora Caron, I have just the samples I was able to obtain before her body was taken away. The only complete set is what I collected during Rita Martinez's

autopsy. I will do what I can with what I have. But I don't know
how quickly I can find answers."

"Do you really think the deaths are linked?"

Apiro sighed heavily. "Of course. Any epidemiologist would
say that three such similar deaths in such a short period is no
coincidence."

"Caused by what? Do you still think it could be food
poisoning?"

"My guess is that all these women ingested something toxic
shortly before they died. But I have no idea what or where. We
can almost certainly eliminate the airplane itself. Señora Caron
and Señora Ellis were on different flights, and Rita Martinez, of
course, never flew anywhere, which rules out the airport. What's
bothering me is that so far it's only women that have succumbed.
Except for some of the hormones, chemicals don't usually
discriminate by gender."

Then a tourist advisory *should* be issued, Ramirez thought.
And one warning Cubans to be cautious as well. He shuddered
to think that a member of his family, or anyone he knew, might
die from their puny amount of rations. Starvation, maybe. But
food poisoning?

"It's an impossible task," said Apiro. "An epidemiological
investigation takes dozens of investigators and resources that we
simply don't have. And there's nothing obvious to look for."

"What are the possibilities?" asked Ramirez. He thought of his
own wife, his children, afraid that any one of them could collapse
and die while he was so far away.

"Some mushrooms produce a toxin. There is also an algae
found in barracuda, which is sometimes served in tourist restaurants under other names. And then there are pesticides, although
those seem unlikely. These days, there is nothing very toxic in
the food chain, Ricardo, which is why this is such a mystery. We

rarely use pesticides now that we can no longer import chemicals easily. Our scientists have developed organic methods of dealing with pests. The new idea of pest control is recycled banana stems covered with honey to collect ants. 'Rational pest management,' they call it, causing me to wonder how one manages irrational pests."

"What about *jutia*? Could they be the connection? At one time, they were being poisoned, weren't they?"

The *jutia* was a large rodent found almost everywhere in Cuba until it was hunted to the verge of extinction, first by mongooses and then by Cubans. The tree rat, as some called it, had returned to parts of the island. It was not unusual to see Cubans walking down the highway with three or four of the dead rodents slung over their shoulders, tied together by their tails.

"Castro halted all extermination efforts a few years ago. Some think it's so the rats can be used as a source of protein," said Apiro. "But it's a good idea. Secondary poisoning could be the cause. These women may well have consumed something that was once poisoned itself. I'll check into it."

Ramirez thought for a moment. "There are rats all over Havana, too. Maybe the deaths are related to the chemicals used to control them."

"We don't control rats, they control us," said Apiro. He laughed, but Ramirez heard the stress in his voice. The frequency of Apiro's small jokes and puns increased with the severity of the situation. It was how he, and Ramirez, survived. "That's another good suggestion, Ricardo. I'll check with the Office of the Historian; I know they have a program to reduce rat populations. Havana is the worst affected because the housing here has deteriorated so badly."

"The Office of the Historian is involved in rat control?"

"To protect Old Havana's cultural integrity. The rats,

apparently, are now considered part of Cuban infrastructure. If we kill them off too quickly, our buildings might fall down." Another staccato laugh.

Ramirez shook his head. Less than twenty-four hours in Canada, and he already missed his country's inane bureaucracy.

"If Rita Martinez hadn't also died, I would think a restaurant was responsible," said Apiro. "But you know how unlikely that is."

It was illegal for *turistas* to eat in private homes. But it was also illegal for Cubans to eat at tourist restaurants.

"Besides," Apiro said, "Rita was working at police headquarters when she became ill."

Ramirez could see why Apiro was having problems connecting the dots, when one victim was Cuban and the other two were tourists. They occupied parallel worlds, ones that rarely intersected.

"Maybe you can get Espinoza to find out what hotel Señora Caron stayed in, Hector. That might narrow down a geographic area at least. But I hope you are wrong about a connection, my friend. Because if you're right, there could be more deaths."

"Not to mention the harm this could cause our flourishing economy," Apiro joked. The strain in his voice caused him to croak.

Ramirez laughed uneasily. "Something like this could ruin us."

THIRTY

Charlie Pike exited from the highway onto a wide, busy street called Bronson Avenue. "The RCMP headquarters is about twenty minutes east of here, off the Vanier Parkway," he explained to Ramirez. "We're going to have to take a detour through downtown to avoid the Queensway. There's a ten-car pileup there; traffic's bumper to bumper all the way to Lees. It's going to be bad today and tomorrow. There's a big storm moving in."

Pike drove north until the road ended at a junction.

"That's the Ottawa River over there," said Pike. "On the other side, that's Quebec. This is all unsurrendered Algonquin territory. Even Parliament Hill."

"Another First Nation?"

"You're learning fast," Pike smiled. "The Algonquins used these lands for hunting and fishing. They never gave them up, never signed a treaty. They have a land claim with the federal government. It's been in negotiations for maybe ten, fifteen years. The federal and provincial governments have it on a fast track. Might get it settled in a century or two if they can keep up the pace."

Pike signalled and turned the big truck right on Albert, then left on Bay. They drove down Wellington, past the Supreme Court of Canada, the Justice Building, and the Parliament Buildings. These were massive structures, strung with bright Christmas lights, as was every tree along the route.

But as they drove past Ramirez's hotel and through the downtown core, it was the advertising that shocked him. Billboards with signs for Coca-Cola, new cars, laser eye surgery, even women's lingerie.

In Cuba, there was no advertising for goods or services. The only billboards on Cuban highways were state-owned. Most had cartoon pictures of either Fidel Castro or George Bush. Bush was usually portrayed with a small black moustache, like Adolf Hitler. Sometimes blood dripped from the corners of his mouth, like a vampire.

Edel and Estella would love to see the Christmas lights, the spires of the Gothic churches. Francesca, she of the handmade Christmas bells and stars that still decorated their small apartment, would be amazed at how much energy was spent on Christmas lights when their own electricity supply was so precious, so often disrupted.

There were only a few people walking about. They were bundled up like the Egyptian mummies on display at the Museum of Universal Arts in Havana.

At home, even this early in the day, the streets would be full of people, tourists coming and going from bars, *jineteras* calling softly to potential customers.

Pike turned on the wipers to clear the falling snow. Ramirez was amazed by the flat, intricate shapes. Tiny lace doilies melted on the windshield.

"It must have warmed up," said Pike. "It was too cold to snow last night. Only minus twenty today, and no wind chill."

"So this is snow. It is quite beautiful."

It did feel warmer, Ramirez thought. Cold, it seemed, was a sensory illusion.

"They say that no two snowflakes are the same. I'm not sure how anyone could ever know that without seeing every single one of them. But yes, this is it, alright. You're here at the very worst time of the year, Rick," Pike said, as the windshield wipers thwacked back and forth. "We have at least three or four months of really cold weather in the winter. But January is always the worst. Well, that and March. And February can be pretty bad, too."

Ramirez laughed. "Appreciating your weather may take me a little time. How long have you been with the Rideau Police Force, Charlie?"

"Since 1995. O'Malley talked me into joining up when he got appointed chief. He was with the Winnipeg Police before he came here. That's in Manitoba. Another province. Believe it or not, it's even colder there than it is here. O'Malley was a beat cop when I first met him."

"You knew him before he took over this police force, then?"

"Yeah, I've known him since I was fourteen." Pike turned to look at Ramirez. He grinned. "He caught me breaking into an apartment. That was my lucky break."

"Lucky? Why?"

"It was his apartment."

THIRTY-ONE

"I was with my best friend, Sheldon Waubasking. We ran away from school up north, hitchhiked all the way to Winnipeg. We were supposed to be staying with Sheldon's sister, but we ended up living on the streets."

Inspector Ramirez looked at Charlie Pike with interest.

"Did Chief O'Malley charge you?" He wondered how someone with a criminal record could become a police officer.

"No. I think he felt sorry for us. He took us under his wing. Although he made me buy him a new radio to replace the one I broke when he hauled me out the window he caught me coming through. Me and Sheldon, we were headed on the wrong path back then; he turned us around. Although back in '84, when all that happened, he scared the heck out of me. He looked like a biker who stole someone's uniform. He was even bigger then, if you can imagine. Built like a bull and just as bald. That scared me, too. My mother was Mohawk, but my dad was Ojibway. The Anishnabe only shave their heads when someone dies."

"Mohawk is another Indian tribe?"

"Part of the Iroquois Confederacy. The Haudenosaunee. They're called the Six Nations, too. Under Confederacy laws,

I'm supposed to be Mohawk, not Ojibway, because my mother was Mohawk. But the Canadian government doesn't recognize Haudenosaunee laws. We don't recognize theirs, either. We use our own passports when we travel."

"It sounds complicated."

Pike shrugged. "I guess so. It's always been that way."

"I like him, your Chief O'Malley."

"He's a good guy. He grew up in Northern Ireland. He told me once that even though he was an atheist, the street gangs there used to chase after him. They'd ask him which god he didn't believe in, the Protestant one or the Catholic one. And then they'd beat him up, whatever he said. I don't think he was joking."

Ramirez laughed. "In Cuba, we believe in every god rather than picking only one. The Yoruba slaves who were brought to Cuba to work on the tobacco and sugar plantations gave their *orishas* the names of Catholic saints so that they could practice their religion under the noses of their masters."

Even Castro was on the fence, thought Ramirez. He was baptized a Catholic. When he marched into Havana as the leader of the revolution in January 1959, he wore a locket bearing the image of the Virgin of Charity. He was excommunicated shortly after he announced his belief in communism.

Pike smiled. "My people did the same kind of thing. When the government said we couldn't have traditional chiefs anymore and had to elect them, the clan mothers told the hereditary chiefs to run for election, and everyone voted for them. The government never knew the difference."

"We have no choice but to vote for our government," said Ramirez. "But it's not that bad. No one is homeless in Cuba. We don't eat well, but usually no one starves. On the other hand, all our buildings are falling down."

"It's the same here, for First Nations people, anyway. The

Crown owns our reserves and the band councils own the buildings. There's never any money to fix them up. In a lot of First Nations, particularly up north, people have to use slop buckets, because they don't have any plumbing. It was a problem when we had the SARS epidemic a few years back. The doctors kept saying 'wash your hands.' But they couldn't."

"We have problems with our water supply, too. And with our power, which often doesn't work."

Ramirez yawned. Pike took a quick look at his passenger. "You look tired, Rick."

Ramirez's eyes had started to droop with fatigue. "Forgive me. I didn't sleep well. And I am worried about events at home but powerless to do anything about them. It is stressful to be so far away from my family in such circumstances."

"Yeah, I know what that's like."

The national police force headquarters showed a Soviet influence, to Ramirez's eyes. It was a square brown building that sprawled across acres of flat land.

"The RCMP are involved in the Indian residential school files because the schools were owned by the feds," Pike explained. "They're the federal police force. When the first complaints about abuse were made, back in the sixties and seventies, they're the ones that investigated, so they have a lot of files. There are class actions all across the country now by former students who claim they were sexually and physically abused at those schools. Twelve thousand claimants so far. They figure eighty or ninety thousand may file for compensation under the settlement agreement the churches have worked out with the government. I guess you know that Rey Callendes was arrested because of the child pornography they found on his laptop at airport security?"

Ramirez nodded.

"After he was taken into custody, the RCMP found his name in the database of those old residential school complaints. And then Celia came back from Cuba with a report that said Callendes was involved in abusing kids there as well."

"Yes," Ramirez said. "He assaulted a child at a boarding school in Viñales. But that was in the early 1990s."

Rodriguez Sanchez.

"Callendes was in Canada long before that," said Pike. "In the seventies. Up in Northern Ontario. He taught at an Indian residential school. There were lots of claims filed about that school. I've heard that every little boy that went there was sexually abused."

Charlie Pike pulled the red truck into the wide driveway that led up to RCMP headquarters. He stopped beside a small white booth in front of a large parking lot. He rolled down his window and gave their names to the security guard. The guard checked a list and waved them through. Another elderly commissionaire, Ramirez noticed. Canada was a country confident enough to be guarded by the frail and the old.

The parking lot barrier arm rose, and they entered the grounds of the RCMP headquarters.

THIRTY-TWO

The fax machine in Hector Apiro's small office beeped. He hopped off his swivel chair and made his way over as a page curled through. He pulled it out of the tray, relieved to discover it was the results of the gas chromatography test on Rita Martinez's remains.

Apiro read through the sheet quickly. He was astonished at its contents.

How could Rita's body possibly have fluoroacetate in it? The chemical was extremely rare. It was used only where the risk of accidental poisoning of humans was minimal, given its high toxicity. It was a rodenticide as well as an insecticide, one that was quickly absorbed from the gastrointestinal tract. Apiro knew of twelve deaths in Brazil caused by the poison after thirsty men drank what they thought was liquor in an old whisky bottle.

It was the perfect poison with which to commit murder, if one could find it.

It dissipated quickly in water. It was colourless, odourless, and almost entirely tasteless, except for a bit of a salty aftertaste. This was the reason it was used to bait and poison small animals. The chemical was virtually impossible to trace in the human body unless one knew exactly what to look for: an elevated level of citric acid.

Apiro had decided to test for it after Ramirez's mention of banana rats and pesticides. This was what Apiro liked best about their friendship. Their back-and-forth, the way one idea fed another. They made a good team, he and Ramirez. Like the paramedics, able to anticipate each other's moves. Except in chess, where only Apiro could foresee what was coming and develop a strategy.

Perhaps Rita Martinez *was* murdered, then, thought Apiro. But how? It was impossible to obtain the chemical in Cuba. Or to make it.

Fluoroacetic acid was one of the most deadly nerve agents on earth. It was manufactured by men who wore spacesuits like Russian cosmonauts. There was no laboratory capable of producing it anywhere on the island, nowhere safe enough.

Well, here it is, thought Apiro, so it has to be somewhere. But where?

If the poison was in powder form, it could kill through inhalation. But then others would have been exposed to it too.

No, thought Apiro. Rita Martinez was stricken in the police station. She must have consumed something there that had the chemical in it.

Which was why he was so perplexed.

The first symptoms of fluoroacetate poisoning usually appeared within a half-hour of exposure and worsened as time progressed. But Rita was almost at the end of her shift when she collapsed. She had to have come into contact with the chemical somewhere within the police headquarters building the night she died. She'd been drinking coffee from the cafeteria, but no one else who drank coffee from the same machine had taken ill. He'd tested her mug; it was free of contamination. Other than her desk, which he had already checked, Apiro didn't know where else to look.

His legs were as heavy as cement. His fatigue was catching up with him. He ran his hands through his greying hair, frustrated.

Apiro sipped his coffee slowly, grateful he'd brewed it to be extrastrong. Another beep drew him back to the present: an incoming fax. He put down his mug and rubbed his legs before standing up painfully.

Apiro suffered from early degenerative joint disease, another symptom of his achondroplasia. It was usually treated with Aspirin, but there was none to be found. Lack of sleep made the condition more painful.

He limped over to the fax machine for a second time. He pulled the sheet from the tray and skimmed through it, thankful the fax hadn't run out of toner, and read through the test results for Nicole Caron.

Startled, he wiped his forehead, his aches and pains forgotten. There were traces of fluoroacetate in her tissues, too. How was this possible?

Apiro sat down so heavily he shook the desk. Coffee splashed everywhere, but he was too distracted to notice. He tried to imagine how a Canadian woman from British Columbia and a Cuban clerk had crossed paths, how they could have been exposed to the same rare poison.

He picked up a pen and began to make a list of possible connections between the two women. Did they share a taxi? Unlikely. Cuban nationals weren't allowed in tourist taxis.

A bus? Almost impossible, for the same reason.

He needed to find out if Nicole Caron had been questioned or arrested, if she had been in police custody at any time. That might explain the women's proximity to each other at police headquarters, but little else.

He thought again about the *jutia*. Had these women perhaps eaten meat from the same source? But if so, what, and where?

Apiro made another note: check to see if any *cederistas* reported seeing a tourist eating at a private restaurant.

And another: check to see if anyone saw Rita Martinez with a foreign woman. If Rita was a *jinetera*, she might not have limited her clientele. Nicole Caron travelled alone; Apiro should not make assumptions about her sexual orientation.

For the moment, he realized, he'd have to leave Hillary Ellis's death out of his search or he could be easily led down a false path. Her death was the anomaly; she became ill on a flight out of Cuba, not while she was still in the country.

Despite the coffee, his thinking was slow and laboured after two full days without rest. He was no longer a young resident, capable of working for sixty hours on his feet. Age was catching up to him.

But he was the only one who could solve this mystery. Lives depended on it. *Eliminate the impossible.* Apiro thought of the risk to the people he loved so much and pressed on.

THIRTY-THREE

Charlie Pike and Inspector Ramirez waited at the RCMP reception desk for almost half an hour before their contact came downstairs to meet them. Pike, Ramirez noticed, seemed unconcerned by the delay.

"I'm on Indian time," Pike shrugged.

The RCMP officer introduced himself as Corporal Yves Tremblay. The policeman wore a beige shirt and navy pants with yellow stripes down the sides of the legs.

Ramirez was scanned with a handheld scanner while Tremblay signed them in. A commissionaire, this time an elderly woman, took Ramirez's passport. She threaded a numbered plastic pass that said "Visitor" onto a metal chain that Ramirez put around his neck.

They took the elevator to the second floor.

Corporal Tremblay spoke with a slight accent which Ramirez assumed was French-Canadian.

"I'm sorry you've been waiting so long, gentlemen. I was on the phone with our legal counsel. He reminded me that there are privacy issues to work around. We have to be very careful about the information we share with you, Inspector Ramirez. It's nothing personal. We have laws in this country that limit what we can do, even in a police investigation."

Tremblay took them into an office. The room had four chairs, upholstered in blue fabric, and a computer on a desk. They sat down. Tremblay didn't offer them coffee, for which Ramirez was grateful. Canadian coffee, he had decided, was toxic.

"We arrested Rey Callendes at the Ottawa International Airport just before midnight on December 29," said Tremblay.

That was the same day Rodriguez Sanchez killed himself, Ramirez noted.

"Father Callendes had a laptop in his possession when he entered Canada. He admitted it was his." Tremblay pointed to the desk. "Here, take a look at what was on it, Inspector. Detective Pike has already seen these images. We burned them onto a CD for you."

Ramirez scrolled through the photographs. Pictures of young boys, some barely older than toddlers. Acts of penetration, fellatio. And in some photographs, the men involved were unmistakably priests, wearing black cassocks.

The children in some of the photographs looked familiar. Ramirez was sure that if he compared them to the Polaroids in his jacket pocket, the ones he had removed from the Michael Ellis file, they would be identical.

"We know that some of these images came from a server in Cuba. That's why we think that some of the children are Cuban."

Ramirez nodded. Photographs like these tended to merge together after time, the horror of them supplanting individuality. But Ramirez could prove where at least some of them had originated. Sanchez's computer. It made him sick to his stomach to think of it.

"Do you know when these pictures were taken?" asked Ramirez.

Tremblay shook his head. "No, only that some of them were downloaded about two weeks ago. Since then, they've probably made their way around the world."

"I have seen photographs like these before, Corporal Tremblay. We monitor the internet in my country for such things." Telling the Canadian police officer the truth, but only part of it—not that the detective who Ramirez had authorized to monitor traffic on the internet had used it to share child pornography.

"There are several hundred images on this CD, Inspector. All of them are equally disturbing. But we can only charge Rey Callendes with unlawful possession of pornography, not the abuse that's depicted in them. And maybe not even that, given his position."

"What position is that?" Ramirez asked.

"He says he is an apostolic delegate. So far, the Vatican hasn't responded to our request to either confirm or deny that assertion."

"What does that mean?" asked Charlie Pike.

"If he's telling the truth, he's a kind of Church envoy. The Catholic Church usually sends apostolic delegates to countries where it doesn't have missions. That would give him the same ecclesiastical rank as a papal nuncio, but without formal diplomatic status. It would make prosecuting him difficult. The Vatican will claim immunity."

"We know that Rey Callendes sexually abused at least one boy at a boarding school in Viñales in the 1990s," said Ramirez, remembering what Sanchez had told Celia Jones. Some of it was recorded on the tiny tape recorder Sanchez had with him while he held Jones hostage. Jones said he had clicked it on and off while she begged to leave a message on it for her husband before she died.

"He always used the same methods," Ramirez went on. "The

children were brought to the rectory, to what they were told would be a special dinner and a sleepover. A bath was followed by a brutal sexual assault. After it was over, he forced his victims to kneel on the floor and pray for forgiveness. It doesn't matter what his religious position is in my country, Corporal Tremblay. Children have special protection under the Cuban Penal Code. My government wants to bring him back to prosecute him for his crimes. And we need only meet the test of probability for an indictment. He could be sentenced to up to twenty years for committing homosexual acts with boys. As well as barred from teaching children or exercising authority over children. Another five years for the pornography."

"That's about what a murderer in this country gets," said Tremblay. "But I doubt he'll be teaching anywhere again. He's seventy-six years old."

The same age as Raúl Castro, thought Ramirez. Another coincidence?

He shook his head. "His age is unimportant in Cuba. We still have the firing squad for crimes like this, if the juridical panel decides special circumstances apply, although that penalty hasn't been applied in the last two or three years."

"And that compounds our problem, Inspector Ramirez. We can't return Rey Callendes to a country that could even possibly execute him. When it comes to prisoner transfers, capital punishment is against our government's current policy. That may change, because the new Conservative government has a different perspective on crime than previous ones, but for now, that's the way it is. The other problem is that we have Father Callendes in custody because he's obviously a flight risk, but there's a limit to how long we can hold him. His lawyer has arranged a bail hearing for next week. If we can't get him transferred in the next few days, he's likely to be released. We're not sure he'll stick around."

Ramirez nodded. "Then we have the same interests."

Tremblay looked at Pike. "Can I speak to the inspector in private, Detective, so we can work out some intergovernmental issues? This may take a little while."

"Sure," Pike said. "I'll wait downstairs in the canteen."

THIRTY-FOUR

Charlie Pike sat in the cafeteria in the basement of the RCMP headquarters, nursing a cup of coffee. He thought of the abuse the old man in the alley had suffered in Indian residential schools, and how closely his story fit with the Cuban inspector's revelations.

"I remember that residential school like it was yesterday," the old man had said, sipping his bowl of soup in the cold air. Steam rose from it, like smoke from a campfire. "My father"—he used the Ojibway word *nimbaabaa*—"was on the trapline. Me and my three brothers, we were all by ourselves when they came to get us. Just our auntie looking after us. My mother died when my little brother was born.

"An RCMP Mountie and the Indian Agent came in a big black car. I was six years old. Never spent a day in school before then. That Indian Agent, he snuck up and grabbed us, one by one, and threw us in the back of the car. The Mountie held my *ninzigo* so she couldn't run after us." *Ninzigo* meant "my father's sister." "He wrapped his arms right around her, tight, like this."

The old man put the soup down. He crossed his arms around his shoulders, like a straitjacket.

"She was kicking and screaming, trying to break free, *mahwee*." Crying. "We were crying too. I didn't even get to say goodbye to my own dad. I don't know if they told him where they were taking us. If they did, he never came to see us. I didn't see my auntie again for two years. That's the first time they let me go home for the summer. I couldn't look her in the eye.

"I spent eight years in that school. I left in '61, when I was fifteen. Couldn't read or write after all that schooling. They put me in junior grades that whole time. I sure knew how to say Jack and Jill went up the hill, though. And how to pray. Oh, my, we had to pray all the time. Over and over again. Or they'd whip us. And we had to pitch hay, us kids, until our backs hurt, every day.

"We had to get up early; go to bed when it was still daylight out. Sometimes I would look out the window and try to see the night sky. They beat me up pretty good for that, those priests, whenever they caught me. Same thing if I tried to talk to my little brothers. Sometimes they used sticks, or those long wooden rulers. But they really liked to use those big old fan belts, the type you get off a tractor. And they hit you hard, those priests. They never held back. You'd be black and blue for days. Made it hard to sit down. We'd try not to cry, to be brave. But it was hard."

"My grandfather, he went to residential school," Pike said. "My mother, too. But they never talked about it."

"We all want to forget, son. I'm so old now, I can't even remember what I'm trying to forget sometimes." The old man laughed. "You know, it's a gift, hearing you use that word, *mishomis*. I love my grandchildren. I never hurt them. I had lots of children with different women, but they all got taken away. I wasn't good to them. I used to drink heavy, trying to forget those priests and nuns. I was so angry; sometimes I took my anger out on them. I know now that was wrong. I got convicted of manslaughter once. I beat a man to death when I was drunk.

I spent time in Stony Mountain Penitentiary. You know that place?"

Pike nodded.

"That's where I found the old ways. Funny, eh? To find out who you are in jail. There are gangs in those jails, but the elders try to teach them a good path. About the medicine wheel, the four directions. *Ekinamadiwin*." The teachings. "The things I'm telling you, they're all we have left. Did I ever tell you the story of where we came from? The first beings the Great Manitou made were evil serpents. But they were destroyed in a big flood. So the Great Manitou created a new being, a man, and brought him a woman. That's how we began. We multiplied, had big families. Do you know why those snakes couldn't multiply?" He laughed, his face lighting up like a beacon. "Because they were adders, not multipliers."

There was something else the old man finally told Charlie Pike as Pike slowly pulled him in from the cold. Not the details—Pike knew he would never speak of them—but enough that he could guess.

"One of my brothers died at that school when I was nine. They told me he ran away, that he fell through the ice. But I saw the bigger boys out back that same night. Behind the school, digging a grave."

Maybe that was why the old man told the stories, thought Pike. Four brothers, one who drowned. A mother who died in childbirth. Like Nanabozho and the story of winter.

But the old man said a priest at the school told him to forget he ever had a brother who drowned. He was never to speak of him again.

"That priest, he had an accent. He wasn't all that old, maybe thirty. Maybe twenty-five. He was nice to me, put his arm around me when I cried. He gave me chocolate candy the day my brother died. I'd never tasted chocolate before. He told me I had to give up my Indian name or I'd go to hell. And that really scared me, that there could be a place even worse than that school.

"He took me to the rectory that same night. He said we'd have a special meal, just him and me. And after that, I knew there wasn't nowhere worse than that school. Whatever I did wrong that day, I still don't know. But I was in hell already. That's when I knew I'd never go home. I had two brothers still alive. I never spoke to either of them again. Too ashamed, I guess."

Charlie Pike finally knew why the old man used drugs. And the pain he tried so hard to forget. Someday, Pike promised himself, he'd find out what happened to the old man's brother, and why a young student in a Catholic school wasn't taken to a Catholic graveyard or sent home to his family for burial. How the child really died.

"That priest's name," the old man said. "I never knew how to say his last name right, or how to spell it. But I'll never forget his first name. We called him Father Ray, us children. Like a little ray of sunshine. Because at first we thought he was kind."

THIRTY-FIVE

"I'm going to be honest with you, Inspector," Corporal Yves Tremblay said to Ramirez after Charlie Pike left the room. "And if you tell anyone what I've said, I'll deny this conversation took place."

Ramirez nodded. He was starting to feel more comfortable. This was familiar territory. Like being at home.

"There is a commission of inquiry under way in Ireland at the moment. They're investigating claims of sexual abuse at the Archdiocese of Dublin."

"Yes, I've heard about it." The one Chief O'Malley had mentioned.

"We have reason to believe that this commission will report that the Catholic Church, at the highest levels, was not only aware of abuse by priests at the residential schools they managed, but covered it up for decades."

"This surprises you?" It didn't surprise Ramirez; he would have expected it.

"Not the cover-up itself, but how far it extends. When complaints were made, Church authorities persuaded the local police to let them deal with it. Then they forced secrecy on everyone involved and moved the offenders elsewhere. The *Crimen sollicitationis* was a secret Church decree that required everyone involved in a complaint about sexual advances by a priest to take an oath of silence. The victims, the priests assigned to investigate the complaints, all the witnesses. Or be excommunicated."

"I'm not sure that I understand how any of this applies to Rey Callendes."

"I'm getting there. Without someone willing to speak openly to us about the abuse they suffered, we can't do a proper investigation. We can't even get search warrants. It's not Rey Callendes we're after, it's the higher-ups who covered up serious sexual and physical abuse for years. But the Vatican claims sovereign immunity. And it's almost impossible to execute a search warrant against a church. Certainly not without reliable information."

"Ah, yes," Ramirez said, "the sanctuary of the church has been a problem in my country as well."

Originally, fugitives from the law could take refuge in a church if they were innocent, but canonical law had long ago extended that right to include the guilty.

"We know that the Catholic Church reassigned priests automatically," said Tremblay, "as soon as they received complaints of sexual abuse involving children. They were sent all around the world. We've obtained access to an internal Church file that proves this was done to shield Church assets from lawsuits. Rey Callendes's name is on documents in that file."

"How did you get it?" asked Ramirez.

"It was leaked to us."

"I see," Ramirez said. "A confidential source?"

"I'd rather not say. But there is a strong Cuban connection. Our problem is that the Justice lawyers can't use any of the documents in that file in either civil or criminal litigation without potentially revealing who gave it to us. But I can assure you, the information is highly credible. It establishes serious criminal conduct dating back to the 1960s. That's the reason you're here."

"I'm still not sure I understand."

"Here." Tremblay handed him a thick file. "You will when you read this."

Ramirez flipped through the pages of internal correspondence between various priests, archbishops, and the Vatican. He was sickened by what he read.

Dozens of allegations of sodomy, beatings, and the vicious rapes of young children. Confirmation of hundreds of cases of abuse in Ireland, Austria, Switzerland, Poland, Brazil, Canada, Cuba. Revelations that would be devastating to the Catholic Church if made public.

He found the document Tremblay had referred to.

It was a report written when Padre Rey Callendes was in Cuba in 1992. It was in English, addressed to his superiors. "An eight-year-old boy has been injured in a sexual attack by another student," it said. "The minor responsible has been transferred for re-education. The boy who was raped is in the Children's Hospital in Havana with serious internal injuries. It is not known if he will survive."

Rubén Montenegro. No mention that Rodriguez Sanchez was the assailant. Or that Rey Callendes had abused Sanchez himself before moving on to a younger boy.

Callendes wasn't a Vatican envoy back then, thought Ramirez. He was a teacher at the Viñales boarding school. But maybe this was where his talent for diplomacy was first recognized by his superiors. The precise, almost clinical, description of the abuse, the rapid response. His fluency in a second language.

Yves Tremblay sat drumming his fingers on the table. Ramirez closed the folder.

"Let me guess. Rey Callendes was one of the priests the Vatican sent to do the internal investigations whenever they received a complaint of child abuse."

Tremblay smiled tightly. "You're quick, Inspector. We've been through thousands of documents disclosed to our government in the civil litigation and couldn't find a connection before. But this proves the Holy See had a policy to deal with these cases. Rey Callendes helped the Vatican move personnel before they could be sued or criminally prosecuted."

"Let me ask you something, Corporal Tremblay. Where was Rey Callendes travelling from when he was stopped at the Ottawa airport? Was he entering Canada or leaving it? Where was he going?"

Tremblay frowned. "He was on his way to Rome from Havana, with a brief stop here to change planes. He had arranged for a two-day layover in Geneva. You didn't know?"

Ramirez shook his head slowly. He had wrongly assumed that Callendes was returning to Havana at the time of his arrest. And that he had left Cuba after the Viñales school was closed in the late 1990s.

We want him brought *home*, the minister had said. Callendes had either stayed in Cuba after the school's closure or had returned for some reason. Either way, Geneva was hardly on the way to Rome.

"The photographs on this laptop confirm what we've been told, Inspector Ramirez. But the more important information, from our perspective, is what's contained in these documents."

"Won't Callendes defend himself by saying that the photographs were gathered in the course of his investigations?"

"He may, although that admission would expose the Church

to liability. He'd have to admit that the Vatican knew about the abuse depicted in these photographs and did nothing to stop it or to report it to the proper authorities. But he could refuse to testify, given the consequences of speaking out."

Excommunication, thought Ramirez. Those were the likely consequences. More threatening to a Catholic than death, because it affected the next life, too.

"Besides, he's in poor health. Some kind of heart trouble. We want to use these documents in a different way, where we don't need to rely on him at all. It could be years before all this is resolved. He could be dead by then."

"What do you have in mind?"

"If we can say we got these documents from Cuban authorities—that is, from *you*—we can use them to get search warrants. Or at least threaten to. We knew you were investigating Rey Callendes, thanks to the contact made with us by your Ministry of the Interior. Frankly, it's why Father Callendes was stopped at the airport in the first place. We want you to swear an affidavit suggesting you gave this file to us, instead of the other way around."

Ramirez sat back in his chair. So it wasn't a request by the Canadian authorities that had precipitated his trip to Ottawa but a request initiated by the minister. The bigger picture was beginning to take shape. The outline, if not yet the details. "And you would use these threats of search warrants for what purpose?"

"As Detective Pike may have told you, Canada is involved in a class action settlement involving thousands of abuse claims at Indian residential schools. The governments built the schools, but the churches supplied the personnel."

"He said the schools were church-run."

Tremblay nodded. "The majority of the claims involve the Catholic Church. The other parties—the United, Anglican, and Presbyterian churches, as well as the Government of

Canada—agreed to a billion-dollar settlement about six months ago. But the Catholic Church has so far refused to pay its share. Negotiations are under way."

"And to encourage a successful resolution, you want me to swear a false statement."

Corporal Tremblay was prepared to doctor evidence; Charlie Pike had been a thief; Detective Ellis was a murderer. Perhaps all Canadian police were criminals, thought Ramirez. There could be more similarities between Canada and Cuba than he had realized. He reached into his jacket pocket for his cigar.

"I'm sorry, Inspector. This is a smoke-free building. If you want to smoke, you'll have to go outside."

Ramirez put the cigar away, disappointed.

"Our Justice Department is chomping at the bit on this one," said Tremblay. "Think about it. No one needs to know where the information really came from. And now that you've read it, it's not like you'd be lying. Well, not really."

"Let me make sure I understand your request clearly. You want me to attest that the Havana Major Crimes Unit provided this information to you, even though you gave it to me. Presumably, you want me to say that it came to our attention during our investigation into Father Callendes so that your courts will think that the information originated in Cuba instead of Canada. Is this correct?"

"We all want the same thing, don't we? We just have to be very careful," Tremblay said. "We can't lie under oath."

Ramirez somehow managed not to laugh. "Such evil deeds does religion prompt," he said.

"I'm sorry?"

"It's a quotation from Lucretius."

The corporal looked confused. Once again, Ramirez missed Apiro. The pathologist would have laughed until he cried.

"Nothing important," said Ramirez. "Sometimes the only way to deal with atrocities is to joke about them."

There was irony in the Canadian policeman's request. And in the half-truths the Minister of the Interior had told Ramirez about the job he was sent to do.

Ramirez thought for a moment. "I think I can do this. But I need something from you in return."

"What?" asked Tremblay warily.

"I have to bring Rey Callendes back to Cuba with me when I leave tomorrow night: my government insists on it. And if I'm going to claim that these documents were under my control, I need to have accurate copies of all of them. As well as the original laptop. Rey Callendes can't be prosecuted in my country without it."

"That's fair," Tremblay nodded. "But you have to get me something in writing from your government that says he won't be executed if we turn him over. If you do that, I can almost guarantee our Justice Department will agree. Believe me, the Canadian government is deeply conflicted about all of this. It has a strong base of Christian support that it doesn't want to lose by going after a priest, but it has a tough law-and-order agenda as well. They'd much rather the priest be your problem. We have a new acting RCMP commissioner, and trust me, he wants Rey Callendes out of here, too. But we need this whole thing papered."

Papered. Ramirez took that to mean that Canadian officials wanted to be able to blame Cuba if their intelligence failed yet again. He didn't see that as a problem. Everyone in Cuba blamed Cuban Intelligence, since it wasn't always intelligent. Or intelligible, for that matter, given the ministry's need to rely mostly on Russian and Chinese sources. The Chinese translation of the English phrase "wet floor," for example, was "execution in progress," which had caused at least one serious misunderstanding.

"I understand your concern. I'm sure we can work things out. May I?"

Ramirez opened the file of Vatican documents again and flipped through them until he came to the memorandum that mentioned Rey Callendes specifically.

He brought his exit permit out of his pocket and looked at the signature more closely. He smiled to himself. The Minister of the Interior *had* been busy.

"It shouldn't be a problem, Corporal."

"Then I think we may have a deal. You can keep that file; it's a copy. And remember, none of this ever happened. Do we understand each other?"

"Completely," said Ramirez, thinking how closely this discussion paralleled his conversation with the Minister of the Interior. Except, of course, for the ban on smoking.

Framing the guilty. Rodriguez Sanchez would have approved.

THIRTY-SIX

"Twelve thousand children," Inspector Ramirez said, shaking his head, as Charlie Pike drove him back to his hotel. It was late afternoon, but the sky was as dark as night. "It's hard to believe. I can't begin to imagine how much they suffered."

His head had reeled at the documentation of nuns and priests who put pins through children's tongues to stop them from speaking their own languages. Who made them eat their own vomit and kneel for hours on concrete floors. And then sexually abused them on top of all that. His eyes had filled with tears at the statement of a little girl who said she knew whenever the priest wanted sex because he would open his desk drawer and bring out a roll of duct tape.

He thought of his own daughter. He would kill anyone who did that to Estella. Or to his son. However old the assailant might be.

"A lot of our people committed suicide because of what happened to them in those schools. We're still losing them."

"They blamed themselves?" said Ramirez. "But they were small children. It wasn't their fault."

Pike nodded. "Quite a few of them never went back to their reserves, because they couldn't face their families. And when they grew up, they abused their own kids a lot of the time. Nobody knew how to be a parent after that. Their only adult role models were people who hurt them."

"What was the purpose of all of this? These were innocent children."

"To assimilate us, I guess. We weren't seen as completely human, thanks to Charles Darwin. They started the residential schools back in the mid-1800s. But the last one didn't close until the 1990s."

"My friend Hector Apiro is a doctor, but he takes issue with Darwin, too. He often jokes that if only the fittest survived, he wouldn't last very long. He has a genetic defect that makes him very short. The way you speak of these schools, Detective Pike—I mean Charlie—it sounds personal. May I ask: did you go to one of these schools as well?"

"I was sent to a day school. I was allowed to go home to sleep at night. But I remember a teacher who called me a '*maudit sauvage*' just before she grabbed a big leather belt to whip me for picking up a toy. I didn't even know what those words meant at the time, I just knew it was bad. Turns out it's French for 'damn savage.' The school I was sent to was Jesuit-run. It was better than most. But that's not saying a lot."

Pike gripped the steering wheel more tightly, but his voice remained calm. Ramirez was impressed by the man's composure.

"Were all the staff like this?"

"No. We had some teachers that were okay, but plenty who weren't. And any staff member who complained disappeared pretty quickly. And the living conditions were always terrible, right from the beginning. At the Duck Lake Agency, where my grandfather was sent to school, twenty-five percent of the children died from TB his first year. The infirmary was overcrowded. They were starving, Rick. They didn't have a chance."

"I can't begin to imagine this," Ramirez said.

The magnitude of it was overwhelming. He tried to think of the grief that would overcome any small village in Cuba if every fourth child forced to go to boarding school never returned. He couldn't fathom it. The depth of loss was beyond comprehension. These were more like war crimes, cultural genocide. Like a natural disaster, with the power of a tornado that destroyed everything in its path. But entirely *unnatural*. Perhaps this was how the Tainos felt as they fled into the mountains, leaving the bodies of their dead children behind.

"Did the parents know what was happening to their children?"

Pike shook his head. "Not often. In Ojibway and Cree cultures, children are raised to be respectful. If they told anyone about the abuse, they would have been disrespectful to their abusers. But even when they tried to tell, most of the time no one believed them. Their parents had been taught to respect the Church. They couldn't imagine that nuns and priests could do that to their children. Children weren't even spanked on my reserve. We learned how we were supposed to behave from the elders. They told us stories, legends. It was up to us to interpret those stories to understand how we were supposed to act."

How heartbreaking, thought Ramirez. Children raised to be kind to the people who brutalized them. Children who sought help, only to see it denied by the adults they trusted to protect them.

"And what about this claims process that Corporal Tremblay told me about? Is it going to resolve these matters?"

"I don't think so. It's not automatic: the claims are adjudicated. Some victims go to these hearings and struggle to tell an adjudicator what happened. It's usually the first time in their lives that they've had the courage to talk about it. Then they find out they're only going to get a part of the compensation awarded to them, because there's nothing coming from the Catholic Church. But it took dozens of years to get things this far, Rick. So I guess you could say this is progress."

Pike didn't sound like he saw it that way.

"You don't support this settlement process, then?"

"Not really," said Pike. "It opens up a lot of old wounds." He pulled his red truck over to the side of the road and put on his hazard lights. "Give me a second, will you?"

Pike got out of the truck and walked over to an old man sitting on the sidewalk. The man looked aboriginal to Ramirez. He leaned against a stone wall, a garbage bag full of clothes beside him. There was a blanket wrapped around his legs, but he seemed indifferent to the cold. Ramirez saw Pike put something in the old man's lap and pat him on the shoulder.

"Sorry," Pike said, when he climbed back into the truck. "I try to keep an eye on him. He's Anishnabe, from somewhere up north. He's homeless, but too proud to live in a shelter. He was abused at Indian residential school, too. I can't find out what his name is; he won't tell me. But he's finally starting to talk to me about what happened. Do I support the claims process? Well, I think people who sexually abuse children should go to jail and see how it feels to be raped by someone bigger. But our courts don't like to sentence old men. Most of the people who did this are elderly. A lot of them are already dead."

"What do you think should happen to the perpetrators, then, Charlie? Jail? Capital punishment?"

"We don't have capital punishment in Canada." Pike turned his head to look at Ramirez and smiled. "Although some people think living in Ottawa is capital punishment."

"But seriously, what do you think should be done?"

Pike sighed. "The Anishnabe would have banished them. Made them live somewhere on their own, away from the community, to think about what they'd done. I guess if they thought they were really dangerous," he shrugged, "the people would have got together to decide who would kill them. The way they used to kill *windagos.*"

"*Windagos*? What are they?" asked Ramirez.

"Monsters that killed people in the winter and ate their hearts. Every time they possessed another person's body, they got stronger, more powerful. You had to kill a *windago* twice or it would come back, and their hearts were made of ice, so you had to cut them out. The *windagos* always took over the bodies of the best hunters and fishermen. If the community didn't do something about them, it couldn't survive the winter."

Ramirez shuddered. "They really existed?"

"Our people believe so. Isn't that the same thing? My dad's great uncle, Jack Fiddler, was a shaman and a famous *windago* hunter. He hung himself after he was arrested for killing fourteen of them. The police let him go outside for a walk. He kept going until he found a tree he liked better than jail."

"When did all this happen?"

Pike thought for a moment. "Early 1900s, I guess. Once he was arrested, it wasn't long before the white men came and took away our land."

"What are shamans?"

"Spiritual leaders. But the Victorians thought they were witch doctors. The Indian Act made most of their ceremonies illegal. A lot of them went to jail."

"That's a fascinating history," said Ramirez. "But very sad."

Apiro would want to hear the details. He was enamoured with the romance of the American Wild West. But the information Charlie Pike was sharing was far from romantic.

"We had the same kind of thing happen in Cuba with the *brujos,* around the same time you mention," said Ramirez. "There were many former slaves in the early 1900s who were born in Africa. The ones who believed in *brujería*, like my grandmother, were often prosecuted as witch doctors, too."

"Well, that's the difference, I guess," Pike said. "We didn't come *from* anywhere. We were already here when the white people came. There's a grand chief in British Columbia who says we should have killed every European who got off the boat instead of offering to trade with them. Sometimes I think he was right."

"The indigenous people in my country were slaughtered by the Spanish when they came to trade with them, too. None of the Tainos survived."

"I don't know how we did," said Pike, pulling his truck in front of the Chateau Laurier. "The Europeans put smallpox in the blankets they traded with us. Wiped out thousands of Anishnabe. Sometimes I try to imagine what this country would be like if we'd just been left alone."

Ramirez picked up the RCMP file and put his hand on the door handle to get out. "That man you gave money to, what do you think he would want done to the priest who hurt him?"

"The old man?" Pike smiled sadly, thinking of the story. "He believes in the traditional ways. He wants to know that spring will come again, even if he doesn't live long enough to see it. If the priest would just apologize, he'd forgive him, I think. Sometimes that's the worst punishment of all."

THIRTY-SEVEN

Celia Jones was seated in a red wingback chair in the hotel lobby when Ramirez walked through the glass doors. He had entirely forgotten that they were supposed to go out for dinner.

"With everything going on, are you sure you still want to come with us?" she asked, standing up. "You must be terribly worried about events at home in Havana. We won't be offended if you want to stay close to the phone."

"I admit, I'm concerned about the situation. But I have to trust Hector to find the answers. I've already warned my family to be careful. All I can do now is wait. Perhaps going out with you this evening will help take my mind off the situation."

After Ramirez checked for messages, Celia Jones drove him to a polished, wood-panelled restaurant where her husband, Alex Gonsalves, was waiting for them at the bar. They moved to a table and ordered a bottle of wine to go with their entrées.

People spoke in hushed tones. A pianist played quietly in the background. The service was so unobtrusive, so smooth, Ramirez hardly noticed they had a waiter.

"How is your steak and salad?" asked Jones.

The meat was tender enough to be cut with the side of a

spoon, but Ramirez was too tense to enjoy it. Each bite was like a mouthful of sawdust.

"Fantastic," he lied. "We don't see beef in Cuba these days. Or any meat, for that matter. Or even many vegetables other than beans. Lucky for us, few Cubans eat vegetables anyway. I think there's a law requiring it, but we try not to enforce it."

Gonsalves chuckled. "Where does the food for the restaurants and hotels come from, Inspector Ramirez? Still from state farms?"

"Please, both of you, call me Ricardo. Yes. These days the farms are worked by oxen and mules, since we have no fuel for tractors. Our harvests are smaller, because we no longer have ready access to pesticides, either. It's actually resulted in fewer homicides." He smiled. "Once the bottles were empty, they were sometimes used as bludgeons."

Alex, Ramirez had discovered, was Cuban. Alejandro. One of the wave of migrants who fled the island in the 1990s. "I finally decided," Gonsalves said, reaching for a dinner roll, "that democracy is essential. Without it, nothing else matters."

Ramirez looked around the restaurant to see if anyone was listening. Discussions about democracy in Cuba were dangerous. But here no one paid the slightest attention.

"Well, I think that democracy is overrated," said Jones. "George Bush got elected with less than twenty-five percent of the votes. And a lot of those were rigged. It's the economic taps being turned off that has crippled Cuba, not its politics."

"You sound like a Cuban politician, Celia," said Ramirez, smiling. "Fidel Castro offered to send observers to monitor the last American election, but President Bush declined his offer. I don't think Señor Bush appreciates Castro's sense of humour."

Jones laughed, wiping her mouth with her napkin. "The offer

alone must have made Bush apoplectic. But if he's the poster child for democracy, maybe you're better off without it."

Gonsalves shook his head. "Until the dictatorship is replaced with democratic elections, the United States will never remove the embargo. And nothing is going to change as long as the US can point to things like the way Las Damas de Blanco have been treated by Castro's government."

"Who are Las Damas de Blanco?" asked Jones.

"I mentioned them to you before Christmas," Gonsalves said. "Remember? The Ladies in White. It's a protest group."

"They march every Sunday, after mass," said Ramirez.

"Some of them were beaten up on December 10. International Human Rights Day," Gonsalves explained.

Ramirez remembered it well. Hundreds of mostly middle-aged women marched in silence, carrying pink gladioli, until they were pushed off the sidewalk by pro-Castro demonstrators. The revolutionaries tore the women's flowers into pieces and threw garbage and bottles at them before the protesters were dragged away by militia and security officers and loaded on buses.

All this happened as foreign reporters watched. Castro had fumed. Not at the arrests, of which he approved, but at the reports of them that hit the international news.

"Their sons and husbands are dissidents," Ramirez explained. "Most were arrested during a crackdown a few years ago for *desacato*—that's contempt for the government—for criticizing programs. I remember one was jailed because he claimed the organ donation program donated too many organs to *extranjeros*."

After dinner, they walked to the National Arts Centre. Jones assured Ramirez that it was only a few blocks away. Ramirez wore the clothing Alex Gonsalves had loaned him. These included heavy canvas boots with a thick rubber sole that looked like it was made from the tires on Charlie Pike's truck. The boots had liners of dense grey felt.

His head and feet and hands were quite warm, and as a result, the walk was not altogether unpleasant. Although after a block or two, he could no longer feel his cheeks and his nose was so dry that it felt like it was made of straw.

The National Arts Centre was another Soviet-style, flat-roofed, brown building that hugged the side of the Rideau Canal. Ramirez was surprised at how plain the architecture was in a country that had the resources to build whatever it chose. There were none of the pinks, yellows, or turquoises of Havana. All the buildings in downtown Ottawa seemed to be brown or grey, or clad with mirrors that reflected other brown and grey buildings.

Hundreds of people skated on the frozen surface of the Rideau Canal. "They're going to designate the canal a World Heritage Site soon. Just like Old Havana," said Jones. "It's the longest man-made skating rink in the world."

Gonsalves explained that the canal was built by Irish stone-masons in the 1800s, during the struggle for control of North America.

"Che Guevara was part Irish, did you know?" said Ramirez. "His father once said that his son had the blood of Irish rebels in his veins. But his mother was Basque."

"Really?" said Jones. "I have to say, Cuba must be one of the most interesting countries on the planet. Tell me more about the *houngans* you mentioned earlier today, Ricardo."

They were approaching the front doors of the NAC. Inside, a line had formed. Seeing a queue made Ramirez a little homesick.

"Here," Gonsalves said. "Give me your coats. I'll take them to the cloakroom."

He walked away briskly. A nice man, Ramirez thought. Principled, and intense, but also kind and good-humoured. A good match to the Canadian lawyer, who Ramirez had come to like greatly.

"*Houngans*? They're witch doctors. They practice a form of voodoo."

"I thought voodoo only existed in Haiti."

"Vodun came to us from Africa, too, Celia, with the slaves brought to work in the tobacco and sugar plantations. My grandmother was one of them. But she was Yoruba, from Nigeria, so she followed Santería as well."

"I remember being told about Santería when I went to Blind Alley. I didn't really understand the beliefs. I remember thinking it was odd that people could believe in it and in Catholic saints at the same time."

"They did that so they could protect their own religion. They gave each *orisha* the name of a saint. For example, Chango, the god of thunder, is also Santa Barbara. She is a good fit for Chango because she was murdered by her father for worshipping the Catholic god.

"Right after her father killed her, he was struck dead by lightning. Because of this, Santa Barbara is invoked against sudden death. Those who pray to her, or to Chango, believe that they will never die without first receiving the sacraments."

"Did your grandmother believe in the Catholic god, too?"

Alex Gonsalves returned and handed them each a stub from the coat check. "It won't be long. They're going to open the doors in a few minutes."

"*Gracias*. No. She preferred to worship many gods," said Ramirez. "She thought it best to keep all channels open. She was often possessed by *orishas*."

"You're kidding. Really?"

"The Santería believe that drumming opens the gateway to the *orishas*. If the drummers are good enough, the *loas*, or spirits, of the *orishas* take over the dancers. My grandmother loved to dance."

"I thought I saw something like that in Blind Alley when I was there," said Jones. "A woman was screaming while people sang and drummed. When I left, I saw something on the ground. I thought it was red paint. Well, actually, at first I thought it was blood. The whole thing was pretty scary."

"The *babalaos* draw those pictures on the ground long before the dances, to persuade the gullible that the *orishas* have visited," said Gonsalves. "When they point them out later, people forget they've walked over those same drawings all day. It's like the doctors in the Philippines—the faith healers—who pretend that bloody chicken livers are tumours they've extracted from people's bodies. People desperate to believe in something will believe in anything."

"I don't suppose Cuban voodoo is the same as it is in the movies, is it, Ricardo? With those little dolls that witch doctors stick pins into?" Jones asked as they joined the lineup.

"I don't know about movies," said Ramirez. "We so rarely see any new ones."

The last movie Ramirez and Francesca had gone to was at a theatre across the street from the Gran Teatro. Ironically enough, it was called *Brujas*. A movie starring Penélope Cruz, so old and out of date that Cruz was only seventeen.

"But, yes, sometimes they'll use voodoo dolls to change someone's behaviour. To get them to quit smoking, for example. Or to give up a mistress. Some voodoo masters claim they can lure someone's spirit into water and kill them by stabbing the reflection. The water turns red and the person becomes a zombie."

"But of course that doesn't really happen. It's all a trick," said

Gonsalves. "There is no such thing as zombies. That's as silly as believing in ghosts."

Ramirez smiled. "I can see you are a scientist, Alejandro, like my friend Hector Apiro. But religion is about faith. Hector says that chess is the only endeavour based on pure science."

"Do you play chess, Ricardo?" said Jones. "I tried to take it up, but I wasn't that good at it. Alex, on the other hand, is a whiz at it, and crosswords. He can figure out all kinds of complicated clues. I'm just not that good at games that require strategy. I'm more sort of 'in the moment,' if you know what I mean."

"I don't play well, sadly. But I find its theory useful on occasion. As Hector once explained to me, in chess, tactics is knowing what to do when there is something that can be done. Strategy is what you develop when you lack tactics. And if you have no time to develop strategy, if you do something unexpected it can sometimes confuse your opponent and allow you to win."

Directed by a young woman in a burgundy velvet jacket, they found their seats.

"Explain something to me, please," said Ramirez, as they sat down. "Charlie Pike told me that the internet is mostly used to circulate pornography. If the rest of what's on the internet is full of misinformation, why do people here rely on it so much?"

"It's an instant source of news and articles. In a few seconds, you can find out almost anything," said Gonsalves. "It's a great tool."

Ramirez nodded. "In Cuba, when we want to know everything about something, we take the more traditional route."

"You go to a library?" asked Jones.

"No," Ramirez said. He smiled. "We ask our wives."

Inspector Ramirez was tired when he got back to his hotel, although the opera had been a marvellous distraction.

Love, murder, and jealousy. Not a whodunit, as Celia Jones pointed out, since the operatic murder of Canio's wife and her lover was committed in front of an audience within the opera as well as the real one.

Leoncavallo wanted *Pagliacci* to be a story about the downfall of a complicated man, one who was wrongly viewed as a clown instead of as a person with feelings. Every time Canio spoke of his jealousy, the fictional audience laughed. Even when Canio discovered that the wife he adored had betrayed him, he had to put on his clown face and perform as if nothing had happened.

Each character was flawed and yet human. One could feel sympathy for everyone involved.

Michael Ellis wears a mask, thought Ramirez. Every day, his mutilated face conceals his true thoughts. Did he, like Canio, take out his anger by murdering his wife? And in seeking his revenge, did he accidentally kill two other women as well?

Ramirez opened the small *frigo* and pulled out a tiny bottle of rum. He winced when he looked at the price list on top of the mini-bar. A month's wages for a single drink. He poured it into a glass he found wrapped in paper on a shelf in the bathroom.

Ramirez sat on the bed and leaned against the plump pillows. He sipped the rum, willing his fingers to settle down, to stop shaking. He tried to concentrate, despite his fatigue after a long day in an unfamiliar setting. If it was hyperthyroidism he suffered from, his condition was getting worse.

The search, he thought. There was something in our search of Señor Ellis's hotel room that ties into his wife's death. Something that shouldn't have been there. I need to remember what it was.

But nothing came to him.

He put down the empty glass and undressed. He crawled beneath crisp, cool white sheets and a warm down comforter.

As he slid into sleep, Ramirez glimpsed a dull blue mist in the shadows of the heavy drapes.

A dignified middle-aged man in a Victorian-style suit with a high-necked collar emerged. A piece of kelp was wrapped around his neck, forming a dark-green cravat beneath his beard. Water dripped slowly to the floor from his sodden clothes. A small girl in a gingham pinafore peeked shyly at Ramirez from behind the man's jacket. In her small fingers, she held a gladiola.

The man leaned against the wall as the small girl walked out. She kneeled before the mini-bar and gently placed the flower on the carpet, as if it were a grave.

She stood up again. The man nodded to Ramirez as if to wish him well. The little girl raised her hand.

They turned their backs and vanished from Ramirez's vision as magically as if conjured from Apiro's Luminol.

THIRTY-EIGHT

Ramirez called Hector Apiro in the morning to find out if he had made any progress. He found the small man at the morgue.

"I'm afraid I have more questions than answers," said the pathologist, "but at least I was able to sleep for a few hours. Getting some rest has helped enormously. I was becoming a menace. Good thing my patients don't care," he cackled. "The poison that killed Rita Martinez and Nicole Caron was fluoro-acetate, Ricardo, not cyanide. It's even more deadly."

"What is it?"

Apiro explained. "It's been used in the past here to kill wild dogs and small mammals. It interferes with the citric acid cycle in animals and in plants."

"You say it's deadlier than cyanide?"

"Cyanide, depending on the amount, isn't always fatal, as I mentioned before. But even tiny amounts of fluoroacetate can kill. Three thousandths of an ounce is enough. I have no idea how these two women could have come into contact with it. I checked with the Office of the Historian to see if it had been used in Old Havana for rat control. They tell me it hasn't been on the island for decades because of the embargo."

"Is it something that someone could make? Or perhaps purchase on the *bolsa negra*?"

"No," Apiro said. "Unless one lived in Africa. It comes from a South African plant called the poison tree. Not very creative, the Africans, when it comes to naming deadly plants."

"Is this the same drug that killed Señora Ellis?"

"I don't know yet. But I have found something odd. I can find no link whatsoever between Señora Caron and Rita Martinez, and believe me, I've tried. But I *have* found a connection between the two Canadian women, and a strong one at that. Señora Caron stayed in the same hotel room at the Parque Ciudad Hotel that was occupied by Señor Ellis and his wife during their visit. Room 612. In fact, Señora Caron moved into Room 612 on New Year's Eve, the same day Señor Ellis checked out."

"That *is* a strong link," said Ramirez, puzzled.

"I can't figure it out. We thoroughly searched that room before he was arrested."

Something nagged at Ramirez even as Apiro said it. The hotel room held the key, he was sure of it. He retraced the room's contours in his mind.

A king-size bed, an upholstered chair, a chest of drawers, a locked wall-safe in the closet. The hotel staff opened it for Apiro's technicians after Ramirez and Sanchez left; it was empty. Ramirez sighed. He had no idea. These women's deaths were giving him a headache.

"At least one good thing will come out of this. Rita Martinez left a signed consent form," Apiro said. "She carried an organ donor card."

"Her organs weren't affected by the poison?"

"No. We have had successful transplants even after poisonings by cyanide and methanol without any hemorrhagic complications. It is not an absolute contraindication, not at all."

Everyone in Cuba was expected to register in the "voluntary" organ donation program Castro initiated in the early 1980s. "Let's see if one million citizens will agree and we can deprive the worms of their food," Castro said, as he became the first volunteer to sign the forms.

Ramirez wondered which lucky Cuban would get Fidel Castro's kidneys or heart. With the amount of rum he had consumed over the years, it was doubtful anyone would want his liver.

But the program had run into problems. There was often no place to store donated organs, given the chronic problems with electricity and refrigeration. That, and the lack of proper medical supplies, meant little Beatriz Aranas was likely to die young.

Which reminded Ramirez: he had completely forgotten to tell Apiro that Celia Jones and her husband wanted to try to arrange the child's medical transfer to Canada so she could be treated. He summarized what he had in mind, remembering the promise he'd made to the couple after dinner.

"It might work," said Apiro. "The embargo has interfered with our ability to get immunosuppressants. Mycophenolate, for example, should be taken daily by transplant patients, but it is hard to find these days. We could argue for a medical transfer on the basis that without the drug she could die. Besides, most transplants are done on *turistas*.

"The real money these days is in foreigners, as you know. The hospitals can charge the *extranjeros* several hundred thousand CUCs for an operation. We had a regional workshop in Holguin last October where participants discussed the ethical issues around it. The consensus was that at the moment the income outweighs the disadvantages."

Interesting, thought Ramirez. Something about that information tugged at him, something about the dead cigar lady, but it slipped away before he could grasp its importance. He looked at his watch. "I'm supposed to fly out this evening, Hector. This worries me. That travel advisory could be issued soon."

"I agree, Ricardo, time is short. And it is much harder to find a toxin in a hotel that has hundreds of people coming and going; there are so many things we need to check, so many items to cross-reference. The Parque Ciudad Hotel is not happy, but I've quarantined Room 612 while we search for answers. I just wish that Hillary Ellis's body had not been cremated. I certainly hope the Canadians tested it for fluoroacetate when they had a chance. The chemical is so rare, the test for it is often not done."

Ramirez shook his head. Apiro was right. Who in their right mind would be so anxious to cremate the body of a loved one?

As soon as Ramirez got off the phone with Hector Apiro, he called Celia Jones.

"Celia, Hector needs copies of the autopsy and laboratory results from Señora Ellis's death. We have to find out if they tested for fluoroacetate in her system." He explained Apiro's findings. "We don't have time to work through official channels. The travel advisory is only hours away."

"I'll do what I can, Ricardo. But as I explained before, Canadian laws are a problem when it comes to personal information. Almost fanatical. I've asked them once already and they refused."

"It could be a matter of life and death. Hector has found a connection. Nicole Caron stayed at the Parque Ciudad Hotel around the same time as Señora Ellis."

He didn't tell her they had stayed in the same room. He didn't want to accuse Michael Ellis of murder a second time, unless he was absolutely sure. Not after the first mistake.

"Oh, wow, I stayed in that hotel, too. That can't be coincidental."

"I don't think so. But we need to get those reports to Hector so he can find out for sure."

"Let me think." A long pause. "Alright. Listen, O'Malley knows the chief medical examiner really well. He and Ralph Hollands are good friends; they always golf together. I'll call O'Malley right away and see what he can do. Maybe he can get them through a back channel, once Dr. Hollands knows what we're up against. What exactly does Dr. Apiro need? Let me get a pen." He heard her shuffling through papers. "I'm back. Go ahead."

"The toxicological reports from Señora Ellis's autopsy and the analysis of her tissue and blood. Gas chromatography test results. If they were done, he says they should have them by now."

"The Chief Medical Examiner's Office is going to be really concerned about the link he's found to that hotel. The Canadian Public Health Agency won't be able to defend itself if another Canadian dies because it hoarded information. The authorities here got hammered for that a few years ago, after the Walkerton crisis. It's a long story, but there was a commission of inquiry into deaths from tainted water and the federal and provincial governments withheld information from each other. But if it's something in the hotel that's poisoning guests, there's no reason for a general travel advisory, is there? Couldn't you just close down the hotel until your people find out what it is?"

"All we know so far," said Ramirez, "is that Hector has found a link to the hotel, but only between the two Canadian women. We have to assume the problem is more widespread because of Rita Martinez's death. So far there's nothing to connect her to the other women or the hotel."

"I'll do what I can."

After he hung up, Ramirez called the Minister of the Interior's office.

After consulting with the minister, the minister's clerk confirmed she would prepare a letter to the Canadian Attorney General for the minister's signature stating that Rey Callendes would not be executed if convicted in Cuba. Apparently, the minister didn't care if that was true or not, as long as there were no political obstacles to the transfer. That made things simpler. She promised to fax the letter to the Canadian authorities as soon as it was signed.

Then Ramirez called Corporal Tremblay.

"We'll have a response for you as soon as the Justice Department confirms receipt of the minister's letter," said Tremblay. "Things should move quickly. I'll call you one way or the other before my shift ends at four. Where will you be?"

Ramirez looked at his watch. It was a quarter to one, and he was supposed to have checked out of his room by noon. "I'm not sure. I'll have to get back to you."

THIRTY-NINE

Detective Fernando Espinoza signed out a police car. "I'm sorry you had to wait so long," the mechanic said, wiping his hands on a rag. "I had to change the oil filter. Actually, I had to invent one." He grinned.

Detective Espinoza nodded. Mechanics were like *babalaos*. They worked magic, transforming bits of wire and cutlery into replacement parts. Very few new cars had been imported into Cuba in forty or fifty years, and yet somehow these wizards managed to keep the old ones running.

Espinoza checked the tank to make sure he had enough fuel for his trip. Nothing would be more embarrassing than to run out of gas the first time he drove an unmarked police car. He didn't want to have to hitchhike back to Havana.

But it was early in the New Year and the tank was full with the month's rations. The young detective was grateful. He did not have sufficient funds to purchase a tank of gas: three pesos was almost a week's wages.

After leaving Havana, Espinoza put on the right turn signal and exited the *autopista*. The highway was almost empty except for clusters of tired Cubans waiting beside the road to catch rides.

It was illegal for a vehicle to drive by the *botellas*, the underpasses where hitchhikers waited, without picking up a passenger. Only *turistas* and police were exempt from this rule of polite behaviour. The hard-packed dirt road wound up the hills to Viñales. He passed the occasional truck loaded with stalks of sugar cane.

The Viñales Valley was a World Heritage Site situated in the Sierra de los Organos. It was surrounded by *mogotes*, small mountains that looked like slightly flattened pincushions. Turkey vultures circled high above the mountains. The occasional mongoose and dozens of tree rats scurried through long grasses at the side of the road.

Espinoza drove past the mountain called Dos Hermanas, or the Two Sisters. The Mural de la Prehistoria painted on its side was commissioned by Fidel Castro. Leovigildo González, a student of Diego Rivera, completed it with the help of twenty or thirty locals, but even then it took years to finish. Castro thought the display would attract foreign tourists. Which it did. They came by the busload to laugh.

Four hundred feet high and six hundred wide, it was supposed to show the evolution of man: a tribute to Cuba's indigenous people, the Tainos. It depicted how snails had evolved into red and yellow dinosaurs, and finally into two long-haired Taino Indians, a man and a woman, their skin bright red. Espinoza thought it was fortunate there weren't any indigenous people left in Cuba to complain.

Oxen worked in the fields below, and the scent of tobacco teased the air. The barns were stuffed with tobacco leaves, drying from the harvest. A slight morning mist curled around the road.

Espinoza drove by the entrance to the Cueva del Indio, an impressive limestone cave with a river running through it. Once occupied by the Tainos, and now by thousands of bats, it was filled with stalactites and stalagmites as well as ancient cave drawings. One had to take a boat to go all the way through it. A local legend suggested that if any water fell on the nose of a visitor, he would have good luck. Espinoza hoped there would be time to explore the cave before he returned to Havana. After what happened to Rita Martinez, he could use a little luck. He felt terrible that she had died.

Three hours after leaving Havana, he entered Viñales. All the houses in the village were painted in different colours. They were neat and trim, one of the benefits of so much tourism in a small village.

He found the orphanage easily. It was on the main road, a low building, surrounded by a metal fence. But he wasn't really sure what he was looking for.

Inspector Ramirez had told him to find a little girl in a wheelchair, but that, and a child's crumpled drawing, was the only description he had. "That picture was in the cigar lady's apartment for a reason, Fernando," Ramirez had said. "I'm sure of it."

Espinoza was doubtful, but it was a nice day to be in the country, in the fresh air, away from the choking diesel fumes of Havana. He pulled the police car over to the side of the road.

Espinoza opened the iron gate and walked into the yard. He had assumed that children would be outside playing, but the grounds were empty. He walked up the path and rapped on a heavy wooden door.

"Yes?" said a woman, opening the door tentatively.

"My name is Detective Espinoza. I am with the Major Crimes Unit, Havana Division. I would like to visit one of your charges. A child in a wheelchair. A little girl."

"Oh, thank God. I didn't think he was going to call you."

"What are you talking about?"

"I would have contacted you directly," the woman said, "but the priest said I should leave that to him. I thought it should be turned over to the police. That's why you're here, isn't it? Because of my complaint?"

"What complaint is this?"

"A complaint I made to the Ministry of the Interior. About my suspicion that the children here were being abused. They transferred my call to someone who told me he would follow up. I told him about the time I saw the former administrator going into the dormitories at night when I was doing the laundry. I heard a little boy crying in the morning, and saw him rubbing his private parts. The church sent an elderly priest to look into it. He was a charming man. He said I must be mistaken but assured me he would look into it. Is that why you are here?"

"What was his name, this priest?" asked Espinoza, writing the information in his notebook. "And what is your name?"

"The priest's last name was Callendes. My name is Teresa Diaz. I work down the street at the veterinary clinic, but I come here on the days that it's closed. I help with cleaning and laundry. I like being with the children, and I need the extra money. Believe me," she rolled her eyes, "it's better than spending your entire day with pigs."

"Rey Callendes?"

"Yes, that was it," she said. She looked relieved. "Thank God. I was afraid for a moment I might have violated the oath he made me take. I had to swear not to tell anyone what I saw. But I felt it was my duty to report it. After all, I'm the captain of the local Committee for the Defence of the Revolution."

"You acted properly, comrade. We appreciate your cooperation."

Rey Callendes, thought Espinoza. That was the priest arrested in Canada for child pornography. He didn't like the sound of this. Children in orphanages were vulnerable to abuse; they were alone. Exposed.

"When was Padre Callendes here?"

"He arrived about two weeks ago. He stayed for a full week. And then they sent a new administrator to replace the one I complained about."

"What was the name of the priest, the one they replaced?"

"Father Felipe Rubido. I don't know where he is now. I assumed he had been arrested."

"Who else knew of your complaint?"

"No one. Although Beatriz's grandmother told me she has also complained to the ministry about the care children receive. She feels that Father Rubido hasn't done enough for Beatriz because her father is in jail. But that's not the government's fault. There isn't enough medication to treat any of the children properly when they get sick. We have the same problem at the veterinary clinic: not enough supplies. I told her I didn't think the ministry could do anything to help Beatriz, and I was right. When the priest came, he said we should pray and the child would recover. But she gets worse every day."

"Who is Beatriz?"

"The little girl you asked for. The one in the wheelchair." She looked confused. "Beatriz Aranas. Why were you asking for her if you don't know who she is? Did the ministry not send you?"

"I see no children. Where are they?" asked Espinoza, ignoring her questions.

"The new administrator has taken them to the Combinado del Este prison for the day. They have no mothers and their fathers are dissidents. That's why they're here. Not orphans, strictly speaking, but they have nowhere else they can live. Once every few months, the children are permitted to visit their fathers. The new padre said he would take them there personally. He's a very nice man. Not like Father Rubido, who was sometimes rude to the staff."

"And what is the name of the girl's grandmother?" asked Espinoza, making a note in his tidy script. "The one who made the complaint you mentioned."

"Angela Aranas. But the children call her Mamita, because she brings them dolls."

Espinoza thought for a moment. "Who was it that you complained to at the Ministry?"

"I don't remember who I first spoke to, but I remember the officer I was referred to. He told me his name was Rodriguez Sanchez."

Detective Espinoza wasn't sure what to do next. He radioed the switchboard at police headquarters and asked to be patched through to Hector Apiro. He told the doctor what he'd found out.

"I suggest you come back to the city, Detective Espinoza. We need to track down this woman's son. He needs to be informed of her death, prisoner or not. Inspector Ramirez will be returning later tonight. If you prepare a written report, I'll make sure he sees it."

"*Gracias*, Dr. Apiro. You know, I think our victim may have had enemies. She complained to the Ministry of the Interior about the conditions here, and she named names. Someone could have killed her to shut her up."

"Perhaps," said Apiro. "I have to leave police work to those more qualified than I. By the way, I found DNA on the knife handle. At the moment, I don't know whose it is, only that it's

male. If you identify a suspect, however, I can match the sample
to his DNA, with 99.999 percent accuracy."

"That's good to know," said Espinoza.

No time for caves, he thought, as he started the ignition. He
grinned to himself. But maybe this time, I got lucky.

FORTY

Inspector Ramirez's phone rang again as he was packing up his few belongings.

"O'Malley managed to get the records, 'off the record,'" said Celia Jones. "Clare has already faxed them to Dr. Apiro's office. But O'Malley says that Dr. Hollands has spoken to the head of the Canadian Public Health Agency, and it doesn't matter whether it was a problem with the hotel or in the city of Havana generally. Our Foreign Affairs Department is going to issue a travel advisory before the end of the business day today. They have no choice now that there have been three suspicious deaths."

"Do you know when exactly they plan to do this?" asked Ramirez.

"Well, it's the Ottawa bureaucracy. And there's a storm rolling in. The people at Foreign Affairs will probably close up around four. Maybe earlier, because of the weather."

"That doesn't give us much time," Ramirez said, frustrated. It was only minutes before one o'clock. That gave Apiro less than three hours to compare and analyze the results.

"I'm sorry. Believe me, I know the effect a travel advisory will have on tourism."

"I am frankly more worried that others may die before we find out what's causing this."

"What time is your flight back to Cuba?"

"Just after nine, but I need to be at the airport by seven. A little earlier if I have Rey Callendes with me, so I can arrange for his ticket."

"When is Corporal Tremblay supposed to let you know about the transfer?"

"He said he would call me by four. But I have to check out of my hotel room right away, and I won't have a number where he can reach me."

Ramirez glanced anxiously at his watch. He'd be charged for another night if he didn't check out soon. The Cuban government was already paying six hundred dollars a night for his visit. Added to that would be an extraordinary amount for the edible contents of the mini-bar, which he intended to empty into his carry-on bag, along with the tiny bottles of shampoo, the wrapped squares of soap, the plastic shower cap, and anything else he could pilfer.

"I know this sounds inappropriate, Ricardo, but I'm still on holidays if you feel like going over to the Rideau Centre before you leave. You did say you wanted to buy soap for your wife."

"I'm afraid I've lost some of my enthusiasm for shopping, Celia. By the way, I forgot to tell you, I brought Señora Olefson's camera with me." He picked up the camera he'd placed on top of the hotel dresser. "It should be returned to her. Can someone pick it up?"

"You can always leave it at the hotel's front reception desk in an envelope with her name on it. The staff are very good at taking care of things like that. You can get an envelope from the business centre in the hotel. But listen, if you have to check out anyway, why don't we go over and give it back to her in person? She lives in Sandy Hill, which is pretty close to your hotel. And I have a cell phone, if anything comes up. It's better than you sitting around the lobby just waiting. Dr. Hollands has my cell number; so does O'Malley. We can give it to the hotel switchboard, too. How about if I pick you up in fifteen or twenty minutes? It sounds to me like you could use a little company. After all, it's your last day in Canada."

"That's very kind of you, Celia. *Gracias.* And I have to give you back the clothing I borrowed, anyway."

"Keep it until we get you to the airport. You'll need it, believe me. I'll get it back later."

Ramirez quickly finished packing. He walked down to the business centre in the hotel's lower lobby, where he photocopied the file of documents he got from Corporal Tremblay. He charged the cost to his hotel room along with the price of a large brown envelope. He slid the copies inside the envelope and wrote a name in large letters on the front.

"May I leave this here for someone to pick up?" he asked the clerk upstairs at the reception desk as she tallied up the hotel room bill on her computer.

"Of course," the clerk smiled, accepting the package. "I hope you enjoyed your stay."

I enjoyed it far more than the Minister of the Interior will when he sees this bill, thought Ramirez. It totalled over fifteen hundred Canadian dollars. He folded the receipt and put it in his pocket.

FORTY-ONE

Candice Olefson wrote crime mysteries, Celia Jones explained, as they drove to the author's townhouse. They drove past the University of Ottawa campus and parked on a wide, treed street lined with snowdrifts. They climbed over one of them and walked up the narrow path to Olefson's home.

"I still can't get over how cold it is in this country," Ramirez said. He was shivering, despite the borrowed toque, mitts, coat, and boots.

"I know. When it gets milder, it actually feels worse because of the dampness in the air. Believe me, it gets to us, too. Canadians spend most of the winter despairing that it will never end."

Ramirez thought of Cuba, where there was only one season, and where so many Cubans despaired year-round.

A woman in her thirties opened the door when they rang the bell. She reminded Ramirez of his wife. She had a round, intelligent face, unlined with worry. Open, friendly.

"Oh my God!" she said, when she saw the camera. "Thank you so much for bringing this back. I never thought I'd see it again. It has so many great photographs that I need so I can finish my book. Please, please, come in. It's nice to see you again, Celia."

The woman shook Celia Jones's hand. Jones introduced her to Inspector Ramirez.

"I'm absolutely delighted to meet you, Inspector," Olefson exclaimed. "I have a character in my books who is a Cuban police detective. Listen, I brought back some coffee with me last week. Along with some very good *añejo*. Nine-year-old Havana Club. Do you have time for a cup of coffee? We can doctor it up with the rum and take the edge off the cold. I'm sure the sun must be over the yardarm somewhere in the world, even if there's no sign of it here."

Ramirez looked at Jones longingly. She nodded, smiling. "Sure. We have time."

"I would love some," said Ramirez. "I have missed Cuban coffee almost as much as my family and friends."

Olefson's house was filled with art, much of it Cuban. An Andy Warhol–style silkscreen, of the type Ramirez had often admired in the Old Havana farmers' market, hung in the kitchen. It was a red-and-white "Cuba Condensed Soup" poster. The label on the Campbell's-style soup can read "America's Favorite Revolution" instead of "America's Favourite Soup" and displayed a photograph of a cigar lady wearing several strands of Santería beads. It was a clever poster. The artist was well-known in Havana, but his work was too expensive, at twenty CUCs per print, for most Cubans to own.

"You collect," Jones said, admiring the pieces.

Olefson stood on the other side of a granite-topped kitchen island. She poured water into a stainless steel coffee maker. The kitchen alone was the size of Ramirez's apartment.

"I love Cuban art. I was lucky enough to visit the National Museum of Fine Arts during my last visit."

Ramirez knew the museum well. The collection of pre- and post-revolution Cuban art was contained in two buildings not far from the police station in Old Havana. One of the buildings, the Palacio del Centro Asturiano, had housed the Supreme Court of Justice for years after the revolution. The other, a much smaller building on Trocadero, was drab and air-conditioned until it was almost as cold as an Ottawa winter. The smaller museum was the inspector's favourite.

"Now, you're someone who might be able to answer a question for me," Olefson said. "One whole room was dedicated to an artist who stuck a sharp-beaked bird's head on all the people he painted. Does that mean something in Cuban culture?"

"I'm not sure, but it may refer to one of our gods, Eshu, who can change his appearance."

"I've heard of Eshu before. He's also a Catholic saint, isn't he?"

Ramirez nodded. "Santo Niño de Atocha, although he has many names. He is responsible for all journeys, so he is the god of travellers and highways, as well as the messenger between the living and the dead."

"Fascinating. Tell me more."

"Well, he carries a hooked stick called a *garabato*, for clearing brush, which he sometimes uses as a cane. He is said to be extremely small and good at medical diagnosis: he saved another *orisha*'s life when he was only a child. But he can be petulant, and he isn't always popular with the other *orishas*. He is a god, some say, who never really grew up."

"A Cuban Saint Christopher," Olefson smiled. "Funny, Saint Christopher is often portrayed with an animal's head as well. Now I'll have to find out why. You know, I loved that little museum. There was one painting in particular I'll never forget. It took up an entire wall. It was a gorgeous mural of Indians and conquistadores. With a priest who looked like he was imploring them to do something, although it wasn't clear what."

"Ah, yes, the Tainos. It's a very old painting. The artist captured their images just before they were slaughtered by the conquistadores. The priest was trying to convince them to convert to Christianity before they died."

"Oh, my, I didn't know that," said Olefson. "It does add a certain pathos to the painting, doesn't it?"

"It's too bad there isn't time to take you to our National Gallery, Ricardo," said Jones. "I didn't know you liked art. It's only a few blocks from the Chateau Laurier. It has some amazing exhibits."

"I'll say," said Olefson. "There's one there right now of a giant baby's head made entirely of resin. Maybe ten or fifteen feet across. Completely accurate in every detail, right down to the eyelashes. Incredible, really. It's so lifelike, you expect it to cry."

She brought over two mugs of coffee.

Ramirez sipped the fragrant brew and almost sighed with relief.

Olefson opened the bottle of Havana Club and raised her eyebrows. Ramirez nodded. She poured an ounce or two in his mug. He took a sip of the hot drink. For the first time in days, he felt warm.

"Let me ask you something, Señora Olefson," Ramirez said. "If you had a character in one of your books who wanted to kill someone from a distance, how would he do it?"

"A hired assassin, that kind of plot line, you mean?"

"I'm thinking more of a situation where the two people are together in one place before one leaves. The murderer is in another country altogether when his victim dies. What plot device would you use?"

"Let me think," Olefson said, sipping from her mug. "I guess I'd use a slow-acting poison. Arsenic, perhaps. I might put it in tea bags, something the victim drank every day. Herbal, probably. Organic. Something seemingly benign always adds a nice touch." She grinned.

"Suppose it is the victim who leaves the country, and the poison acts very quickly. And that the killer has found a way to leave it behind so that it is consumed later on, when he has a strong alibi. Any ideas?" Ramirez asked, interested in her answer.

Celia Jones raised her eyebrows. She pulled her stool closer.

"Alright, I'll play this game," said Olefson. "Hmmm, this is a challenge. It would have to be in something that the victim used regularly. Something so obvious that anyone looking at it would miss it altogether. Perhaps something that could be absorbed through the skin, like soap or shampoo. Is it a man or a woman who's the intended victim?"

"A woman."

"Then something only a woman would use, and wouldn't be likely to share. Like mascara. Or lipstick."

That made sense, Ramirez thought. The CIA had once tried to kill Fidel Castro by contaminating his favourite cigars with a botulinum toxin. They tried to poison his personal scuba-diving equipment as well. They had even recruited one of Castro's mistresses to murder him. They gave her poison tablets to conceal in a jar of face cream, but the pills dissolved.

Legend had it that Castro knew of the plot and handed her a pistol so she could kill him directly. "I can't do it, Fidel," she reportedly said. And then they made love.

"It would definitely have to be something that only the victim had access to. You wouldn't want to accidentally kill the wrong person," Olefson said, putting her mug down on the granite countertop. "Do that, you'll get caught."

Inspector Ramirez drank his coffee slowly, savouring the taste. He let his mind wander back to the Parque Ciudad Hotel as Jones and Olefson discussed the author's extensive art collection. "I've run out of space," he overheard Olefson say. "Once you start collecting something, you can never have too much of it."

According to Apiro, Hillary Ellis and Nicole Caron had stayed in the same hotel room as Michael Ellis, but Señor Ellis never became ill. Was it because he'd put something there to kill his wife that he knew to avoid? Or was there something toxic already in the room that didn't affect him because he was a man? But Apiro said chemicals didn't discriminate by gender.

Ramirez mulled over Olefson's comment that she would put poison in something so obvious that anyone looking at it would miss it.

Had he missed something obvious? He had personally searched the hotel room. And Hector Apiro and his team had processed it as a crime scene.

Ramirez tried again to remember what the room looked like when he and Sanchez first walked in. The drapes were pulled tight. There was a pair of men's trousers on the ground and a suitcase in the closet; the wall-safe was locked.

Sanchez had pretended to search beside the bed, sliding the evidence that framed Ellis under the mattress while Ramirez was looking in the bathroom.

What was in that bathroom?

Ramirez shut his eyes and walked the crime scene again in his mind.

Shampoo and scented soap. He remembered the soap. He had smelled it, surprised to find out that tourists were provided with perfumed soap.

A man's shaving kit. Toothpaste. Those could be eliminated

easily. Michael Ellis's personal belongings would have been gone by the time Nicole Caron moved in.

Soap and shampoo would be replaced every time a tourist checked out. And the maids would hang fresh towels.

Charlie Pike said that people on some Indian reserves drank only bottled water because their water was deadly. Could the two women have died from drinking tap water from the faucet?

Not likely, or other hotel guests would have become ill as well. Something nagged at him. What else was in that hotel room?

A chest of drawers. A television. A mini-bar. Ramirez had opened the small *frigo*'s door and closed it again when he saw it held only the usual contents. Rum, Coke, bottled water. Cans of orange juice and beer.

He thought of the mini-bar in his own hotel room, of the bottles of *agua* sitting on top, and of the little dead girl who'd placed a flower before it, like a grave. She'd provided him a clue, one he'd missed.

"May I borrow your cell phone, Señora Jones, to call Cuba?"

"Oh, heavens," said Olefson. "You'll be charged a small fortune in long-distance fees. There's a land line in the den. I have a plan that makes it almost free."

The den was a handsome room lined with wooden bookcases and more paintings. Ramirez picked up the phone. He dialed the police headquarters switchboard in Havana and asked Sophia to transfer his call to Hector Apiro.

The pathologist answered on the first ring.

"I've just received the Canadian documents, Ricardo. Thank you. There were traces of cyanide in Señora Ellis's tissues. I think she may have died from cyanide poisoning, although the levels were very low. But there was no fluoroacetate in her system whatsoever."

"Well, that may be, but I think Señor Ellis tried to kill her, and I think I know what killed Nicole Caron. You need to go to the Parque Ciudad Hotel as soon as you can and test the bottled water in the room's mini-bar. I think Michael Ellis put fluoro-acetate in it. His wife was cautious about drinking tap water. But she would have assumed that the bottled water was safe. Anyone would. If I'm right, the maids replaced the empty bottles when he moved out, removing the evidence. It's brilliant, really. But he forgot that the maids wouldn't take away full bottles. They would leave them for the next guest. I think Nicole Caron opened one of them, not realizing it had been tampered with."

"Perhaps. But even if there was something wrong with the bottled water, Ricardo, that could have nothing to do with Rita Martinez's death. She was never in that hotel room."

"So far as we know. Once we're sure of the source, I think we'll find the connection."

"I will go over there right away. We'll treat it as a crime scene. I'll seize the fridge as well as its contents," said Apiro. "And I'll check for prints on the bottles as well. But remember, Hillary Ellis wasn't exposed to fluoroacetate. Even if you're right, it doesn't explain how she ended up with cyanide in her system."

"Perhaps Señor Ellis tried to kill her twice," said Ramirez, thinking of Charlie Pike's *windagos*. "Or tried two different ways to do it, and only one of them worked."

"I suppose the Canadian tests could be wrong. And he certainly had motive. His wife was scratching the paint with his best friend." *Rayar la pintura.* Ramirez smiled at Apiro's use of slang. It was no doubt a phrase Apiro had picked up from Maria Vasquez.

"But it may be impossible to prove," Apiro continued. "Unless I find a contaminated bottle in that *frigo*, he may have committed the perfect crime. And Ricardo, it will take me at least eight hours to complete gas chromatography on the contents of those bottles. Fluoroacetate has a long retention time. I can run some other tests, but they won't be determinative of what's in the bottles, only what isn't."

Ramirez looked at his watch. He had less than two hours before the travel advisory would issue. Apiro didn't have enough time. Unless Ramirez could somehow prove the deaths were really murders. Then he remembered the black audiotape in his pocket.

"There may be a way, Hector. We can prove there was a link. We know Señor Ellis had opportunity. And as you say, he had motive."

FORTY-TWO

Miles O'Malley, Celia Jones, and Inspector Ramirez sat in the police chief's office. The tape recorder clicked off. O'Malley shook his head in disbelief.

"My God. I remember that night like it happened yesterday. I kept asking myself what we could have done differently, how we should have handled that call. I've questioned myself every time I've seen Michael's disfigurement, every time I see that photograph of Steve Sloan in the lobby."

"There was nothing you could do, Chief O'Malley," said Ramirez. "Your officer's death had nothing to do with you or your department."

Ellis had admitted to Ramirez on the tape that he killed Steve Sloan after Ramirez produced what he said was an expert report from Hector Apiro to the effect that Ellis's scars were self-inflicted.

It was a ruse. But it worked. Ellis admitted he hadn't told his wife he was infertile. When she became pregnant, he knew she was having an affair.

"Steve and I were working the night shift," Ellis said on the tape. "It was about two in the morning. Communications, that's our Dispatch, told us to be careful. A man on the third floor was schizophrenic, off his meds. That was all the information we had. No one mentioned he had a knife. We were pulling up in front when I told Steve that Hillary was pregnant. I saw the guilt in his face. I couldn't believe it. That someone I loved so much had betrayed me."

Sloan acknowledged the affair as he and Ellis took up their positions on either side of the suspect's door. "She seduced *me*," he said, "honest to God."

The door opened and a man with a hunting knife lunged at them. Sloan shot the man once in the chest. And then Ellis shot Steve Sloan in the groin, just below his police vest.

"I knew I'd screwed up," Ellis said on the tape. "I had one chance to save myself, whatever was left of my life, my marriage. And there was the baby to think of. That was all I had left."

He told Ramirez he took Sloan's gun and put it in his own holster, then pressed his gun into the suspect's hand. "The suspect was dead: I took his knife and pulled it down my face. It was almost a relief that it hurt so much."

Ellis had carved up his own face to cover his crime. Or so he'd said.

Ramirez believed that the real reason Ellis mutilated himself was his anguish at what he'd done. A split second of rage—a moment when he let his emotions get away from him—had forever altered his life. And ended Sloan's.

"The lad confessed to you, Inspector. I can't believe it." O'Malley shook his head.

"If Señor Ellis was angry enough to kill his partner over that affair, he may have been angry enough to kill his wife, too."

"But in God's name how? Where did he get the poison, if you can't bring it into Cuba or buy it there?"

"I think he *did* bring it into Cuba," said Ramirez. "Or rather, his wife did."

It had bothered him all afternoon. Something Señora Olefson said that kept circling around his brain. An exhibit in the National Gallery. A resin sculpture of a baby's head so real it could almost cry.

A smart killer would put poison in something a woman would never share, Olefson suggested. Ramirez had walked through the hotel room in his mind again and again until he saw it.

"There was a package of birth control pills in the bathroom in his hotel room. I don't think the pills were in *his* baggage: the sniffing dogs at the airport picked up nothing. But I never checked the surveillance tapes to see if Señora Ellis's bags had been searched. Even if a dog had found the pills in her luggage, the guards would assume that it had reacted to the medication. Prescription drugs are allowed into our country."

"You think she brought in the very poison that killed her, without knowing?"

"If I'm right, it could explain what happened to Rita Martinez as well. May I make a long-distance call? I think I can find out quickly."

O'Malley nodded and handed Ramirez the phone.

Ramirez called the Havana switchboard, but Sophia said Apiro had asked not to be disturbed.

Ramirez left Apiro a message. He asked Sophia to place a second call, to Conchita Alvarez, the new clerk for the exhibit room.

"Please check the Michael Ellis evidence box for me, will you? I think you'll find that the birth control pills listed in the log are no longer there." He held the phone to his ear, waiting.

Celia Jones raised her eyebrows. "What do you think happened to them?"

"I would prefer not to say anything yet, in case I'm wrong. But this will only take a moment. Conchita is looking."

A minute or two later there was the distant metallic buzzing of a voice on the end of the line.

Ramirez nodded. "*Gracias.*" He hung up the phone. "Rita Martinez was a single woman. She was on her way out for a drink with an attractive young police detective. It is almost impossible to get proper contraceptives in Havana. Our condoms are made in China. Like much of what we import from that country, they are made poorly. They are full of holes."

Rita was a girl who liked to go out. She had stolen the pills from the exhibit room, where she probably also stole the money for her new breasts. The same way Sanchez got fresh batteries and Apiro and Ramirez supplied themselves with rum.

"Rita took the pills," he continued. "She died because she wanted to protect herself from becoming pregnant, not knowing that they had been replaced with a poison meant for someone else."

"Good God. This is incredible," said O'Malley. "Unbelievable. I've known Michael for years."

"There may have been another reason for the murder, Miles," said Jones. "Not just revenge. Mike changed his departmental life insurance policy a couple of weeks ago, just before they left on holidays: He increased the coverage to two million dollars if Hillary died accidentally. It's circumstantial, but with everything else on that tape, it's got to be enough to arrest him."

"That confession of yours wasn't beaten out of the man, was it, Inspector Ramirez?"

"No," Ramirez shook his head. "He spoke freely. He wanted to get it off his chest."

"Yes, I can imagine that. Steve Sloan and Michael were best friends. As thick as thieves, those two. I can almost understand him being angry enough to kill Steve, once he found out his wife was screwing around with him, and particularly if she was careless enough to get pregnant. It's the way Michael covered it up for so long that shocks me. He completely took me in."

O'Malley walked back to his large desk and sat behind it, vigorously rubbing his bald head with his thick fingers. "I never would have thought he had it in him. But that wife of his. A woman like that attracts men the way flowers attract bees."

It seemed to Ramirez that O'Malley had missed the point. The police chief clearly had no idea that Señor Ellis was homosexual, even though Apiro had recognized it immediately.

"It seems obvious," Apiro had commented after listening to Ellis's taped confession. "Most men whose wives have been unfaithful get divorced rather than shooting their wife's lover in the *cojones*. And to show such concern for his friend's baby? Describe it as all he had left? All he had left of Señor Sloan is what I think he meant. I think it was not the fact that Hillary Ellis slept with another man that enraged Señor Ellis but *who* she slept with. His own lover. Steve Sloan."

"No point in beating yourself up, Miles," said Jones. "Mike was in counselling for months after the shooting. Dr. Mann didn't see anything to suggest he was capable of this. There's no way you could have known this was going to happen. SIU investigated; they cleared Mike completely."

"I suppose you're right. I feel wretchedly sorry for the Carons. And for your clerk's family, too, Inspector. They were the truly innocent victims in all of this. Not to mention Steve Sloan. He was a good man, even if he did make a mistake. There's a fine line between love and hate. I'm sure it's the same in your work. Most of the homicides we deal with are domestics."

"Yes, we see it all the time," Ramirez acknowledged. "Most murders occur within families. But they are usually impulsive acts, following petty arguments, disagreements. And they often involve excessive drinking. A poisoning, on the other hand, is deliberate."

That was the one thing that bothered Ramirez about all of this. Michael Ellis's emotional reaction to the affair, the split second of rage that resulted in Steve Sloan's death; these were things he could understand. But the use of poison required cold-blooded premeditation.

Like O'Malley, Ramirez hadn't thought of Detective Ellis that way. Ellis struck Ramirez as someone who, even if he thought about killing someone, would change his mind if given time to reconsider.

Once Michael Ellis had killed Sloan, he had done what he could to salvage the lives of those around him. His concern was for Sloan's unborn child. And when Ellis confessed, Ramirez was convinced it was to ease his conscience. Why had he not confessed to poisoning his wife at the same time? Could it have been because he didn't know if she had taken the bait?

The murder Ellis had admitted to had nothing to do with Cuba; that was the reason Ramirez let him go. But the one involving his wife *was* within Ramirez's jurisdiction. Perhaps O'Malley was right. Perhaps Señor Ellis had taken Ramirez in, too.

"Once you've killed one person, I don't think it takes as much soul-searching to kill another," said O'Malley. "Or a dozen, for that matter. Particularly in Canada. The penalty under our Criminal Code is exactly the same for killing twelve people as it is for one: life in prison. Well, we'll let the Crown figure out the details. Celia, you get on the phone with Andrew Britton and make sure we have whatever we need from the inspector before he heads back to Cuba. Your government will cooperate with us, won't it?"

"They will if the travel advisory isn't issued." Ramirez looked at his watch. Less than five minutes left.

"Sweet Jesus, I forgot all about that. I'll take care of it right away. Clare," O'Malley called out. "Can you get Ralph Hollands on the line for me? Or someone at PHAC? Inspector, I'm not sure I should thank you for bringing that little tape with you. I honestly wish I hadn't heard it. But the only thing that's really changed is that now I know something that I didn't before. Andrew Britton's a good Crown, and a good man. He'll make sure Michael gets a fair trial before he's convicted."

FORTY-THREE

Maria Vasquez and Hector Apiro sat together in his office. Apiro was happy to see Maria but also apprehensive. He took her slender hands in his. "I can spare perhaps a half-hour, no more. But there is something I need to talk to you about. I confess, I don't know how to tell you."

"You're not breaking up with me, are you, Hector? Because of the rice?"

"Of course not. No, nothing like that," Apiro smiled. "Never, Maria. You returned to my life like a gift. I will never stop being grateful for that."

Maria's smile lit up the room.

Apiro had thought long and hard about Ramirez's investigation and whether to tell Maria about the photographs of Arturo Montenegro taken by his attackers. If the photographs were on Rey Callendes's laptop, then they had most likely been circulated to others. It seemed to Apiro that in the relationship he and Maria were trying to build, it was best to have no secrets. He wanted to break it to her gently, but there was no kind way to tell her such terrible news. He launched right in, sickened by the expression on her face as she struggled to comprehend what he was saying.

"Oh my God, that is so awful." Maria's eyes filled with tears. "He was a sweet child, Arturo, always trying to do the right thing. How could those men do those things to him and then send such obscenities to others?"

Apiro patted her hand, not exactly sure what he could do to take the pain away.

Maria was right. The child's anguish had been recorded, preserved forever. It would be seen, over and over, and provide pleasure to other cruel men.

"I can't imagine it myself, Maria. Ricardo says the photographs he saw are beyond belief. Some of the children were little more than toddlers. Still in diapers."

"And these were religious men? How is that possible?" Maria made the sign of the cross.

"There is evil in the world. It has always existed and always will. Perhaps something in our DNA. Some remnant of our life as wild creatures."

"But these men, Hector, they took advantage of small children sexually so that they could take pictures of it. They turned the children into objects and collected them like stamps or baseball cards. Did they trade them, too? Not even wild animals are so cruel."

"I don't know, Maria. I try *not* to know. But Ricardo is in Canada now to take custody of the priest who had these photographs in his possession. Rey Callendes will face justice in Cuba. Ricardo should have him back here tonight."

"Rey Callendes?" asked Maria, stiffening. "Rey Callendes was involved in these photographs? He is the priest you're referring to?"

"Why, yes. The photographs were found on his laptop. He was on his way to Rome."

"Why in God's name would Ricardo want to bring that man back to Cuba?"

Apiro was surprised by the fear and anger that had crept into Maria's voice. She crossed herself again. "You know him?" he asked.

"He taught at the school in Viñales when I was a student."

"I see," Apiro said. He hesitated. "Did he hurt you?"

"No." She shook her head as tears rolled down her cheeks. "Not that way, Hector. No one did, not once I returned to the school from the hospital after Rodriguez Sanchez raped me. But Father Callendes liked little boys. I heard them coming back from the rectory, after his 'special dinners' with them, weeping with pain and shame."

Apiro stood up awkwardly. He bent towards her, patting her hair. She put her arms around his waist and sobbed. Minutes passed before she spoke again.

"He treated them kindly at first. When he finally attacked them, they didn't know what to make of it. Some of them believed that this is how adults show their love. They were so confused. And those who fought back ..." Her voice trailed off.

"What happened to them?"

She took a deep breath and wiped the tears from her eyes, smearing mascara across her cheeks.

"He passed them over to other pedophiles on staff. Men who were not quite so patient. Violent men, who beat the children into submission. We were trapped there, you know, all of us. We couldn't have visitors. Our parents weren't allowed to come and see us. We were permitted to write letters, but I am sure no one saw them. We all said the same thing: please, please, let me come home. When no one came to get me, I thought that either my parents no longer loved me or my letters were being intercepted. My mother and father were good people. I believed they would do something to stop these men. And so when I was fourteen, almost fifteen, I tried to run away from the school, to get back home. To tell my parents what was going on."

She began to cry again, placing her head in her hands.

Apiro sat down again. He pulled his chair beside hers and patted her on the back. "Maria, some burdens are too heavy to carry alone. You don't have to tell me, but I'm here if you want to talk about it."

She nodded. She spoke softly, her voice breaking.

"Rey Callendes came looking for me. He found me on the highway. I was waiting by the overpass for a ride. He told me he would take me back to my family in Havana if that's what I really wanted. I believed him. I got into the van. I was so excited to be going home; I can't tell you how happy I was. But he drove off the highway and down a deserted road deep in the woods. He pushed me out of the van into the dark. He knew I could not survive more than a few days without water. He said he would tell my parents that I died in the mountains, running away. And then he drove off, leaving me alone in a forest full of wild animals and snakes."

"How did you manage to survive?" asked Apiro, stiff with anger. No one will ever hurt her again, he vowed to himself. I swear it on my life. An oath to a god I don't believe in. In the name of the child we can never have.

"A tobacco worker from the valley below was hunting *jutia* a few days later. He found me. I had fainted from exhaustion and dehydration. I think he was disappointed to find out that I wasn't a tree rat. He managed to rouse me and gave me water. He took me to the tobacco huts in the valley. I hid in the bottom of his cart on the way; I was frightened of seeing anyone from the school. The workers were kind to me. They shared what little food they had. I was covered with insect bites and scratches from stumbling around in the woods. I was nearly frantic with fear.

"I begged them not to tell anyone I was there. A few days later, one of the men took me to a *botella* where they waited to make sure I was safe until I got a ride into Havana. But when I calmed down I realized my parents would never believe me. They were very religious, and they trusted the Church completely. I was afraid they would send me back to the school again, the way they sent me back before. I knew if that happened, Rey Callendes would kill me to cover up his lies. And so I came to the hospital to find you. I trusted you because you had been my doctor after Rodriguez hurt me. You had always been so kind to me. And I needed somewhere to hide."

Apiro's heart sank. "This wasn't the reason you wanted the surgery, was it, Maria? Because if it was, I have committed a terrible wrong. One that can never be undone."

"Not at all, Hector. Don't be silly." Maria smiled at him, wiping her eyes. "I'm happy with what I am now, believe me. I am who I was always supposed to be. But if I had a gun, I swear to God, I would kill that priest myself. Imagine, leaving a young child in the woods to be torn apart by animals. And then telling my parents I had died."

"Some things are too terrible to forgive."

Apiro tried not to imagine her terror in the deep woods, blind in the dark, hearing the scuffling of forest creatures. "But you must tell Ricardo what happened, so he can charge Callendes with this. The attempted murder of a child to cover up sexual abuse: these are special circumstances that will guarantee he faces the firing squad."

"Oh, Hector, I can't tell Ricardo what happened to me. Or he will know who I really am."

FORTY-FOUR

While O'Malley spoke with Dr. Hollands, Celia Jones contacted Andrew Britton to explain what was going on. Ramirez waited, trying to be patient, but found himself frequently checking his watch.

"Andrew will be here shortly," Jones confirmed. "He wants to make some inquiries about the SIU investigation before he heads over. We can wait for him in my office."

A few minutes later, O'Malley knocked on her door. "Good news, Inspector. Ralph Hollands says there won't be a travel advisory given all this new information."

"Thank you," said Ramirez. He exhaled, relieved. "Sincerely."

"I've got to get back to work," said O'Malley. "But you're in good hands with Celia. I'm just down the hall if you need me for anything."

Fifteen minutes later, Andrew Britton called up from reception. As he entered Jones's office, he shook the snow from his hair. He removed his rubber overshoes from his black leather loafers before he sat down.

For the second time that day, Ramirez and Jones listened to the small tape spin through Ellis's confession.

"I need to go over the contents of this recording with you,
Inspector Ramirez. The admissibility of this confession is going
to be crucial. I hear Detective Ellis is going to be picked up soon,
is that right, Celia?"

"There's already a patrol car at his house, Andrew. There's
been one there all week, because of the media. They're waiting
for Tactical Squad before they go in, in case Mike has his gun
with him. But the constable O'Malley just spoke to says that no
one has come or gone from his house today, except for someone
delivering a prescription about an hour ago. My God, I still can't
believe Mike did this."

Britton shook his head. "I know. I worked with him on a few
files. I always thought he was a good cop. But two million dollars
is a lot of incentive. We'd better get started; I know the inspector
has a flight to catch. Inspector Ramirez, I understand that you
taped Mike Ellis's confession on December 31. Where exactly
were you when you did that?"

Britton pulled a notebook with a hard black cover out of his
leather briefcase. He began to jot notes in it with an expensive-
looking gold pen.

"In an interview room in the Havana police headquarters."
Apiro had actually done the taping, but Ramirez didn't think it
mattered. "What are his chances of being released on bail?"

"Slim," Britton answered. "It's not easy to get someone out on
a murder charge at the best of times, although it happens. The
court will look at whether he's a flight risk, and whether he poses
a danger to the community. They will also be mindful of the fact
that, as a policeman, any time he spends in remand could put his
life at risk. And they'll look at the strength of the case. That's why
this confession is so important.

"We can't do anything about that clerk of yours who died,
or Nicole Caron; they died in your country, not ours. As for

Hillary Ellis, we don't have anything linking Mike Ellis to her death, except for those stupid printouts that June Kelly gave Chief O'Malley. I'd be laughed out of court if I tried to use those. I don't know what your laws are in Cuba, Inspector, but up here, there's case law that says if you plan to kill one person, and kill another by mistake, it's first-degree murder."

"Yes, it's the same in my country."

"If your pathologist confirms there's fluoroacetate in those birth control pills, you might be able to charge Ellis with the deaths in Cuba and try to bring him back for trial. Canada would want assurances he wouldn't be executed before they'd consider it. But we can't do anything about that right now. Not without a whole lot more evidence."

Not likely a prosecution the Ministry of the Interior would wish to pursue, thought Ramirez. Tourists didn't like to hear of other tourists being murdered, whatever the cause.

"I thought you were going to charge Señor Ellis with murdering his wife?" Ramirez asked.

"We have to do this in stages. Until we get copies of those laboratory reports from Cuba, Steve Sloan's murder is the only count we can allege. And it's pretty weak. Motive and opportunity, yes, but we still have to prove he did it."

"What do you mean, it's weak?" said Jones. "We have a taped confession, for God's sake."

"The Special Investigations Unit already cleared Ellis once, remember? His confession is the only thing that ties him to Sloan's murder. All the other evidence SIU collected contradicts it."

"But that's because he covered it up. What about the gun?" Jones asked. "According to what Mike told Inspector Ramirez, he switched guns with Sloan. If he still *has* Sloan's gun, that would prove he did it, wouldn't it?"

"Mike was issued a Glock when he was promoted. I checked that before I came over here. We don't know what happened to the gun he had before. It was seized by SIU for testing. They say it was returned to the Rideau Regional Police in case they needed it as evidence, but there's no record of it now."

Ramirez wasn't surprised the gun was missing. Lots of guns had walked out of the Havana exhibit room.

"He made no mention of removing any evidence when he spoke to me," said Ramirez. "I think he would have said something."

"Oh, shit," said Jones. "This is making me nervous. So the confession really is all we have. What happens if Mike gets bail?"

"Celia, I think we have enough to hold him on Steve Sloan's murder while we gather more information. And we can probably convict him, too, if we can find a way to get Dr. Apiro up here to testify at his preliminary hearing and trial. If your government will cooperate by letting him come to Canada, that is, Inspector."

"Testify about what?" Ramirez asked the prosecutor. He wondered what Apiro could possibly say about a murder investigation that had nothing to do with him.

"You refer to Dr. Apiro's expert opinion on that tape," Britton said. "It's pretty obvious that Ellis only confessed because you told him that Dr. Apiro was certain those scars on his face were self-inflicted. Without Dr. Apiro here to verify his opinion at trial, it's all hearsay. Our court won't accept it as evidence. And Irv Birenbaum will never consent to it being admitted if he can't cross-examine the expert on his opinion."

"Do you think Irv will act for Mike?" asked Jones.

"They're good friends, Celia. I would think so."

"Is this Irv a defence lawyer?" Ramirez asked.

"Best in town. He acts for all the police who get charged," Britton explained. "Even on disciplinary matters. And he's known for getting them off. He cross-examines every witness for days until they're practically begging him to tell them what he wants them to say so they can finally get off the witness stand."

"I am afraid there was no expert report," said Ramirez, frowning. "It is a technique I often use with tourists who I know can't read Spanish. I use an official-looking document and tell them it's an expert opinion, to encourage them to talk. Hector Apiro never examined Señor Ellis. I made it up. I think I may have used an office-supplies order form that day." He shrugged helplessly.

"Then we have a serious problem," Britton said tightly, clicking his gold pen repeatedly.

FORTY-FIVE

"Did I do something wrong?" Inspector Ramirez asked Celia Jones. "In my country, there is nothing to prevent the use of trickery when it comes to questioning suspects."

"It's a little different here," Jones said. "We have a Charter of Rights that gives suspects the right against self-incrimination. But I think Andrew may be overstating it. You're a Cuban police officer. You made it very clear to Mike that you had no jurisdiction over him or his offences. He spoke to you voluntarily. He never once asked for a lawyer."

"Look, let me get us some coffee," said Britton. "It's going to take us some time to think this through. What do you take in it? Milk or cream?"

Rum, Ramirez thought, but he doubted the Canadian police had any to spare from their exhibit room. "Cream if you have it."

"I'll go with you, Andrew," said Jones.

She returned a few minutes later with three orange-and-white paper cups in a cardboard holder. Ramirez looked at the lid on the tiny container of coffee creamer she handed him. "Edible oil substitute," it said. Ramirez wondered what he'd be ingesting, what substance had been substituted for edible oil. He pulled off the lid and poured it in his coffee.

Andrew Britton swung the door closed behind him. He threw some sandwiches covered in plastic wrap on the table.

"I have a list of things I need to ask you, questions we can anticipate the defence raising at Ellis's bail hearing. Here, have a sandwich. They're chicken, from the vending machine downstairs. Air Ontario doesn't serve food on its flights anymore. You won't have time for dinner."

"That's very kind of you. Thank you. Yes, my flight leaves this evening. But I have yet to hear from Corporal Tremblay of the RCMP whether I will be bringing Rey Callendes with me." Ramirez looked at his watch. It was almost five, and Tremblay hadn't called.

"Inspector Ramirez is supposed to be escorting a prisoner back to Cuba," explained Jones. "That priest in the newspaper. The one who was arrested at the airport last week with a laptop full of child porn. Do you have Corporal Tremblay's phone number? I'll call him for you, Ricardo, while you and Andrew talk."

Ramirez handed her Tremblay's business card and she walked into the hall. A few minutes later she returned.

"Good news, Inspector. Corporal Tremblay says it's no problem. He was waiting to hear from Justice. The Minister has agreed to return Rey Callendes to Cuba for prosecution. Tremblay will bring him here and turn him over to you within the hour. He said to tell you he'll bring the laptop with him. He also says he has an affidavit for you to swear. I can do that for you; I'm a commissioner of oaths."

"If he needs it notarized, I have my seal in my briefcase," said Britton. "I'm assuming a squad car can take you and the prisoner to the airport from here?"

"Shouldn't be an issue," Jones assured him. "Worse comes to worst, Charlie Pike's around."

Ramirez was relieved to know he had accomplished at least one of his objectives. He was still trying to figure out how to ask Celia Jones to swear a false statement before he left. The more he got to know her, the less likely it seemed she would agree.

Ramirez removed the plastic wrap from his sandwich, thinking how casually Canadians dealt with meat. He had eaten chicken only twice the entire year before. At home, a chicken sandwich would be cause for celebration. But there were no smiles on the faces around the table. Including his.

"Did you give Ellis his right to legal counsel?" Britton asked, his pen poised over his lined notebook, his own sandwich untouched.

"He had no right to counsel in Cuba, Señor Britton," Ramirez responded. He took a small bite. It didn't taste like chicken, and the substance around it didn't quite taste like bread. He wasn't exactly sure what it was.

"None?"

"Only at trial," Ramirez said. He wiped his mouth with a napkin and took a sip of the lukewarm bitter coffee.

"Did he ever ask for a lawyer?"

"In that interview, no."

"What does *that* mean? Was there another interview that I don't know about?"

Jones explained. "Mike was initially arrested for sexually assaulting and murdering a young boy, Andrew. Arturo Montenegro. That's why I was sent down there by O'Malley. Inspector Ramirez was investigating the crime. But it turned out that Mike was framed by one of the detectives in the Major Crimes Unit. A man named Rodriguez Sanchez."

"A detective in your own section? And this interview that you referred to, Inspector Ramirez, was it in relation to those charges?"

"Yes," Ramirez conceded. "Señor Ellis asked for a lawyer when he was being questioned by Sanchez and myself about the boy's death. But he had no right under our laws to have one. He was informed of that at the time."

Jones nodded. "I heard the tape of that first interview with Mike." She glanced at Ramirez uneasily. "But there were times when the tape recorder was shut off."

"Is that correct?" Britton asked, clicking the top of his pen even more rapidly.

"Yes," Ramirez nodded. He had shut off the tape because he had brought a bottle of *añejo* from the exhibit room into the interview so he could add some to his coffee. He needed it to control the trembling in his fingers.

Rodriguez Sanchez had made a second, complete recording from the other side of the mirrored glass while he watched Ramirez question Ellis. But Ramirez wasn't sure where that tape was anymore. Unless it was the tape that Sanchez had recorded over in the mountains when he kidnapped Celia Jones. The one still sitting on Ramirez's desk.

Sanchez had turned the recorder on while he described his own abuse at the hands of Rey Callendes, as if he was recording evidence, thought Ramirez. Sanchez had even asked Celia Jones if the statement of a dead man was admissible as evidence in a Canadian court, the way it was in Cuba.

For the first time since Sanchez's death, Ramirez wondered why.

"What's bothering you, Andrew?" asked Celia Jones, interrupting Ramirez's thoughts.

"I don't like this, Celia," said Britton. "Was Inspector Ramirez a person in authority? If he was, that confession is inadmissible. Ellis wasn't given his right to counsel. Quite apart from the fact that the tape is incomplete, which is a whole other problem in itself."

"Come on, Andrew," said Jones. "Mike was in a foreign country at the time. The Charter of Rights isn't carried around the world with each Canadian citizen as part of their baggage. The court sees incomplete transcripts all the time. That's not an admissibility issue. It only goes to weight."

"Courts are a crapshoot," Britton replied. "You know that as well as I do. I'd be a lot more comfortable if Inspector Ramirez had asked Ellis if he wanted a lawyer before he spoke to him."

"That's setting the bar too high," Jones protested. "We can't ask foreign law enforcement agents to apply Canadian laws. The most we can ask is that they apply their own properly."

"I'm not disagreeing with you, Celia," Britton said, "but there is a difference here. We want to charge Ellis with a crime he committed in *this* country. Irv Birenbaum is going to say that if Mike Ellis had been given an opportunity to speak to a lawyer earlier, this statement would never have happened. Correct?"

"If I had told him he had a right to a lawyer," Ramirez acknowledged, "he would not have confessed to me, that's true. I told him the truth. We don't rely on confessions in Cuba as evidence. We consider them unreliable."

"Exactly my point, Inspector. That's why he agreed to talk to you. And now we want to use his statement, which you told him was inadmissible, and which you agree is unreliable, as evidence against him. That's a big problem under Canadian laws."

"But we weren't *in* Canada."

Ramirez was confused. He wondered how Canadian police could ever get confessions if they told all suspects they had a right not to talk to them.

"If I had told him that he had a right to counsel, Señor Britton, I would have been lying to him. Even Cuban nationals are not entitled to legal counsel before an indictment is filed."

"But Celia had come to Cuba to represent him before you questioned him about Sloan," Britton said. "She could have advised him."

"Not really, Andrew," Jones said, her voice rising. Ramirez could hear her mounting frustration. "I would have been in a gross conflict of interest. I'm the departmental lawyer, for Christ's sake. O'Malley had told me to go after Mike if I found out he'd done anything wrong. I couldn't have given Mike advice if I even suspected he'd murdered Steve Sloan."

"Were you Mike's lawyer when you went down there or not?"

"I suppose, technically, I was acting for the department."

"Great." Britton threw his pen up in the air. "If we do arrest him, Ellis will be on the streets the moment Irv gets disclosure."

FORTY-SIX

Mike Ellis stood in the kitchen and watched the snow fall. The trees in the backyard were covered with a thick layer already. He shook his head, his eyes wet.

June 2, 2006. He had tried so hard to forget that night, it had become all he could think about. Most nights, he'd attempted to drink himself into oblivion. He'd failed at that. He'd sworn to quit drinking when he'd come home from Havana. And now he'd failed at that, too.

He had told Inspector Ramirez everything in Havana. He had waited for retribution—for lightning to strike him dead. Or for heavily armed officers to carry him back to the same cramped cell where he had spent four long days locked up with Cuban dissidents.

Absolutely nothing happened. No one arrested him. No one stopped him from catching his flight back to Canada. No police cars waited on the tarmac.

Inspector Ramirez had given Ellis what he'd never expected. Not exactly absolution, but something close to it. Ramirez had listened, sympathized, and let him go.

He gave me a second chance, thought Ellis. Maybe I owe it to Steve to take it, now that Hillary's gone and I'm alone.

He looked around the dirty kitchen. It was littered with empty bottles: beer, whisky, rum. For days, he hadn't eaten much except stale crackers and yoghurt, afraid to go out in case the media ambushed him. He ran his fingers over the scruff on his face. He grimaced when his fingers felt the raised scars.

Steve would have wanted him to live, to enjoy his remaining time on the planet. "Only comes around once, buddy," he had said. "You can't keep lying your whole life about what's important to you. About who you are."

"Fuck, Steve, what were you thinking? Why did you sleep with her?" Ellis had wept as he held Sloan's head in his hands and watched the light in his eyes fade. "I can't believe you did that."

"I don't know. Just to *know*, I guess. I couldn't figure out why you couldn't just up and leave her. But we're even, buddy. I can't believe you just shot me either."

Sloan held up his fingers. They were covered with dark blood. Arterial blood. They both knew he was dying. "I guess I wanted to know why you wouldn't leave her."

"For me" was left unspoken, and then Steve Sloan died.

Ellis threw the empty bottles in the blue recycling bin. He gathered up the dishes and piled them in the dishwasher.

He ran upstairs to the bedroom and pulled Hillary's clothes out of the cupboard. He rummaged through the pockets before he threw them in a heap on the floor. He'd call Goodwill to pick them up. Someone would want them. They were expensive dresses with Holt Renfrew labels, dry-cleaned skirts, silk blouses.

He found an empty condom package in the pocket of the navy blue dress Hillary wore each spring. He picked the dress up and recognized the smell of Steve's aftershave.

He buried his face in the soft fabric, inhaling the faint perfume. He finally put the garment down. He looked at the floor and slowly picked up the torn package.

Tears spilled down his face as he realized that Steve would have used protection. Maybe Hillary never was pregnant, never miscarried at all. She could have said all that to get even with him once she suspected he'd had an affair of his own, to make him feel guilty. She could have lied.

FORTY-SEVEN

"Are you serious, Andrew?" said Celia Jones.

"Absolutely. There are too many things wrong with this confession for it to be the only evidence in a murder case."

Andrew Britton began counting points on his fingers, the way he often did in court.

"Mike Ellis was questioned after he was misled as to the use to be made of his statement. He wasn't told that the interview was being taped surreptitiously. He was interrogated only days after another detective in the same police station, in the same section, framed him for a crime he didn't commit. Inspector Ramirez here, made up expert evidence with the precise intent of persuading Ellis to confess to him. And Irv Birenbaum will argue that God only knows what was on the missing parts of that first tape. Any one of those amounts to 'oppression' under *Oickle*. Put them together, we're screwed."

"That's a Supreme Court of Canada decision," Jones explained to Ramirez. "It says that evidence obtained by police trickery has to be excluded."

"The Crown can't do indirectly what it can't do directly. I don't care what Cuban laws are, we can't use information here that was gathered illegally there. We better hope we get more evidence than this. Maybe something proving that Ellis killed his wife."

There was a rap on Jones's office door. "Come in," she called. Miles O'Malley stood on the other side. He looked tired and disappointed.

Andrew Britton continued. "Because if we don't, Mike Ellis is going to walk."

"I'm afraid Michael won't be walking anywhere, Andrew," said O'Malley, shaking his head. "He's in Emergency at the Civic. In critical condition. He may not make it through the night."

"*What?*" exclaimed Jones.

"Tactical broke down the door when he didn't respond to the doorbell. He was lying on the kitchen floor, unconscious. An overdose of that medication he was taking for his nerves. A suicide attempt, from the looks of it. Well, I guess that's another sign of guilt, isn't it? I'll have to go over to the Kelly residence and tell Mrs. Kelly she was right. You know how much I'm looking forward to doing that."

"Oh, shit," Jones sighed. "She'll just go running to the press. We're still trying to figure all of this out. Let me deal with her."

"You'd best talk to her soon, then. I sent a patrolman over to the General to pick up her daughter's belongings in case we needed them for the investigation. He's just brought them back. There's nothing in them. There's no point dropping them off at Michael's residence, after what's happened. And it's the mother who's acted as the next-of-kin anyway. Can you return them to her? If we don't, you know she'll be screaming about a cover-up on the evening news."

"I'll take care of it, Miles. I'll drop them off on my way home tonight."

"There's a box and a carry-on bag; they're in my office. Thanks, Celia. My God, this is a year I'd already like to start over.

It's as if the universe has decided to play games with us. Every now and then, I think maybe God exists after all. And gets his fun kicking the shit out of us, one by one."

Jones looked out the window. "If I'm going to do that, I'd better go now. It's getting late, and with the bad weather the traffic will be crazy. If I don't leave soon, I'll never get home tonight."

"Go ahead, Celia," said Britton. "There's nothing more you can do here. I'll wait with the inspector and swear up that affidavit for him. Can we stay here and use your office?"

"Of course. Thanks, Andrew." She stood up and removed her parka from a hook. "Ricardo, it's been really great to see you, despite everything that's happened. I'm glad we had a chance to show you around Ottawa. Please don't worry about these charges. It's not your fault that the laws in your country are different from ours. We'll work it out."

"Thank you, Celia, for all your courtesy. Please tell Alejandro how much I enjoyed meeting him. I hope the day will come when both of you can visit Cuba. When you do, we will break the law together: Francesca will cook you a private dinner in our home. And I promise, I will keep in touch about the other matter. As soon as we have a free moment, Hector and I will start working on it."

"Thank you for that," Jones said, smiling. She leaned over to kiss him on the cheek. "We'll keep our fingers tightly crossed. I'll speak to you next week, Andrew. See you Monday, Miles. And for God's sake, call me if anything else happens. I have my cell with me; it's fully charged. Goodbye for now, Ricardo. Have a safe trip home."

"Tell me, Andrew," Ramirez said to the prosecutor after Jones left. "If a child is adopted in this country, what are the legal implications for the biological family?"

"I'm not a family lawyer, but from what I can remember, it's as if they never existed. I think they issue a new birth certificate in the adopting family's name. Why do you ask?"

Before Ramirez could answer, someone knocked on the door. Charlie Pike stood on the other side with Corporal Tremblay and an elderly man. Under his heavy coat, the old man wore the black suit and white collar of a priest.

He looked surprisingly ordinary, thought Ramirez. Nothing about him hinted at the terrible things he'd done. A small man with reddish skin, he appeared confident, relaxed. Not like a prisoner, but like a person one might trust.

Tremblay walked in and handed a brown package to Ramirez. "The laptop, Inspector. I'll need you to sign for it. And I have a statement for you to swear to as well. Mr. Britton said he would notarize it for you, is that right?"

Andrew Britton nodded.

"I'll wait outside with Detective Pike and the prisoner while you do that. To avoid problems, our lawyer said I have to transfer custody of Rey Callendes to the Rideau Regional Police first. Then they'll transfer him into your custody, Inspector."

More paperwork. To avoid liability, thought Ramirez. Everyone in this country was concerned about liability. It was the only advantage of living in Cuba, where people knew better than to use the courts.

"I've got the transfer papers here," said Charlie Pike.

"Good. Here's the affidavit," said Tremblay, and handed it to the prosecutor.

"Not a problem," said Britton, looking at his watch impatiently. "That's why we've been waiting."

FORTY-EIGHT

Celia Jones stood on the doorstep of the big house. She tried to balance the large cardboard box on her knee with one hand. With the other, she had pulled Hillary Ellis's heavy green Roots bag all the way behind her through the increasingly dense snow.

She was trying to execute two contradictory actions: ringing the doorbell with one hand while holding a box that required two. She finally gave up and put the box down, keeping it off the wet snow by resting it on top of one of her boots.

She rang the doorbell. The door had a knocker shaped like a mortar and pestle. Cute, she thought. She looked at the neighbouring homes as she waited. The Kellys lived in a nice part of the city, on a very good street.

Island Park was full of stately older brick and stone homes. The adjacent areas, Wellington Village and Westboro, were rapidly changing. The turnover started after a Mountain Equipment Co-op store was built, and continued with the construction of the new Superstore. Nearby retail couldn't easily compete. Mom-and-pop convenience stores were being rapidly replaced with yoga centres, condos, and trendy restaurants and bars.

Even so, it was one of the prime locations to live in Ottawa. It was a neighbourhood of embassies and private mansions. Expensive real estate.

It was a busy street, though, at this time of day. Island Park was a main artery between Ontario and Quebec. To the north, it led directly to the Champlain Bridge, which crossed the Ottawa River, linking the two provinces.

Traffic was already building from the Queensway to the Ottawa River Parkway as thousands of public servants lined up to take the bridge home to Gatineau and Aylmer. With the falling snow, cars inched along, bumper to bumper.

She rang the doorbell again and then hammered the pestle.

When no one answered, she was tempted to leave the packages behind and run, the way she had when she was a teenager. She and her friends would leave paper bags full of dog shit on people's front steps on Halloween night, set fire to them, and flee, giggling.

She tried again one last time. The door finally swung open. A white-haired man with a sweet face looked out the door at her, puzzled. She struggled to keep the box upright as the carry-on bag tipped over.

"Yes? Here, let me help you with that."

"Mr. Kelly? Thanks very much. My name is Celia Jones. I work with the Rideau Regional Police Force. Chief O'Malley asked me to drop these off for you. They have your daughter's belongings in them. Her things from the flight. They were left behind at the hospital. We thought you might want to have them. I'm so sorry for your loss."

"Thank you for bringing them by," Kelly said. "That was kind of you. You should be home with your family, getting ready for supper, this time of day. Particularly with that storm moving in. Thanks for doing this, young lady."

He reached for the cardboard box.

"I'm sorry, I do have to go over a bit of paperwork with you before I can release them. To make sure everything is in there that should be. If that's okay? It won't take too long, I promise."

"Come on in. May I call you Celia?"

"Yes, of course. Thank you."

She was grateful to get out of the cold and snow.

She hated snow, had hated it ever since she'd lost the man she tried to talk down from an icy ledge when she was a police negotiator. Not because he didn't come down, but because he did. Just not the way he was supposed to.

The mental image of the man, folded in half in the snow, the baby he'd been holding spiralling, head first, slipping from her grasp. It made Jones think of how close she came that day to dying. And then the hostage-taking in Cuba. She pushed these thoughts from her mind.

Nothing to worry about here, anyway. And she'd be home soon. Alex probably had dinner started. He loved to cook, and he was good at it. They would have *fabada* tonight, he had promised. A Cuban stew made with large white beans, *fabes de la Granja*. He had soaked them overnight and would fry them up with bacon, morcilla, and chorizo. She planned to stop at the LCBO on the way home and get a nice bottle of robust red wine.

Walter Kelly picked up the carry-on. Jones lifted the box and carried it inside.

She pulled off her high-heeled boots and left them on the mat in the foyer. She followed Kelly into the spacious designer kitchen. The grey quartz countertop, she noticed, was littered with empty bottles; they seemed out of place in the immaculate home. Some were Havana Club, but there were also some glass bottles with white labels and black print.

"Please, Celia. Sit down." He pointed to the wooden stools around the large kitchen island.

"Your home is lovely. Someone has exquisite taste." Jones put down the box.

"Thanks very much. That's my wife's doing," Kelly said.

He pulled open a drawer and took out a linoleum knife. He cut through the tape on the lid of the box.

Jones opened the flaps and took out a list of items from the brown envelope inside. She reached for a pencil in her purse. She removed each article from the box, marked it off the list of Hillary's belongings, and placed it on the kitchen island.

A woman's leather billfold containing a driver's licence, Ontario health-care card, Visa credit card, two hundred Canadian dollars in twenties, a taxi receipt, a Blockbuster movie rental card. A tube of red lipstick. A bottle of prescription medication in Mike Ellis's name.

She looked at the label on the bottle as she put it down. It was for diazepam, prescribed by Richard Mann.

Jones wondered why Hillary Ellis had Mike's pills. And then she noticed the dispensing information: Kelly's Pharmacy on Wellington Street. The street bisected Island Park Drive; the drugstore was only a few blocks away. Well, that made sense, she thought. Mike would have called Walter Kelly if he needed any medication; he and Hillary lived close by.

"I'd forgotten you owned a pharmacy, Mr. Kelly."

"Please, call me Walter. Everyone does. Yes, we've had it for years. 'Your Friendly Neighbourhood Pharmacy,' that's our motto. But we're closing it down soon, getting ready to retire. This business with our daughter really hit us hard. And retail is getting tougher all the time. That Superstore on Richmond Road almost killed us."

"I can imagine how difficult that must be. Not to mention the shock of what happened to your daughter. Again, I'm so sorry. It must be very hard for you both, particularly coming so close to Christmas."

"It's everything, Celia. There was a time when we enjoyed working in the drugstore. Now it's become a chore. We're hoping to sell the business, maybe leave Ottawa altogether. We're thinking of going somewhere warmer. Like Florida."

"I'm really sorry to hear that. I drive by your drugstore all the time. Now I'll have an excuse to stop in to say hello. At least while you're still there."

She smiled at the kindly old man. She removed a turquoise silk top, a beige skirt, and a pair of silver sandals from the box. A woman's bra, size 36C. Underpants, polyester, pink, medium. A book, *The Taming of the Shrew*.

She was unzipping the green Roots bag when a woman shouted from upstairs. "Who was that at the door, Walter? Has that asshole son-in-law of ours OD'd yet?"

Jones jumped, a little startled. The indomitable Mrs. Kelly, no doubt. The "untamed" shrew.

"Someone from the Rideau Police, dear. She's still here."

June Kelly clumped down the stairs. Celia Jones looked from husband to wife and back again. No information about Mike's suicide attempt had been released to the public. No mention of drugs or an overdose. There was no way that June Kelly should have known anything about it.

No visitors all day. Except for a prescription delivered about an hour ago.

"She's not here about that, June," Kelly said, and Jones heard the warning in his voice. "She came to return Hillary's things."

Jones stood up slowly. She pretended to look out the window. "You know, I think I should maybe leave. You're right; that is a bad storm moving in. Traffic looks snarled. My husband is expecting me for dinner. He's cooking tonight. I'm supposed to pick up the wine. It looks like all of Hillary's things are here."

She kept her back to the counter. Kelly still had the linoleum knife. He was gripping it a little too tightly for her liking. He didn't look quite as kindly anymore.

"Aw, shit," said June Kelly. "You should have said something, Walter. We can't let her go. Now she knows."

Jones looked again at the glass bottles on the counter, saw the small black skull and crossbones on the labels. The Kellys were the residual beneficiaries under the insurance policy. They would get the two-million-dollar payout if the principal beneficiaries, Mike and Hillary Ellis, died.

"It was you, wasn't it?" said Jones. "You poisoned Mike. The medication that was delivered today was from your pharmacy. You put something in it."

Walter Kelly narrowed his eyes and gripped the knife tightly. "There must be a syringe around here somewhere, June. You go find one for me, alright? A hundred-cc needle should do it. That's enough to cause an embolism."

June Kelly nodded and made her way back up the stairs as her husband extended the blade.

FORTY-NINE

Ricardo *is* good, thought Hector Apiro. He had picked up
Ramirez's message after Maria left, and made his way to the
exhibit room.

He found the green plastic disk taped to the bottom of Rita
Martinez's desk drawer: a package of birth control pills, with
several pills missing.

Apiro now stood in the laboratory, the contents of the
mini-bar in Room 612 at the Parque Ciudad Hotel lined up in
neat rows along the counter. He started with the bottled water as
Ramirez had suggested.

He dusted each bottle for prints but found only smudges,
nothing useful. He was almost relieved. Elimination prints would
have been problematic. Probably dozens of tourists had pulled
bottles in and out of that mini-bar as they considered their selec-
tion. The maids would have moved things around each day as
they replaced missing bottles.

For the next half-hour, Apiro checked each bottle of water
carefully, using the tests he had available. He found nothing out
of the ordinary in any of them. They seemed to contain only
water.

That left the beer, the cans of Coke, the orange juice, and the rum.

He opened a bottle of Havana Club and used a pipette to extract a drop, which he put in a test tube. He applied various reagents as well as metallic sodium and watched the fluids react.

By the time Apiro was finished his tests, he was certain that the small brown bottles of rum held something besides alcohol. It would take hours to be sure, but given the circumstances, he felt sure it was fluoroacetate.

Apiro sat down on a stool and lit his pipe.

Why would Michael Ellis bother to put poisoned birth control pills in the bottles of rum in the mini-bar when his wife would have died simply by taking her medication as prescribed?

Perhaps Ramirez was right and Ellis wanted to make sure of her death by finding more than one mechanism to kill her. But Apiro had never liked the concept of overkill.

Why poison the rum at all?

Water, Apiro could understand, but there was nothing in the Canadian tests that pointed to Hillary Ellis having any dependence on alcohol. Her liver wasn't fatty, and her enzyme levels were normal.

He shook his head. It made no sense. Something was wrong.

According to the medical reports provided by Celia Jones to Ramirez when he was investigating Ellis for Arturo's murder, Señor Ellis was infertile. Then why was his wife taking birth control pills?

Apiro spread out the various test results from the three dead women. He lined them up in rows as if they were cards in a game of solitaire: two red queens, one black. He scanned down the pages and then across them, comparing results.

His eyes stopped on one test from the blood samples the

Canadian medical authorities had removed from Hillary Ellis's remains.

A woman on birth control pills should have a decreased level of follicle-stimulating hormone, or FSH. Unless, of course, she was menopausal, which would result in higher levels of FSH than normal.

At only thirty-nine years of age, Hillary Ellis was unlikely to be going through menopause. The Canadians had tested her blood and urine for FSH, perhaps to rule out adrenal disease or disorders of the hypothalamus. But her FSH levels were normal. She definitely wasn't taking birth control pills, then, thought Apiro. And she hadn't for some time—at least four to eight weeks.

He put his pipe in the glass ashtray and pulled his latex gloves back on. He walked over to the counter and picked up the plastic envelope in which he had placed the package of birth control pills.

He opened the envelope and turned the package over. The label on the back was from a pharmacy in Ottawa. Kelly's Pharmacy. The drugs were dispensed in Hillary Ellis's name.

Apiro shook his head, puzzled. Señora Ellis had a prescription for birth control pills that she took all the way to Cuba but never used. Did she know her husband's pencil had no lead? If so, why bother?

Apiro sat down once more to think about this. He drew on his pipe again, watching the smoke float to the ceiling.

According to the hotel records, the maids had replaced only one tiny bottle of rum during Nicole Caron's stay in Room 612. Apiro picked up the test results from Caron's tissue samples and reviewed them again.

She had a very low level of blood alcohol, not enough to be intoxicated. But it meant she had consumed at least one alcoholic drink. The maids had replaced the empty bottle of rum at two in the afternoon, less than an hour after Nicole Caron collapsed on the sidewalk in front of the hotel.

A free afternoon in Havana, thought Apiro. A hot day, a cold drink. But that one small bottle could have held enough fluoroacetate to kill a village.

Ramirez had it backwards, Apiro suddenly realized. Michael Ellis hadn't murdered his wife; Hillary Ellis had tried to kill *him*.

Michael Ellis didn't drink water when he was in Cuba, he drank rum. A good two bottles of it in the bar on Christmas Eve after his wife left him alone in Old Havana. *He* was the one with the drinking problem, not her.

She had knowingly brought the poisoned pills into Cuba. It made sense, now that Apiro thought about it. Señor Ellis would not have hidden birth control pills in his wife's luggage; Customs officials might have asked her questions about them. Besides, they were prescribed in her name. No, she must have brought them herself, knowing full well what they were. That was the only way to explain it.

She had put the fluoroacetate in the rum in the mini-bar after she returned to their room to pack, anticipating that her husband would start drinking when he returned. But he went out that night to get drunk instead. He was taken into custody the next morning in connection with the death of Arturo Montenegro. Those two events—his going out to drink and his arrest—had saved his life.

Apiro had to reach Ramirez.

He hopped over to the phone on the wall. He dialed the number he had used previously, but Ramirez had already checked out of the Chateau Laurier. There was no answer on Celia Jones's cell phone either.

He tried to think where else he could try. Then he remembered that Ramirez had phoned him once from Chief O'Malley's office, a call that Sophia had transferred to the morgue. He called the switchboard and asked the operator if she could kindly locate the Canadian police chief's number and patch him through directly as the matter was urgent.

Chief O'Malley answered on the second ring.

"Forgive me for interrupting you, Chief O'Malley. My name is Hector Apiro. I'm the pathologist with the Major Crimes Unit in Havana. Is it possible for me to speak to Inspector Ramirez before he leaves for his flight?"

"He may still be here, Doctor. If so, he won't be for long. I'll transfer your call. If no one answers, then I'm afraid he's already gone."

When the phone rang, Andrew Britton picked it up. He handed it to Ramirez. Apiro filled Ramirez in while Britton fidgeted.

"That *is* very interesting, Hector. Was the prescription issued in her name?"

"Yes," Apiro said. "Dispensed by Kelly's Pharmacy in Ottawa. And Ricardo, a pharmacist would be able to get fluoroacetate easily. It would be almost impossible for someone else to insert pills into that plastic case without breaking it. They're designed to be tamper-proof. To keep children from being poisoned."

Kelly. Ramirez had heard that name before. But where?

He put the phone down and signed the affidavit without reading it. Andrew Britton witnessed his signature and crimped the document with a round metal notary seal, imprinting his name in raised letters.

"Thank you very much, Señor Britton," Ramirez said. "I appreciate that you stayed behind to take care of this."

"I have to go back to the office tonight anyway, Inspector Ramirez. The weather's too bad right now to take a chance on the

Queensway," the prosecutor said as he stood up. "I don't think we're going to get very far with the charges against Mike Ellis. Just so you know. But at least that travel advisory wasn't issued."

"That's a relief, trust me," said Ramirez. "Please, let me help you gather your papers."

He pulled the Crown attorney's documents towards him. As he did, some fell from the desk to the floor. When Britton bent down to pick them up, he lost sight of Ramirez momentarily. Ramirez felt guilty for a moment as he palmed the notary seal, but that was probably his Catholic upbringing.

"Again, thank you for your help, Mr. Britton. I'm sorry if I did something wrong under your laws. In my country, it would not have been a problem."

"Don't worry about it. Like Celia said, it's not your fault. We'll find a way to get Ellis. I hope your flight doesn't get grounded by bad weather. That snow is getting worse. Have a good flight back to Havana. Day like this, I wish I was going with you."

Britton closed his briefcase and shook Ramirez's hand. The two men walked down the hall to the elevators, where Corporal Tremblay and his prisoner waited with Charlie Pike.

"Chief O'Malley asked me to arrange a ride to the airport for the two of you," Pike said to Ramirez. "The weather is getting pretty bad. So far no flights have been delayed, but I was thinking maybe I'd better take you there myself. My truck can get through just about anything, and I have a cherry—that's a portable flashing red light—and a siren if we need it."

"That would be very helpful, thank you."

Ramirez handed Yves Tremblay the notarized statement. It had felt strange to swear a document on the Bible, to the Christian God, after all the messengers Eshu had sent Ramirez's way. But then again, the document wasn't true, which was something that Eshu might find amusing.

What was it Francesca had said about *The Beggar's Opera*? Ramirez cast his mind back, trying to recall. That she wouldn't believe they were really going to the opera until she heard the Peachums plot to kill their son-in-law for his money.

"Corporal Tremblay, I need to speak with Chief O'Malley briefly before I take custody of the prisoner," said Ramirez. "Can you stay a few minutes longer? I do apologize for making you wait."

Tremblay nodded unhappily. His working day was supposed to be long over. Ramirez could see through the windows how the traffic had slowed to a near standstill. Cars crawled forward a foot at a time.

"I promise, this won't take long." Ramirez walked the few steps down the hall to the police chief's office. Clare Adams was putting on her coat and gloves.

"May I see Chief O'Malley for a moment before I leave?"

"He's getting ready to go home, but I'm sure he won't mind," she smiled. "Go ahead, Inspector."

Ramirez poked his head through the door. "Excuse me for disturbing you, Chief O'Malley, but what was the last name of Hillary Ellis's mother?"

"Kelly," said O'Malley. He pulled on a dark-green parka with grey fur around the hood, then took a black toque out of the pocket and pulled it over his ears.

"Do you know if she owns a drugstore?"

"The family does. Why do you ask?"

"Chief O'Malley, I think your patrol officers may want to treat Señor Ellis's home as a crime scene. Someone from your technical services should check the pills in that prescription bottle of his to see what they really are. They should be extremely careful how they handle them. If the bottle contains what I think it does, it could be lethal."

"What's going on here, Inspector?" O'Malley frowned.

"I've just spoken to our pathologist, Hector Apiro."

"Yes, he called here. I put him through."

"Well, Dr. Apiro thinks that Hillary Ellis poisoned the rum in the hotel mini-bar. She planned to murder her husband. Señor Ellis has a serious drinking problem. She probably expected him to start drinking as soon as she was gone. But he went out to get drunk instead, and we arrested him the next morning. By the time he was released from custody, he was determined to quit drinking altogether. Nicole Caron checked into Room 612 on the same day that Señor Ellis checked out. She drank rum from the mini-bar. She died shortly after."

"My God," said O'Malley, astonished. "But if Hillary Ellis was trying to murder Michael, then who the hell killed *her*?"

"She may have poisoned herself by handling the pills. The drug is highly toxic; it could have been absorbed through her skin. Or the test results could be wrong. But the birth control pills were obtained from Kelly's Pharmacy; that's clear from the label. Dr. Apiro says Señora Ellis could not have tampered with the pills herself; the packaging was intact. Fluoroacetate is hard to find, so she had to have help. The logical person is her mother."

"She was certainly quick enough to blame Michael for her daughter's death," said O'Malley, shaking his head. "I thought she was crazy when she went running to the media. But I suppose that could have been a smokescreen. Something to distract us."

Ramirez nodded. "Something else troubles me. I had assumed that Señor Ellis had his wife's body cremated to hide the fact that she died from a rare poison. But he was in Havana when that decision was made. It was Dr. Apiro who pointed out to me that cremation made no sense if the family itself was alleging murder."

"It was the mother who demanded cremation," said O'Malley. "Michael didn't even know about Hillary's death. The General Hospital dealt with her when they couldn't find him."

"I think Señora Kelly conspired with her daughter to murder Señor Ellis in Havana. And I think she tried to kill him again today by putting fluoroacetate in the prescription that was delivered to his door this afternoon. With everything that's happened, the first assumption would be suicide."

"Oh, Christ," said O'Malley, slapping his forehead. "Celia went over to their address about an hour ago to drop off Hillary's belongings." He dialed her cell phone number. "I'm only getting her voice mail, but you heard her: she said she was going to keep her cell phone on." He tried Jones's home number. "No, nothing important, Alex. Just wondered if she'd made it home yet. ... Yes, I know. Probably the snow."

He put down the phone. "I need to get someone over to the Kellys' right away to check on Celia's welfare. Sometimes she's too goddamn smart for her own good."

"Nothing's going to be moving very fast in this weather, Chief," said Charlie Pike, appearing at the door. "Dispatch says all the squad cars are tied up at accidents. Celia's probably stuck in traffic somewhere and can't answer the phone. I'm sure she's fine. But I can stop by the Kellys' when I'm taking Rick and the prisoner to the airport and check on things. It's not too far out of the way."

FIFTY

"You really don't want to do this, Walter." The words sounded lame coming out of Jones's mouth. From the look on Walter Kelly's face, he really did. June Kelly re-entered the kitchen gripping a long syringe.

"It won't be painful, Miss Jones. I promise you that."

Not a good sign, thought Jones. The fact that he was no longer calling her by her first name was a way of depersonalizing her.

"An air bubble in the main artery will stop your heart in seconds," said Walter Kelly. "Carrying that heavy box in this cold weather can do that, too. Think how many out-of-shape men die this time of year starting snow blowers or shovelling snow. I know it's not perfect, but it's the best we can do on short notice." His wife nodded. "No one will suspect us. We're old; they think we're stupid. That stereotype has worked pretty well for us so far."

"Now, look, let's not be hasty about this. I work for the police, remember?"

Jones felt behind her. She ran one hand along the cabinets, trying to find something to defend herself with.

"She's their lawyer," June Kelly said. "I saw her name on the door to her office. It was near that police chief's. She won't have a gun. You grab hold of her, Walter. Let's get this over with." She pulled the plunger back on the syringe.

Walter Kelly moved closer; Jones backed away. She wished she'd kept her boots with her; the heels could do some damage. As it was, she had nothing. She kept talking while she tried to think what to do.

"I could just walk away right now and we can pretend none of this ever happened. It's not going to work. You'll be charged with murder. Believe me, it's not worth it."

"Sure it is," said Walter Kelly. "Two million dollars. We need that money. I'm over seventy years old. I want to retire someday. That's the irony of owning a drugstore: we don't even have drug benefits."

Jones tried to remember her training as a hostage negotiator. But it hadn't worked all that well in the past. For the second time in two weeks, she was a hostage.

Stall. Always use first names in a hostage taking. It makes the hostage human, appeals to their better instincts.

Well, forget that. This pair had no better instincts. They'd tried twice to murder their son-in-law for his insurance proceeds, and they probably killed their own daughter.

Jones's cell phone rang. It was in her purse beside her stool. If it's O'Malley, she thought, he'll know something's wrong when I don't answer. Please, please be O'Malley.

"Hear those sirens outside?" she said. "That's Chief O'Malley. He knows I'm here. I hit the alarm on my phone before I stood up. I have GPS tracking. That's the ringing you heard. The phone rings when they get a fix on my location. Triangulation."

She didn't have an alarm on her cell phone, but she doubted that a pair of septuagenarians were any more tech-savvy than she was.

"So you poisoned Hillary, too. They found cyanide in her

body. I'm guessing, June, that's why you didn't bother looking after their townhouse when they were away. Because you knew she wasn't coming home."

June Kelly looked puzzled. "What the hell is she talking about? What did you do, Walter?"

"I didn't do anything."

I don't have a weapon, but maybe I have a defence, thought Jones. Ramirez had suggested it. *Confound the opposition by doing something unexpected.*

She bent forward and grabbed the prescription drug bottle from the kitchen island. She spilled the contents into her hand: tiny white pills. She edged back along the counter, holding them out in her palm so June Kelly could see. Give her the details, she thought. Tell her a story.

"Look at these. That's how Hillary died, isn't it, Walter? She took one of Mike's anxiety pills on the flight home. This is supposed to be his prescription, but she had it in her belongings. Why would she have Mike's pills? I think you told her to take them with her. You knew she'd get nervous if she went through with it, if she poisoned him. The diazepam was supposed to calm her down. But they weren't diazepam at all, were they? They're cyanide. You killed your own daughter."

"Christ almighty, Walter. You killed Hillary?" June Kelly's face drained of blood.

"Of course not," said her husband. "I would never use cyanide. It's too easy to trace. I only gave her the birth control pills. The way we agreed."

Jones heard sirens in the far-off distance. She hoped they were headed in her direction, that it wasn't Patrol going to some accident because of the storm.

"The way we agreed?"

"We talked about it, June. C'mon, drop it."

Jones saw the confusion in the old woman's face. There's something wrong with her, Jones thought. She doesn't know what he's talking about.

"I'll bet that cremation was Walter's idea, too," said Jones. "Maybe you'd finally had enough of it, Walter. All the fighting. Mike told me how much June and Hillary hated each other."

"Well, Mike fucking Ellis doesn't know what he's talking about, does he?" June Kelly said, waving the syringe. "Hillary lied about most things." She turned to her husband. "We have to go through with this, Walter. The way we planned if things didn't go the way we wanted."

She's sending him a message, thought Jones. But what is it? She looked at his face, saw him nod slightly. Whatever it is, he's received it.

"Now, June," said Walter Kelly, nodding slowly. "Calm down. You know that's not true." He looked at Jones. "Alzheimer's, Miss Jones. My wife never used to swear either. Aggression is one of the symptoms. She's going to need home care. I can't look after her much longer by myself. It's too expensive. She dispensed those drugs to Hillary, not me."

"Why would you say that?" said June Kelly. "There's nothing wrong with me. It's Hillary. She steals from the drug-store. Diet pills, speed. She's anorexic, you know. She almost died from it."

"That happened decades ago, Miss Jones. My wife remembers most things from the past, but her short-term memory is shot. She gets easily frightened, paranoid. But we were there for our daughter when she needed us. For heaven's sake, the man had a gun. She begged us to help. The rat poison was June's idea. We always keep some around." Kelly had tears in his eyes.

Was he telling the truth? The tears looked real enough, but for some reason Jones didn't believe him. She tried to identify the inconsistency, the lie.

"That's crazy, Walter," June Kelly said. "Why would I kill our own daughter? We were going to split the money with her. A million dollars was supposed to be more than enough to cover our debts." She looked at her husband. "Wasn't it?"

Jones had no choice. She didn't know what was going on, but if the old woman *was* paranoid, she had to use it. Maybe Walter Kelly had acted alone. Either way, she had to turn the wife against the husband, buy some time.

"You heard him, June. Walter said you needed *two* million. Chief O'Malley told me how upset you were the day you came to the police station. But according to O'Malley, Walter sat there and rolled his eyes. How much can you really trust him?"

The old woman looked back and forth between the two of them, uncertain.

Jones pressed. "Where did those computer printouts come from, anyway? Walter probably told you he'd look after their townhouse while Mike and Hillary were gone. But he didn't lift a finger. He didn't even bring in the mail. I think he went there to use Mike's computer. He's the one who told you Mike was going to kill your daughter, wasn't he? Well, he lied to you."

"For God's sake, June, I didn't do anything to Hillary. I'm telling the truth. The lawyer's making things up."

"How long do you think you'll have before Walter decides he'd like that two million dollars all to himself?"

"Walter, you didn't do it, did you? We could have managed. She was our little girl."

"Of course I didn't kill Hillary."

"Then why did you say two million?" June Kelly demanded. "The lawyer's right. Walter, what in God's name did you do? Did you put cyanide in those pills? Tell me the truth, goddamnit."

"She's nuts. I didn't do anything to that prescription. I gave

Hillary the birth control pills. It was up to her to put them in his rum."

"Then why is *she* dead and he isn't?"

"I don't know, June. Something went wrong."

The needle in June Kelly's hand wavered. She wasn't sure who was telling the truth.

That's because no one is, thought Jones. We're all lying.

FIFTY-ONE

Charlie Pike drove his big red truck down what was normally a sidewalk on Island Park Drive. It had completely disappeared under drifting snow. As he got closer to the Kellys', he pulled the truck back onto the boulevard, honking at vehicles to get out of his way. Ramirez and the priest were wedged beside him in the front. The priest looked terrified.

Pike managed to control the vehicle through a number of skids. At least there were no pedestrians to avoid, he thought, spinning the steering wheel. The snow was pelting so hard it came down at an angle.

The portable cherry on the dashboard flashed red. Cars moved aside as far as they could; the truck skittered in between them. Pike missed a few by mere inches. The priest crossed himself.

Pike finally slid into the Kellys' wide driveway. The big truck fishtailed when he pumped the brakes hard. Celia's car was parked in front of the garage. It was almost buried in snow.

Pike pulled out his portable radio. "We're here. So is her car," he said to Communications.

"Ten-four. We have a squad car on the way. They're at the

intersection of Island Park and the Ottawa River Parkway. Don't go in there without backup. They'll be ten-twenty in a couple of minutes."

Pike clicked the radio twice. He never used the ten-code; he could never remember the numbers. He turned to Ramirez. "You wait here with the prisoner. I'm going to make sure she's okay. Here," he said, handing Ramirez his gun, "keep an eye on him."

"You keep it," Ramirez said, handing it back. "Old people can be vicious."

Pike walked up the path towards the front steps. He slid his gun back in his shoulder holster.

He didn't need to be a trained tracker to see the faint impression of a woman's boot prints leading to the front door—one set going in, nothing coming out. A lot of snow had fallen since those boots went inside. It shouldn't have taken that long for Celia to return Hillary Ellis's belongings.

He didn't want to ring the bell and startle the elderly couple. If Ramirez was right, it could cause a hostage-taking situation. But the few minutes it was supposed to take backup to arrive could turn into five or ten in this weather.

Pike didn't want to be too late.

There were wooden sandwich boards protecting pyramidal cedars at the side of the house. Each was made of two pieces, hinged in the middle; they looked like small teepees.

Pike pulled one over to what looked like the dining room window and stood on top of it. He balanced lightly on his toes as he peered inside, using his hands to transfer some of his weight to the windowsill so the boards he was standing on wouldn't collapse.

He could see Celia through the dining room doorway. She was backed against a kitchen counter. An old man held a knife. He waved it in the air.

There was no sign of Mrs. Kelly. *Shit*, Pike thought. I can't wait for backup. I've got to go in now.

He examined the window. It was old. Wooden frame, no bars. Plenty big enough for him to climb through. He took off his jacket and wrapped it around one elbow to protect himself from the broken glass.

"Enough of this," said Walter Kelly. "Forget the needle. Like I said, June can be aggressive." He swung the knife. Jones ducked; he slashed at the air.

In the dining room, glass shattered. It sounded like an explosion. Charlie Pike rolled in through the broken window and onto the hardwood floor.

"Jesus Christ, Walter," June Kelly screamed. "Someone's breaking in."

"Watch out, Charlie," Jones shouted. "June's behind you. With a syringe."

As Walter Kelly turned to look, Jones grabbed a heavy glass bottle from the kitchen counter, dropping the white pills. They bounced on the floor, scattering.

Walter Kelly spun around again with the knife just as Jones swung the bottle. It hit the side of his head with a dull *thunk*. He fell down, heavily.

"You stay back, or you're next." Jones held the bottle out in front of her like a club. "And keep that fucking needle away from me."

Walter Kelly groaned. Blood trickled from his ear.

"You killed him," June Kelly said. She looked panicked, her skin like crumpled paper.

"No," said Jones. "He's making a sound. That means he's breathing."

Pike stood up and wiped the snow from his shoes. He shook

off the shattered glass. He picked up his jacket and pulled it on. "Are you alright?"

"I'm fine," Jones said, as she started to shake from adrenalin. "Am I ever glad to see you. Give them their rights, will you, Charlie? And arrest them for conspiracy to attempt murder, kidnapping, and, I don't know, possession of a dangerous weapon. Two counts. A linoleum knife and a syringe. Just be careful with the old woman. Document everything. She may have dementia."

"You have your cell phone, Celia? Mine's in the truck. Call an ambulance, will you? Backup's on the way."

As Pike knelt to check on the old man, Jones made the call. Then she put the phone back in her purse, trembling. She felt sick to her stomach. She picked up one of the white tablets from the floor. She wiped it off, walked over to the sink, and poured herself a glass of water. Her hands were quivering.

She shook her head and took a mouthful of water. She swallowed the tiny white pill.

"What are you doing?" said June Kelly. "You said those were cyanide."

"Yeah? Well, you should know better than to trust a lawyer."

FIFTY-TWO

"Come with me, dear," Chief O'Malley said, holding June Kelly up gently. One of his homicide detectives waited by an unmarked car. "Not too tight with the handcuffs, John. Be kind. She's lost a daughter."

Celia Jones watched Mrs. Kelly get into the police car. Walter Kelly was already on a stretcher in the back of an ambulance. Protocol required the couple be kept apart, questioned separately. Jones had the sense they'd turn on each other pretty quickly.

"Old people," O'Malley said, shaking his head. "Mr. Kelly says his wife has Alzheimer's. He claims she acted on her own."

"It's an act, Miles." That was the signal, Jones realized. "When they heard the sirens, they knew they might not get away with it. They were practicing, the same way they practiced on the bottles. I was their dress rehearsal. At first he said he dispensed the birth control pills. Then he blamed her."

"No one will suspect us," Walter Kelly had said. "We're old; they think we're stupid."

"I'd like to know how long she's been displaying those symptoms," Jones said. "My guess is weeks, if not days. There's no way he'd let her handle any prescriptions if she really had

Alzheimer's. But it's the perfect defence. If she had it, no court would convict her. And no judge would ever let her testify against her husband."

One of them had decided to take out their daughter, maybe both. She wasn't sure which one. They both had motive and opportunity.

"We'll have to leave that one to the doctors to sort out," said O'Malley. "If you're right, she's set things up nicely, what with her complaint to us and all her media interviews accusing her son-in-law of murder. But with the evidence we have, Walter Kelly is likely to spend what's left of his life in prison either way. He's seventy-two years old. He might never get out."

"Well, you know what Fidel Castro would say. Do your best." O'Malley chuckled.

He was handling both suspects with kid gloves. He wanted no allegations of manhandling. June Kelly had already demonstrated how savvy she was at media relations. The white vans with giant satellite dishes would be pulling up any minute.

The case against the elderly couple wasn't entirely circumstantial, not with the bottles of rodenticide that Walter Kelly had experimented with.

But Ricardo Ramirez was right about one thing, thought Jones. A bottle made a pretty good bludgeon.

"Are you going to be okay, Celia?" asked O'Malley. He put his arm around her shoulders. "Was it a good idea to take that pill? How did you know it wasn't cyanide?"

"I was in Cuba with Mike Ellis last week. He told me he popped these things like candy. I don't know *how* I am, Miles. I thought being a lawyer would be a desk job. I didn't know it would be so dangerous. I'm thinking I should take up something safer. Like sword-swallowing."

She tried to laugh, but her mouth was dry. Possibly the sedative. Or maybe the fear that crept through her as she realized how close she'd come to dying yet again.

"I want you to see Dr. Mann next week. And take some time off. I'm going to get a squad car to drive you home. Someone will come by to get your witness statement later. I don't want you driving."

Jones nodded. She felt weak, and a bit disoriented. "That's probably a good idea."

"Give me your keys. I'll get someone to drop off your car later."

"Thanks, Miles." She fumbled in her purse and handed them over.

"By the way, Andrew Britton called me a few minutes ago, about Michael. It's not good news, I'm afraid."

"Is he dead?"

Jones tucked her hands in the pockets of her parka. She wasn't sure if she was shivering from shock or the cold. O'Malley wiped the snow from his eyelashes.

"No, he seems to be recovering now that the Civic Hospital knows what they're dealing with. They've pumped his stomach and have him on intravenous fluids. But Andrew says he's talked to the Chief Crown Attorney, and there's no prospect of charging him for Steve Sloan's death. Not unless we can find that gun. The Cuban confession will never be admitted as evidence at a trial here without it.

"We can't even know for sure that what Michael told Inspector Ramirez was true, given everything that happened to him down there. He'll be free to leave the hospital as soon as they're ready to discharge him. He'll have to resign from the department, of course. I can't have a man on the job who killed his partner."

O'Malley looked down at his rubber overshoes. Jones knew how disappointed he was. He treated his men like family. He'd always been fond of Mike.

"You mean, he'll get away scot-free? That doesn't seem fair."

"Not completely. We'll keep investigating. Meanwhile, when you get back to work, maybe you can get hold of the insurance company that carries our policies and make sure they get a copy of that confession."

"I can't do that," said Jones. "Privacy laws. But balance of probabilities, that's all the insurance companies need to deny a payout. The same burden of proof as the criminal courts in Cuba. They'll do their own investigation once they hear about all of this."

She looked at the reporters lined up along the sidewalk with their microphones, already broadcasting news of the arrests. "They'll tie that money up for years."

"You know, Celia?" O'Malley smiled. "I'm starting to think Cuba is my kind of country."

June Kelly waved at O'Malley from the back seat of the police car. A little old grey-haired lady, thought Jones. Counting on charm, and her acting ability, to keep her out of the penitentiary. Irv Birenbaum or one of his associates would have her released within a day.

FIFTY-THREE

Charlie Pike pulled his truck in front of the Ottawa International Airport. Ricardo Ramirez stepped out, followed by the priest. Ramirez removed his parka and the other pieces of borrowed clothing and handed them to Pike.

"Can you return these to Celia? And thank her for me?"

"Sure," said Charlie Pike. "Before you go, Rick, do you mind if I take a minute to talk to Rey Callendes in private?"

"Of course not," said Ramirez. He helped the handcuffed priest climb back inside the cab of the truck.

Ramirez waited on the sidewalk, his carry-on bag beside him on the ground. He stuffed his hands into his coat pockets. But an amazing thing had happened in his two days in Canada. He no longer felt the cold.

"Tell me something," Charlie Pike said to Rey Callendes, turning sideways to face the priest. "You taught at a school in Northern Ontario in the 1970s. There were four boys there from the same family. One of them drowned. Do you remember their last name?"

"I don't remember too many of the children," said Callendes.

"After a while, they all looked the same. We had a lot of runaways in those schools. Sometimes they never made it all the way home."

"You might remember the oldest boy," said Pike. "He says he was nine years old when you raped him. It was the same day his little brother drowned. Look, I don't care what you did to him; he doesn't have much time left. He's dying from hepatitis. If I knew his name, I could try to find his brothers so he can see them before he goes."

The priest flinched. "I don't know what you're talking about." He slid across the seat and pulled on the door handle.

"It's a chance for you to make things right," said Pike. "He blamed himself his whole life for something that wasn't his fault. He never went home after that happened. He couldn't face his family. You could help give him back something that you took away from him. Something important."

The priest turned around and looked at Charlie Pike. Pike saw something pass through his eyes. A shadow. Too fleeting to read. But he hoped it was shame.

"There were four boys from one family, come to think of it. And, yes, come to think of it, one of them drowned. I can't remember the English names they were given. We tried to discourage them from using their Indian ones, you know. But I think his name was Manajiwin. An Ojibway word. I never knew what it meant."

"I do," said Pike. His eyes prickled with tears. "It means 'respect.'"

FIFTY-FOUR

The plane was in the air. Rey Callendes sipped from a glass of water. Ramirez had removed the priest's handcuffs. These planes had only plastic forks and spoons, no knives. He doubted Callendes was a danger to him or any other adult, but he kept his eyes out for children.

The priest smiled slightly, holding up his plastic water glass. "Are you sure it's safe for me to drink this?" By the time they had reached the airport, the television screens throughout the terminal were showing footage of the arrest of Walter and June Kelly.

"Yes, I think so," said Ramirez. "Although I'd stay away from the coffee."

"You understand, Inspector Ramirez, that if you deliver me over to Cuban Intelligence, they'll simply let me go. They wanted me to leave Cuba. I was trying to, remember? I would be in Rome already if the Canadian authorities hadn't stopped me at the airport."

Ramirez nodded, slowly. "The Minister of the Interior called you when he found out Rodriguez Sanchez had died, didn't he? You arranged to fly out the same day. I thought that it was a coincidence. I don't like coincidences."

The old priest simply smiled. He looked out the window, holding his glass carefully. He tapped it with his index finger.

Ramirez was starting to connect the dots. A pornography ring, by definition, involved others. Not just Rodriguez Sanchez and Nasim Rubinder, but dozens, maybe hundreds, even thousands, of men.

The wonder of the internet: the instantaneous circulation of photographs of children being violated. The globalization of evil. Empires had destroyed the Tainos, had tried to destroy the Ojibway and the Cree. This one destroyed children.

Ramirez had been sent to Canada to make sure Father Callendes came back to Cuba. That he came "home," as the minister had said. The term implied that Rey Callendes, when he returned to Cuba, would be among friends.

If the Canadian authorities had continued their investigation into the images on Rey Callendes's computer, the distribution list for that pornography would almost certainly have led to men who preferred to be anonymous. Men powerful enough to approve a special travel authorization from Cuba to Canada in only three days, not the months usually required.

Ramirez thought about it. The only way the minister could have known what was at risk if the Canadian investigation proceeded in that direction was if one of the addresses on that laptop was his. Or one of his superiors. Or perhaps both.

Ramirez smiled. He sat back in his upholstered seat and pulled a cigar from his pocket. He rolled it around in his fingers. It was too bad the airlines had banned smoking, too.

He was finally starting to grasp the big picture.

FIFTY-FIVE

It was Saturday morning. Inspector Ramirez sat in Hector Apiro's office, enjoying a mug of his exquisite Cuban coffee.

"You have no idea how much I missed all this, Hector."

"All of this?" Apiro laughed, waving his arm around the room, indicating the dilapidated furniture, the cracked windows, the piles of books, the papers stuffed everywhere.

"The warmth of our conversations. The beauty of the ocean. My family. Even our bureaucracy."

Apiro inclined his head. "Perhaps some of your nostalgia is due to the investigation you became involved in."

Ramirez nodded. "Yes, the stories of child abuse broke my heart. My grandmother was wrong. She thought that only religion prompted good people to do evil things."

"Perhaps that's because she had no money."

"You were completely right about appearances being misleading, Hector. Walter Kelly, from all accounts, was supposed to be a nice, quiet man. But he was ruthless. I'm still not convinced he didn't kill his own daughter. I suppose we'll never know for sure."

Apiro put down his mug and reached for a file on his desk.

"Before I forget, that young detective on your squad left this for you. Detective Espinoza."

Ramirez flipped through Fernando Espinoza's report. It was interesting, for a number of reasons. "He did well," Ramirez said. "So the old cigar lady was the mother of a political dissident."

"Yes," Apiro said. "Paulo Aranas. He was jailed three years ago for criticizing the government about the organ donation program. He had no idea that his mother was dead. He was quite distraught, as you can imagine. Despite her age, he said he always thought she would live forever."

"The fact he is in jail explains why no one filed a missing person report about her."

Apiro nodded. "That boy, Espinoza? He is very good, Ricardo. He managed to keep Rita Martinez alive for almost twenty minutes until I arrived. He's young, but his instincts are impeccable. Did you know he had medical training?"

"No, I didn't. But I'm hardly surprised; so many do. And what of Señora Aranas?" asked Ramirez. "Have you had a chance to determine the cause of death?"

The old woman had been waiting for him at the Havana airport. She now sat impatiently in the corner of Apiro's office, crossing and uncrossing her legs. She stopped fidgeting and leaned forward, listening anxiously.

"Yes, I got around to it last night, finally. So much for telling Maria I wouldn't work nights. But then, she often works nights, too," Apiro laughed. "I think Señora Aranas died from a chokehold, Ricardo. The hyoid bone, which elevates the larynx, was fractured."

"Chokeholds are supposed to be used to restrain someone, not kill them," said Ramirez, as he considered this surprising information. "Most law enforcement officers and security agents are trained to use them to subdue suspects. The military, too."

"If one of them was responsible, that could explain why they tried to cover up the cause of death by using the knife. I'm quite sure it was intended to be a diversion."

"How long does it take to choke someone to death?"

"At least a minute or two. She was probably unconscious within seconds. If the chokehold had been released, she would have recovered without any ill effects. But the fracture shows that the pressure was far more than what was needed to subdue her, if indeed it was needed at all, given her age.

"The cause of death was asphyxia. The chokehold was the mechanism, not the cause, if that makes sense. Her carotid sinus may have been stimulated by the choking, causing bradycardia. But that's unlikely, given the petechiae I found in her lungs. Those indicate that her heart continued beating for a minute or two longer. She actually died of a heart attack. When she was stabbed, her heart had already stopped pumping, which explains why there was so little blood around the wound and on her clothes."

Ramirez nodded, chewing his cigar thoughtfully. He assembled the pieces, the old woman's messages, the clues he had ignored.

Did you ever want something for someone else so badly that you were willing to risk your own future?

The old woman had nodded in the exhibit room and pointed to her throat. She was trying to show him she'd been choked. Ramirez had misunderstood. And her deliberate refusal to communicate initially was probably her way of showing him how she'd been silenced.

Her son, Paulo, was arrested because of his concern that the organ donation program favoured foreigners over Cubans, and his fear that his little daughter could die because of it. Angela Aranas wanted better medical care for her granddaughter too. It might have cost her her life.

She had complained loudly to the wrong people, at a time when there were foreign journalists in Havana. A lot of money was at stake in that program; Apiro had explained just how much.

Security forces knew who she was. She was dressed in white, this mother of a jailed dissident. Not because she was a witch, or a cigar lady, or even an initiate into Santería, but because she was a Dama de Blanco. One of the Ladies in White.

Ramirez should have seen it: the way she'd paced behind the minister with her flower in her hand; the way she'd thrown it on the ground and stomped on it. She'd tried to show him what had happened, how security agents had reacted on International Human Rights Day.

Mamita Angela had marched silently in protest, in support of her son, until someone grabbed her and choked her and dragged her away.

What else had she tried to tell him?

FIFTY-SIX

"I meant to tell you, Hector, I had a detective from El Gabriel in my office before I left for Canada. Juan Tranquilino Latapier. He was smart, intuitive. A good investigator. And yet when I called there this morning, the station commander told me they had no such officer."

"But I met him," Ramirez had said to the station commander. "He was working on a murder involving a little girl named Zoila."

"We have no such case," the station commander said. "There has been no child murdered in El Gabriel for as long as I've been here, and that's almost twenty years. And I've never even known a police officer with that name."

"Juan Tranquilino Latapier?" said Apiro. "Perhaps someone was teasing you, Ricardo. That's a very famous name. But Latapier was no detective."

"You know him?"

"I know *of* him."

"Who is he?"

"You mean who *was* he. He was the first Afro-Cuban lawyer in all of Cuba. He represented three men who were executed for a child's murder. But that was a long time ago. At least a century ago. In fact, this could be the month of the anniversary."

Apiro pulled a book from the shelves and turned to the index, then flipped through its pages. "Yes, as I thought. It was January 2, 1906."

"Really?" said Ramirez, drawing on his cigar. "Tell me more about his case."

"It involved the supposed murder of a toddler named Zoila Gallardes. When her body was discovered, her heart and intestines had been torn from her remains. Eduardo Varela Zequeira, a white reporter, asserted that she had been murdered by three *brujos*—Pablo and Juana Tabares, and Domingo Bocourt, a former slave. Residents began to organize as vigilantes. The mayor accused the men of being *brujos* and demanded Bocourt and the others be charged. There was widespread hysteria. It was a fascinating case, Ricardo. I reviewed it in my studies in forensic medicine. It is extremely easy to confuse the bites of an animal with the wounds made by a knife. In fact, when I was still in Moscow, there was such a case in Australia. A wild dingo carried off a child. The mother was wrongly convicted then, too, but the mistake was eventually discovered."

"You think an animal killed Zoila?"

"Oh, yes, I am sure of it. The little girl's death occurred at a time when *jutias* were still plentiful. You will recall that mongooses were brought to the island to control them. The mongoose travels in groups, like hyenas. It is vicious enough to kill a cobra. When they were introduced into the West Indies, they killed off all the small mammals. And when they had destroyed almost all the *jutias* here, they began hunting for other food. Zoila was playing in her family's backyard. She had no chance against one mongoose, much less a group of them."

"Did Latapier argue this at court?"

"No, no, no. Originally, Latapier tried to defend Bocourt by arguing that he was insane, that as a *brujo* he was not in possession of his senses. But he lost that argument. As I recall, as he learned more about *brujería*, he tried to present new evidence to reopen the convictions. His last argument was an allegation that the local mayor had tried to protect whoever had sexually abused the child, and that the death was linked to that of another little girl who was raped and murdered. A knife had been left behind, stuck in her heart. He argued this was done to cast blame on the *brujos* and away from those who were truly guilty. But the appeal was unsuccessful. His clients were garrotted. This was long before firing squads became popular."

"It's interesting that the facts are so similar to the ones in our file."

"That's probably the reason someone pretended to be Latapier. It sounds to me like someone was having fun with you. A rather sophisticated joke, at that. But he was an interesting man, Latapier."

Apiro read aloud from the book: "'He was a supporter of José Martí, deported in 1895 for revolutionary activities. He returned to Cuba during the armistice and obtained his doctorate in law. He was the object of extraordinary racism in his lifetime. One newspaper, for example, reported that his success demonstrated that, with proper encouragement, a black brain could function almost as well as a white one. He married a white woman, a Basque.' Interesting: her last name was Aranas, too, according to this article. 'His children bore her name, not his, in the Basque tradition.' This says they had four children: a daughter and three sons."

"I remember reading about this case now," said Ramirez, nodding slowly as he considered this information. That was why the name Zoila had been familiar. "Fernando Ortiz refers to it in his textbook. The one on racism."

"That's correct," said Apiro. "Ortiz sat in the courtroom, watching the court proceedings every day. He thought Latapier was brilliant. The trial and appeals gripped all of Cuba."

"Do you have a copy of Ortiz's book, Hector?"

"Of course. Over there. Help yourself." Apiro pointed to a hardcover book resting on the buckled shelves.

Ramirez pulled it down. He opened the cover tentatively, half expecting to conjure Juan Tranquilino Latapier from its pages. But Latapier had returned to his own time. A black-and-white photograph confirmed that the man Ramirez had met was not a police detective but a lawyer who'd been dead more than fifty years.

Just over a century had passed, Ramirez realized, since Juan Latapier had stood before the Supreme Court of Cuba, presenting his new evidence. It was an argument he was destined to lose, but one that would change the country.

Because an academic named Fernando Ortiz was watching, mesmerized, taking notes of Latapier's impassioned appeal. Notes he would use to write a book that would influence Castro and forever change Cuba.

FIFTY-SEVEN

Ricardo Ramirez snapped the book shut and put it back on the shelf. This was a new development: a messenger who could communicate with speech, not merely gestures. Had Ramirez conjured Juan Latapier from the recesses of his memory? If not, and there were others like him, how would Ramirez ever discern who was alive and who was dead?

He wondered if he was losing his mind. How would he know? Or did mental illness creep up on a person silently, like a pickpocket?

"How is Señor Ellis?" asked Hector Apiro, interrupting his thoughts.

"Recovering quickly, from what I hear."

"You know, I've been thinking more about his wife's death. The Canadian doctors assessed her levels of luteinizing hormone when they tested her for infertility. They were normal then. But by the time of her death, those levels were grossly impaired. All of this points to anorexia. Her folate levels would have been below normal levels, even below those of most Cubans. That's probably why she died."

"Are you saying she died of starvation, Hector?"

"Well, indirectly, perhaps. She consumed a relatively small amount of cyanide somewhere and yet it turned out to be fatal, the result of poor nutrition from excessive dieting. It's ironic, isn't it? A Canadian woman, surrounded by abundance, starving herself to death. As for her husband, it helped that the Canadian authorities knew so quickly what they were dealing with. You probably saved his life."

"I'm not sure how grateful he will be. His career is over. And he may yet be charged with his partner's murder."

"As he should be, Ricardo. He should have killed him in his spare time." Apiro chuckled. "Given his employment, he took a big risk committing his crime while on the job."

Ramirez took a deep breath. He told his friend how he'd stolen money from the exhibit room and then found himself unable to spend it. "I ended up giving it away."

Apiro smiled. "You see, my friend? That is your good Catholic conscience catching up to you. That sense of guilt, the belief that there will be recriminations, even when no one is looking. As if a god, if one existed, would have nothing better to do than follow people around, making lists of who has been naughty, like the Christian Santa Claus. I think you are too hard on yourself, Ricardo. Even Castro siphons money into Swiss bank accounts. Rumour is, he uses diplomatic pouches. It's money for the revolution, he claims. But there is no revolution in Geneva that I know of."

Geneva, Ramirez thought. Diplomatic pouches. He hadn't thought of that. He wondered how many Swiss bank accounts Rey Callendes had opened. And how many secret safety deposit boxes in Geneva were full of CDs loaded with child pornography.

"It was such a small amount, Hector. I think that's why I felt guilty."

"Would you have felt any better if it was larger?"

"No," Ramirez acknowledged. "If I had taken more, there would have been no turning back."

"Who did you give the money to?" asked Apiro, as he added a shot of rum to Ramirez's coffee.

"A homeless man. An Ojibway. Anishnabe, I believe, is the correct term."

The old man was sitting on the sidewalk, wrapped in his blankets, when Ramirez left the hotel to watch for Celia Jones's car to pull in. He barely looked up when Ramirez dropped the folded bills in his lap. Five hundred U.S. dollars, in fifties and one-hundred-dollar bills.

"I can't accept this," he said to Ramirez softly. He tried to hand the money back. His hands looked like scarred leather, the blue tattoos on the backs of his fingers the same colour as the raised veins.

"Please, take it. It has no value to me. It is worthless in my country."

"God bless you," the man said to Ramirez quietly. "*Miigwetch.*"

His toothless lisp made Ramirez think of his little daughter and how much he missed her. He was moved by the fact that a man so abused by God still believed in one.

"There's no need to thank me," said Ramirez. "Thank the revolution."

FIFTY-EIGHT

It was 11 A.M. when the phone on the wall in Hector Apiro's office rang. Ramirez tensed. Apiro jumped off his chair and picked up the phone.

"It's for you, Ricardo. I think you know who it is."

"Welcome home, Inspector," said the minister's clerk. "The minister wants to see you in his office immediately."

"It's time," said Ramirez as he hung up. His heart jumped a little at the risks they were taking. "Do you still think Rey Callendes was the poisoned pawn?"

Ramirez and Apiro had worked through the evidence together until Ramirez could finally see all the pieces on the board. The possibilities, the counter-moves. They had no tactics left. Only strategy.

"I think so, Ricardo. But remember this. You have the initiative. Play the man, not the game. Good luck. You know what to do." But the small man looked worried nonetheless.

"The statement from Celia Jones. Affirmed and notarized, as you requested, Minister." Inspector Ramirez put the document on the polished mahogany desk.

"Well done, Inspector," the minister inclined his head. "How did you get her to sign it?"

"I didn't," said Ramirez.

The politician frowned. "Is the signature genuine?"

"It's as real as the ones on the Vatican documents."

Ramirez hoped Andrew Britton would be able to replace his notary seal, which now sat on Ramirez's desk. His slide down the ethical cliff had gathered momentum. But then, at least *he* hadn't lied about his actions. Whereas the Minister of the Interior had.

The minister flinched. "Vatican documents? I don't know what you are talking about."

"The documents you had couriered by diplomatic pouch to Canada. The ones leaked to the RCMP. Your handwriting is on one of them. I recognized it immediately. That looped *y* is distinctive. Hard to miss."

"Ridiculous."

"Not at all. I had much of this backwards," said Ramirez. "I thought that Sanchez and Rubinder took photographs for their personal use. But pedophiles don't do that, do they? They share their photographs. It's like art to them; they're collectors. They can never have enough of it." Like Candice Olefson and her paintings.

"At first I thought Rey Callendes was stopped at the Ottawa International Airport because of the Indian residential schools claims, but apparently very few priests have been investigated criminally in Canada, much less charged. The crimes are too old. And that confused me. Until I realized you made sure the Canadian authorities knew to stop him. It wasn't Father Callendes you wanted back. It was his laptop."

"I am sure I don't know what you're talking about, Ramirez. But you're walking on dangerous ground, making accusations like this."

"Oh, I think you do. It took me a while to understand the

thinking behind it. After all, I'm no politician. May I? This could take a while."

Ramirez sat down in one of the minister's deep leather armchairs. He reached in his pocket for a cigar, the first one he'd dared to light. But his pockets were empty; he had smoked his last cigar in Apiro's office. He reached for the humidor on the mahogany desk and removed one of the minister's. Once again, it seemed small compared to the cigar lady's.

"I've always been partial to Montecristos." Ramirez struck a match and inhaled. "Ah, the taste of a good cigar. It really is good to be back home."

He wondered if it would be inappropriate to ask for a glass of rum. Then again, this was how co-conspirators dealt with each other, wasn't it?

"About Rey Callendes. You see, I thought he was on his way to Cuba when he was arrested in Canada. But he was headed in the other direction, for the Vatican. He told me on the flight here that you personally informed him about Sanchez's death. I think you warned him to get the laptop out of the country before someone in my office thought to look more deeply into Sanchez's activities. That's why my authorization was approved so quickly. To distract me."

Ramirez had allowed the minister to divert him from the person he should have been investigating—Rey Callendes—by sending him to Canada, putting him up in a nice hotel, letting him put expensive meals on his tab.

"But sending Callendes away so quickly after Sanchez's death was a poor move. The Kotov syndrome, Apiro would call it. It was a bad decision, made under the pressure of time. You realized as soon as he left that you didn't trust him. He could use the information on that computer to his own advantage. Perhaps to blackmail you, or the government.

"So you contacted the Canadian authorities to warn them there was a pedophile with a stopover in Ottawa and that they should check his laptop. Normally, they don't look all that closely; trust me, I was there. But that created a new problem: if the RCMP examined the computer too carefully, they might find the distribution list for all the recipients of those pictures. You realized you needed to get it back. Which meant creating another diversion."

Ramirez exhaled. The smoke corkscrewed overhead.

"This, I think, is where it gets interesting. Once Callendes was arrested, you realized it would create an international scandal. This was something you could use for other purposes. You created a set of false Vatican documents and had our embassy leak them to the RCMP, with the help of Cuban Intelligence."

An oxymoron, Ramirez thought. But he might as well blame Cuban Intelligence, even though the minister's own clerk had been seconded to the task. She wrote English fluently, but seemed unable to spell some words correctly. The faked memorandum stated that Rey Callendes would "lick" to inform his superiors of events at the school in Viñales. Well, perhaps he had.

But the minister knew what happened to Sanchez at that school: all of the facts were in Ramirez's draft report to the Attorney General. The fake memorandum was easy to manufacture once the minister had that information. And the other documents? For all Ramirez knew, they were genuine. Maybe true.

"It was a good ploy," said Ramirez. "The Canadians were after the Catholic Church in a civil action for a lot of money. There's a multi-billion-dollar settlement that the Catholic Church has refused to contribute to so far. They were almost too happy to give us Rey Callendes back if I would only confirm the authenticity of the Cuban documents they'd received. That was easy enough for me to do, once I realized you were the one who gave them the documents in the first place."

Ramirez could tell from the minister's face that he had scored.

"Rey Callendes shared a lot of information with you over the years, despite his oath of silence. He knew a lot about the cover-up of claims of child abuse, didn't he? He held a position of considerable power. My fault, I didn't realize he was a bishop; I thought he was a pawn. Once you had Callendes back in Cuba, it gave you something to trade with the Vatican, because they want him back too."

"Complete nonsense. You accuse me of forging documents? I'll have your head for this," the minister sputtered.

"The RCMP officer working on this matter is the one who told me the documents were leaked. He mentioned a Cuban connection. When I realized he meant you, I wondered why you'd done it. It made sense when I learned the Catholic Church is facing an enormous wave of lawsuits. Twelve thousand claims in Canada alone. More legal actions forthcoming, I imagine, once the Dublin inquiry releases its report. The world is like a giant chessboard when it comes to protecting Church assets. But you already knew that. You knew that if the Canadians relied on those documents in their court action, it would frighten the Vatican into moving quickly. I seriously underestimated you. My apologies, Minister. You're not stupid at all."

"Your logic escapes me," said the minister, ignoring the insult. He pulled a cigar from the humidor on his desk and rolled it back and forth in his fingers.

"Ah, that's what Apiro says sometimes, too. That I use faulty logic. But it allows me to be creative. Here's my thinking. Cuba needs money. The Catholic Church has money. Cuba wants the Catholic Church's money. Is that logical enough for you?"

"You think I would blackmail the Catholic Church?"

"Not blackmail it. But certainly make it think it was about to be torn apart. After all, if the CIA could create an exploding cigar, Cuban Intelligence could create an exploding file. The prospect of the Church being sued for billions of dollars around the world would send it into a panic. All that money at risk. But Cuba would be a safe place for the Vatican to hide its assets. Too harsh? Alright, let's say *protect* them. Not only do we have no extradition treaties, but there is no reciprocal enforcement of civil judgments with other countries. Once the money is invested here, it's safe from foreign judgments."

The minister forced his face into a tight smile. "Certainly imaginative. And insubordinate as well, Ramirez. I should have you arrested." He reached for the phone on his desk.

"Yes," Ramirez nodded. "You probably should. But I think you should hear everything I have to say first. I'm sure the distribution list encrypted on that computer is a long one. In fact, I'm quite interested to see just how far it reaches. The internet is a wonderful thing. One of its many uses, I learned in Canada, is for the dissemination of child pornography."

The minister collapsed in his chair. "What do you think you know, Ramirez?"

Ramirez thought back to the old cigar lady, the photograph she had stopped to examine in the hallway. She had given him another clue, he realized. Another one he had misunderstood.

"Rey Callendes was the priest who administered last rites to the counter-revolutionaries after the revolution, wasn't he. He's seventy-six, the same age as Raúl Castro. I should have recognized him in that photograph hanging in the hallway, but forty years does a lot to a man.

"Che Guevara was responsible for deciding who were war criminals and who would be executed. He was Argentinean, not Cuban, and therefore extremely efficient. But he was raised a Catholic and probably had a guilty conscience, something I have recently experienced firsthand. The least he could do was let a priest meet with the prisoners to give them the sacraments. Rey Callendes knew just how summarily some of those prisoners were killed, and who fired the bullets. Bullets kill, you know. Another logic tree. People fire the guns. But guns make bullets go very, very fast.

"I'm guessing some of our leaders were a little overly enthusiastic when it came to sending Batista supporters over to the other side. Rey Callendes kept that information to himself. Which allowed him, once he was assigned to the boarding school at Viñales, to rape little boys with complete impunity. He knew he would never be prosecuted, that the presidential palace would protect him at all costs because of what he witnessed in the mountains.

"His work allowed him to identify men of like mind. He even brought in his friends, like Father Felipe Rubido, to work with him. When complaints began to circulate about abuse in the Catholic schools, Fidel Castro closed them, but he didn't close the orphanages. I never thought to ask why Sanchez had maintained such a close connection to Viñales even after he had been sent for re-education to another school.

"At first, I couldn't understand why you insisted on making Sanchez a hero when we both knew what he was. I wrongly assumed that Sanchez no longer had any contact with the priest who had molested him. But he didn't hate Rey Callendes; he loved him. He supplied Callendes with photographs of little boys."

"So Father Callendes has certain tendencies," said the minister. "So what? You already knew that. It was in your report. And so what if Callendes had photographs on his laptop? There's nothing revolutionary about that."

"Good pun," Ramirez smiled. "I have a friend who would appreciate your sense of humour. But as Orwell said, in a time of universal deceit, even telling the truth is revolutionary. If I had

been thinking clearly, I would have realized that a child pornography ring, by definition, involves more than two people. Which
brings me back to the information on that computer. With the
greatest of respect, Minister, and I mean this sincerely, you've
been juggling a lot of balls."

Apiro would have laughed. The minister stiffened with rage.

"You fool," spat the minister, banging his hand on the desk.
"You have no idea what you're involved in. Why do you think
we sent *you* to Canada instead of Luis Perez? Because you're not
yet corrupted." Despite the minister's intent, Ramirez didn't feel
insulted for not having achieved the prosecutor's high level of
corruption.

"Yes, we leaked documents to Canada," the minister continued,
"but you're the one who swore under oath that they were true.
The Canadians have already threatened to issue search warrants
based on the reliability of those documents. When the story
of the Vatican's cover-up hits the wire services, lawyers across
North America and overseas will be signing plaintiffs up by the
thousands. The damages will be huge. Our consulate is talking
to Vatican authorities about the considerable investments they
might make to help our economy."

Religion and money, thought Ramirez. There would never be
charges against Rey Callendes. The whole thing had been a sham.
A passive sacrifice, Apiro would say. The minister had moved
Ramirez to avoid giving up his own man.

"You were afraid that if Rey Callendes was charged in Canada,
he might tell the RCMP about the prominent men here who
engage regularly in the sexual abuse of children and photograph themselves while they're at it. And that would shut off
the economic tap. The Vatican wouldn't dare send money to a
country run by men linked to a child-sex scandal; that's what
they're trying to escape."

Ramirez leaned back, enjoying the cigar enormously. Despite its small size, it was one of the best he'd ever had.

Money laundering. Bank accounts in Geneva. Political intrigue. Yes, Havana was returning to the good old days of Batista. And the embargo hadn't even been lifted. But Catholic money could flow more quickly than American investments. And, even better for the Communist Party, it lacked the taint of capitalism. It didn't require democratic change.

"Billions of dollars are involved, Ramirez," said the minister. "That's money we need for reconstruction, food, fuel. With that kind of money at stake, you should understand that any one man is dispensable. And *we* have the laptop now."

"Before you get too far with that line of thinking, you should know I figured most of this out before I left Canada. I understood the importance of that laptop. That's why I asked the Canadians to turn it over."

"Its contents have already been destroyed by our intelligence section."

Ramirez shook his head. "You really place much more faith in the Cuban Intelligence Service than I do." Duplicates, triplicates, those files were probably all over Havana if Cuban Intelligence had taken control of them. "But you forget, there were *two* laptops. The one Callendes had and the one I assigned to Sanchez. My fault, really. I gave Sanchez a secure laptop to monitor the internet.

"The encryption on it wasn't difficult to decipher. A silly password, really. But it produced a very interesting list of names. I have someone in my office working through them now. I'm quite sure we've found the location of some of those pictures as well. My new detective, Espinoza, made a trip to the Viñales orphanage this week."

The politician turned pale. He slumped lower in his chair. He was looking older with every passing moment. Ramirez almost felt sorry for him. But all he had to do was think of the abuse in those photographs to overcome any sympathy he might have.

"What is it you want, Ramirez? Money?"

Ramirez had thought about asking for the minister's resignation. But Apiro agreed it was better for them to have him exactly where he was.

"Actually, I do have a list of demands. I plan to charge Father Felipe Rubido with the sexual assault of minors. I want those charges to proceed without political interference. If that's not done, trust me, the names on that list will be posted on every lamppost in Old Havana. I'm sure that many citizens will be interested in them. The tourists certainly will be. Quite a few of our visitors come from Ireland."

Banishment, thought Ramirez. That's what I should do to these monsters. That's what Charlie Pike and his people would do to protect their community.

But Ramirez had nowhere on the island he could send them without the consent of the monster on the other side of the desk.

The minister nodded, almost too enthusiastically. He's back in his element, Ramirez thought. Wheeling and dealing. Any minute now and he'll light up his cigar and break out a bottle of old rum.

"Someone in Security Services was responsible for the death of an old woman on International Human Rights Day. Her name was Angela Aranas. That section reports directly to you. I want the names of the man or men responsible so I can lay charges, just as I would in any other case. Things, again, are to take their usual course. No interference. And I want a meeting with the acting president. Call it insurance. I learned a lot about insurance in Canada. I won't mention our discussion to him, I give you my word. I have my own reasons for wishing to speak to him that are unrelated to this. Do we understand each other?"

The minister sighed. "And that's it? That's the price of your silence? Nothing for you, Inspector?"

Ramirez smiled. "I want only what I'm entitled to. I want my wife to be happy. I want a raise."

FIFTY-NINE

Inspector Ramirez sat in the reception area, nervously awaiting the arrival of the acting president. He tried to keep his fingers still. *Win the king and you win the game.*

"Comrade Ramirez," Raúl Castro said. He was smaller than Ramirez remembered, as if shrinking beneath the burden of power. He bore no resemblance to his famous brother. He had a slightly Asian look, which Ramirez thought more likely accounted for his nickname. But then, Raúl and Fidel Castro had different mothers. And possibly different fathers, if the rumours that Raúl's biological father was one of Batista's staunchest loyalists were true.

"It is good to see you again," said Castro. "This meeting— I was told you want to keep it confidential? Between the two of us?"

"Yes, thank you."

The acting president nodded to his bodyguard, who left the room.

"Please, come in." He led Ramirez into another office. It was modest compared to that of the Minister of the Interior. "Have a seat. Shall I send out for some coffee?"

Ramirez shook his head. "I know you are busy. I wanted only a few minutes of your time."

"I assume you are here about Rey Callendes. This business with the Catholic Church," Castro sighed. "Can you understand why there can be no charges against him? Twenty years ago, ninety percent of our foreign exchange came from sugar sold to the Soviet Union. Now it comes from tourism. To develop that industry, we need money. Long-term loans. The Church plans to invest here."

"So I understand."

"Father Callendes has already booked his flight to Rome. He leaves this evening at seven-thirty. I have assurances from the highest levels that he will be dealt with appropriately."

"They've said that before. But they've never done it."

"I think they will this time, Inspector," Castro said. "The Church is under enormous pressure. You must understand that my views of the Church are not those of my brother. He's always been bitter about being excommunicated for his political beliefs. But Cuba is changing rapidly. The Church can be a moral compass as we seek a new national identity. I met recently with the Vatican's secretary of state. He shares our view that the American embargo is ethically unacceptable. He assured me that the Church wants to help mediate a resolution. In fact, the Vatican is considering a large donation to the Golden Age orphanage, to be announced in Havana very soon."

An orphanage, thought Ramirez. How very generous of them.

"And what about the fact that the Canadians were told Rey Callendes would face charges here?" Ramirez said. "How will they react when they hear of his release?"

"We'll tell them the truth, that the Vatican will deal with it. I'm told the Church will excommunicate him as a warning to others. This is a punishment far more severe than anything the Canadians, or we, for that matter, might impose. Canada is important to us. We have more trade with them than we do with even the Chinese. Just behind the Netherlands, in fact. But we haven't executed a priest in Cuba since 1870. I could not allow Rey Callendes to be the first, not in the midst of such delicate financial negotiations. And not with the debts that we owe him."

Ramirez raised his eyebrows.

"Don't look at me that way, Inspector. Hypocrisy was President Kennedy ordering a thousand of our cigars the day before he signed the trade embargo in 1962. One must be pragmatic. It is not the Church that committed genocide against this country, but the United States through the economic war it unleashed over forty years ago. The Church can assist us with financing we cannot easily obtain elsewhere. And if it happens to be in its own interest to move money around the world, better the money comes here than languishes in a Swiss bank account. Besides, I have never really trusted the Swiss, not since they let the Americans set up that Special Interests Section in their embassy."

Ramirez inclined his head. "I appreciate your candour. And what about Father Rubido?"

"Proceed with your indictment. He will plead guilty, and the Vatican will ask for his extradition. I assume you prefer this approach to our turning the file over to Luis Perez?" Castro smiled slightly.

Ramirez nodded. It was what Apiro had predicted would happen.

"Good. Was there something else you wanted to discuss, Inspector?"

"I have a favour to ask."

Castro raised one eyebrow. "I expected you might."

"There is a disabled child in the Viñales orphanage. A little girl. She has a severely damaged heart. There is a Canadian lawyer,

Celia Jones, who has been a great help to us. She is a friend to Cuba. Her husband is a cardiologist. They want to bring the child to Canada for medical treatment. And if she survives the surgery, they want to adopt her."

Castro frowned. "We don't like foreign adoptions, Inspector. Is there no extended family to take the girl?"

"The child's grandmother died on International Human Rights Day, following the protest by the Ladies in White. Someone in Security Services got carried away. The father is a political dissident. Charges will be laid. The foreign media are likely to pick up the story, given the Canadian interest in this child. A request is being prepared for a medical transfer. If she is adopted in Canada, under that country's laws all ties to her original family will be severed. She'll have a new name, that of her adoptive parents, even a new birth certificate. There will be no way to trace her back to Havana. This may be a situation where it could be expedient to let the child go. A quick adoption may make political sense."

The acting president thought for a moment before he smiled. "Very well. Good advice, Ramirez. I'll sign the papers when they're ready."

"I happen to have them here," said Ramirez, producing a set from his jacket pocket. He was becoming quite proficient at forging Celia Jones's signature. "The child will need a medical escort to Canada. And authorization for the escort, of course. The Canadians are willing to pay all expenses. I was wondering if Hector Apiro could take her."

The old man nodded. "Very well. I hear he has a new woman. That will ensure he comes back. We don't like to lose doctors, Ramirez. Although we don't mind lending them out. Anything else, Inspector?"

The acting president got to his feet.

"Just one thing. A suggestion as much as a question. You've heard of the Russian author Nabokov? His favourite character, Luzhin, committed suicide. I wondered how you would feel if Rey Callendes did the same."

SIXTY

Inspector Ramirez closed the door to his office and sat behind his desk for a few moments. He steeled himself to make the calls, to finish what Rodriguez Sanchez had started.

Ramirez had promised the acting president he would not take further steps to investigate the Catholic Church's activities in Cuba. He intended to keep his word. But that didn't prevent others from doing so.

Besides, an international media scandal was in Cuba's interest. Even the Minister of the Interior had figured that out. Catholic money would flow quickly once the Church began to panic.

The first call he made was to an ecstatic Celia Jones.

The second was to the number on the small white business card he pulled from his jacket pocket.

"This is Jennifer White speaking. How can I help you?"

"There is a package in your name at the Chateau Laurier reception desk awaiting pickup. A large brown envelope. It is full of documents you may find interesting."

Yes, Rodriguez Sanchez had abused a small street child, Arturo Montenegro. But unlike the others, Sanchez recognized that what he did was wrong. He took his own life because of his shame.

The password on Sanchez's laptop was "la China roja." Sanchez wasn't sharing child pornography as Ramirez first believed. He was collecting information to build a case against some of the most powerful men in the world. Whatever else he was, whatever his crimes, Sanchez was always a good detective.

I'm sorry, my friend, thought Ramirez. I wish you had trusted me enough to tell me what you'd found.

But then Sanchez would have been forced to confess his own crimes to Ramirez, his superior and his friend. Sanchez had been trapped between conscience and guilt, jealousy and shame.

It wasn't Ellis who wore Canio's mask, Ramirez realized. It was Rodriguez Sanchez. He had hidden his rage at Rey Callendes, the man who had abused and betrayed him, while he developed the means to destroy him. Not with a gun, but with a mouse.

And a small black tape recorder.

Ramirez found himself whistling an aria from *Pagliacci* as he hung up the phone.

SIXTY-ONE

The paramedics had arranged with Hector Apiro to bring Beatriz Aranas to the airport directly from the hospital. The small doctor had Ramirez's carry-on bag stuffed with the warm clothes Maria insisted he bring with him. He carried his black medical bag. In his pocket was a hideous red wool hat that Ramirez said he would need to protect his ears from the cold.

In a third bag there were items from the exhibit room that Ramirez asked him to deliver to the Rideau Regional Police Force for use in the charges filed against Walter and June Kelly. They included the opened package of birth control pills.

Apiro sat on a bench in the airport terminal, waiting patiently. He watched the entrance to see who would arrive first, the paramedics or the priest.

"*Prohibido,*" a young *policía* said, pointing to the bottled water.

"I know," Apiro nodded. "Don't worry, officer. I won't be taking it on the plane."

The priest stepped out of a taxi, carrying a small brown suitcase. Apiro took a deep breath, knowing Ramirez would never approve of what he planned to do. He picked up his medical bag and approached the elderly man as he entered the terminal building.

"Padre Callendes," he called out. "My name is Hector Apiro. You may remember me, at least by name. We never met, but I was the physician who treated a small boy for his injuries at the Viñales boarding school in 1992, back when you worked there. Father James O'Brien was the principal at the time. A terrible incident, actually. The worst beating I had ever seen." He lowered his voice to a whisper. "Not to mention the sexual assault."

"Ah, yes. I do remember that," the priest frowned, "but only vaguely, after all these years. As I recall, the assailant was a minor. Too young to be charged."

"Yes, that's the case exactly. The little boy was hurt so badly, he almost died. He was in my clinic for months while he recovered."

"A very sad case, indeed," the priest nodded.

"May I walk with you, Father? I have an ethical issue. I would welcome your guidance in resolving it."

"Yes, of course," said the priest, looking around for the security checkpoint. "But I have only a few minutes before my flight leaves. I'm sorry, what was your name again?"

"Hector Apiro. I'm not surprised you don't remember me. It was so long ago. The older boy who committed this terrible crime was sent to another school to be re-educated. But I'm sure you remember him. Rodriguez Sanchez? He went on to become a detective in the Havana Major Crimes Unit. I knew him well; we worked together often. I should explain. I am the pathologist to the unit. I work part-time, on call."

"I'm afraid I can't say whether I knew him or not," said the priest. "You know the rules about confidentiality, Dr. Apiro. But I'm surprised you remember this so clearly. It must be at least twenty years ago."

"True," said Apiro. "But I have personal reasons to keep it fresh in my own mind. You see, I am in love with a woman who was very close to the little boy who was Sanchez's victim. Rubén

Montenegro. Several years after that assault, Rubén went missing. He tried to run away. He died in the mountains, or so you told his parents. But I am surprised you don't remember Rodriguez Sanchez. He died recently, too, after disclosing his own abuse by a priest at the same school. In fact, the more I hear about that boarding school in Viñales, the more horrified I am. There is a cycle of violence that begins with such terrible acts, don't you think, Padre? One that almost inevitably leads to further acts of violence."

"I'm no expert on the human condition, Doctor," said the priest, running his finger around his white collar, "but like all good Catholics, I abhor violence."

"Really?" said Apiro. "I'm sure the Tainos would be surprised to hear that."

"Pardon me? My, it is hot in here, isn't it?"

"Please, take this," said Apiro, handing him the bottle of water. "The taxi ride must have been uncomfortable. And it is illegal, now, to bring bottled water on flights. Even though the tap water in Havana is not always safe to drink."

"Why, thank you," the priest said. He twisted the cap off the bottle and took a deep draught. "I'm sorry. An old man loses his memory."

"About my ethical issue, Father. Is it true that suicide is considered a crime in the Catholic Church?"

"I hope you're not considering suicide, Doctor."

"Oh, not me. No, not at all."

"There are suicides in the Bible. Samson and Judas, for example. But God can redeem any sinner, so I think the question you have to ask is whether the suicide pleases God. Samson allowed himself to be compromised. His suicide was a chance at redemption, an act of contrition. One can willingly give one's life to save others, for example, and commit no sin."

The priest took another drink from the bottle. He stopped for a moment to put his bag on the ground, wiping his forehead with the back of his sleeve.

"Yes," said Apiro, smiling. "Your temperature tends to elevate as your blood pressure goes up. And it is very hot, isn't it? It's supposed to be even hotter where you're going, if you believe such things. By the way, Father, the pictures of those children were shocking. Even for me, and I see terrible crimes all the time."

"I don't know what you're talking about, Dr. Apiro. Pictures?"

"I think you do, Father. And the fact that there are photographs of Maria's little brother in the hands of pedophiles around the world wounds her deeply. Whatever hurts her, hurts me, too."

"Maria?" The priest looked puzzled. He took another swig of water. His forehead was beaded with sweat.

"Maria Vasquez. I'm sorry, I forgot to mention I was once a plastic surgeon. Maria is the woman who plans to live with me. I suppose the Church would consider that living in sin, but, regrettably, we can't marry. She's Catholic, and Church doctrine insists that marriage must be between a man and a woman. Lucky for me, I'm not religious. Do you understand who she is yet, Padre? I would spell it out for you, but as you mentioned, there are laws in this country concerning confidentiality. If I told you, I'd have to kill you." He cackled. "But trust me, Rubén Montenegro didn't die in the mountains, despite your best efforts."

"I'm afraid I have no idea what you are talking about," Callendes said. A note of fear had crept into his voice. "Rubén Montenegro is dead. He disappeared. I do remember him now, come to think of it."

"Amazing how your memory is returning. But he's very much alive. In fact, he is out looking for a bed for us at this very moment. Mine is too small. I live in a small world, by definition.

Not only did I treat Rubén Montenegro after Rodriguez Sanchez attacked him so many years ago, but I also did the autopsy on the little boy who died on Christmas Eve as a result of a child-abuse ring that Detective Sanchez was also involved in. Another coincidence: that boy was Arturo Montenegro. Rubén's little brother."

The priest stiffened. "They were related?"

"You see! You *do* know them. Perhaps you can think about that on your flight. Thanks to the Minister of the Interior, the Vatican is quite worried about this kind of thing. Word is that Rome has plans to excommunicate you the moment you step on European soil. I never thought of it, but that's a form of banishment, isn't it? It would deny you the sacraments, regardless of your prayers. Perhaps you'll have time to consider praying to Santa Barbara. But I wouldn't take too long, if I were you. I deal with death every day. We never have as much time as we think."

"I don't know what you mean," the priest said. He swayed on his feet. He looked around for a bin for the empty bottle. He put his hand over his heart and coughed.

"I'll take that bottle back, thank you. As you probably know, we believe in recycling here. Have you ever heard of the Greek sacrifice in chess, Padre? It's where one deliberately sacrifices a bishop in order to protect one's pawns. It's one of my favourite moves. Apparently one of Raúl Castro's as well. He told Ramirez what time you were leaving today. I'm sorry, I *did* warn you not to drink the water."

The priest looked at the bottle in Apiro's hand, confused. "Was there something in that?"

"Yes," the small doctor shrugged. "But you have a choice as to what to do about it. There are paramedics coming any minute. They're bringing a patient I'm escorting to Canada. Why look, there's the ambulance now."

Apiro pointed to the yellow van that had pulled up in front of
the glass doors.

"They can take you to a hospital for treatment. But if you
go, I'm quite sure you won't leave Cuba alive. Cuban Intelligence
believes you leaked highly confidential documents to the media
in Canada, together with information proving they were forged
by the Ministry of the Interior. I'm not sure how many friends
you have left in the minister's office. On the other hand, if you
take your flight now, you'll probably collapse in a few hours. The
pilot will land the plane somewhere and they'll take you to a
foreign hospital. By then, you'll most likely be brain-dead, but
able to donate organs so that others may live. This seems to me
to be a choice even your Catholic god might respect. Not suicide,
according to your own analysis, but rather more selfless."

The old priest's face collapsed as he worked through his
options. He grabbed his arm; a shooting pain from his heart ran
down his shoulder to his elbow. He nodded slowly. "How much
time do I have?"

"A few hours at most." Apiro handed the priest a blank organ
donor card. "You might want to complete this."

Callendes bowed his head, accepting his fate. Apiro had
offered him the possibility of another life, of divine forgiveness.
Whereas Cuban Intelligence could offer him nothing of value.

"They're calling my flight. I should go now, Doctor." The
priest's face had turned grey, his damaged heart no longer fully
pumping blood to his extremities. "I assume you know Inspector
Ramirez?"

Apiro nodded.

"There's an old man in Ottawa. An Indian. His name was
Manajiwin. His brother died in one of the schools I worked in.
Tell Inspector Ramirez it was no accident." The loudspeaker called
all passengers on the flight to Rome to the departure gate. "I'm

sorry, there's no time to explain. As for Rubén …" he hesitated. "May God be with you. With both of you."

"I'd wish you the same, Father, but I don't believe in God," said Apiro. "Trust me, that makes this much easier."

Hector Apiro rolled his carry-on bag out to the pavement. The paramedics were already pushing the little girl's wheelchair over to the van.

He tossed the empty bottle into the recycling bin. Water bottles were hard to come by, and there was nothing wrong with this one. There had been nothing in it except water. It wasn't always the truth that was important, after all, but what people believed.

I was wrong, thought Apiro. Words *can* kill.

SIXTY-TWO

Inspector Ramirez was in his office completing the paperwork from his trip when the phone rang. The clerk transferred him directly to the Minister of the Interior. Ramirez resisted the temptation to ask her if she was "licking" the New Year.

The minister got directly to the point.

"Rey Callendes died of a heart attack on his flight to Rome, Ramirez. He had a donor card with him, apparently. I'm told his organs are now travelling around the world without him."

"A heart attack?" Ramirez was surprised. He had planted the idea in the acting president's mind, as Apiro had suggested, of Callendes being removed altogether, but without really expecting Cuban Intelligence to act on it.

"Cuban Intelligence insists they had nothing to do with this. I don't believe them, of course. But I must say, Ramirez, his death solves a number of political problems. I want you to notify the Canadians. Tell them the man was old and in poor health. There was no time for us to proceed with an indictment."

"Of course," said Ramirez. "I'll take care of it."

"They don't need to know he was on a flight to Rome when it happened. The airline is happy to keep this quiet. They have no interest in the public knowing two passengers have died in less than two weeks. Father Callendes lapsed into a coma, apparently. A lapsed Catholic at the end, after all." The minister laughed nervously. "Believe me, the Vatican was robbed."

Like the *windagos*, the Catholic Church collected souls, thought Ramirez. With each one, it had become more powerful, until it threatened the community.

So someone found a way to get to the priest. Interesting that the monster's heart had been cut out, along with his corneas and all his other re-usable parts. No fear of this one coming back.

Still, Ramirez wondered who in Cuban Intelligence had managed to pull it off. It was hard to arrange a heart attack when one lacked the necessary drugs.

Well, whoever did it, it was well-played. The priest died in international airspace. No one would assume jurisdiction, not in this case. And there would be no autopsy; the organ donations would take care of that.

Ramirez called Corporal Tremblay first to inform him. Then he dialed Detective Pike's number, but Pike was out.

"Charlie," he said to the tinny recorded voice that responded. "It's Ricardo Ramirez. I wanted to let you know that Rey Callendes died of a heart attack today." Ramirez looked out the window at the swaying palms, at the colourfully dressed tourists flooding the sidewalks. "It's a beautiful day in Havana. Blue skies, not too hot. Please tell your friend that it looks like an early spring."

Inspector Ramirez pushed the stack of papers to a corner of his desk where he could pretend he didn't see them.

When Hector Apiro got back from Canada, Ramirez had decided, he'd talk to him about his hyperthyroid condition.

Maybe ask Apiro to arrange for an MRI, a complete scan. Check for tumours, cancer. Just in case.

After all, the trembling was getting worse, and there were only six crates left of that old *añejo*.

But right now, it was time to go home.

For the moment, Francesca was happy. She had bags of cashews, chocolate bars, and tiny bottles of perfumed shampoo. As for *tacos*, well, maybe that was something Maria Vasquez could help her to find.

They had a little extra money, thanks to the small increase in his salary. Women's shoes seemed a good investment, if they made his wife happy. "A happy wife makes for a happy husband." Another of his beloved grandmother's sayings.

And the next week was going to be busy. Once the minister identified Angela Aranas's killer, or at least whoever he planned to scapegoat for her death, Ramirez would have to indict him. If it was a police officer, it would be bad for morale. If it was a Cuban Intelligence officer, on the other hand, no one would much care.

Ramirez walked outside into the warm night air.

The dead cigar lady materialized at his side. She escorted Ramirez back to the parking lot where they had first met. Only a week had passed, but it seemed eons longer. A few days in Canada added a whole new meaning to the word *infinity*.

"Good evening, Mamita Angela," Ramirez said, looking around to make sure no one watched him speaking to himself. "Your time with me must be coming to an end. I had most of it wrong, didn't I? No wonder you frowned at me so often. This case was complicated."

The old woman smiled slightly.

Yes, a knife had been plunged into her chest. But not to

disguise the fact that she had died from a chokehold. The more he thought about that, the more Ramirez was convinced he'd been mistaken. Like with so many other things in this investigation.

The knife had been stabbed into the old woman's body so forcefully it went all the way through her heart, making it useless for donation. It was a message to her jailed son. The old lady had told him as much, when she drew an X over her ruined chest.

Besides, the inspector doubted that anyone in Security Services could come up with a plot so complex as to link the old woman to *brujería*.

Instead, Ramirez believed that a grieving, superstitious old woman had put on a white dress to please the gods. She shaved her own head, trying to contact the *orishas*. She threw shells on the floor, trying to divine her granddaughter's future, to learn if the child would survive.

She crafted a Chango doll out of fabric remnants, and prayed to it for the child's recovery. Chango was also the god of strength, after all.

When the future was not as she wished—or perhaps when she foresaw her own death in the seashells—she cast him in the corner. Had Chango then turned on her?

It didn't matter, really. Any way you looked at it, she'd died of a broken heart.

The old woman had pointed to the knife in her chest over and over again, and Ramirez hadn't understood. The *veve* Luis Martez saw in Blind Alley; she had painted it on the stones. Another message from an old woman unable to speak out openly.

But she had found a way to communicate even after her death, through Juan Tranquilino Latapier. A self-made *ahijado*, she'd created a channel of her own. Latapier was the one who had pointed the police investigation towards Viñales.

Because of it, a beloved grandchild now had a chance at a healthy, if somewhat colder, life in a foreign country, in a family, Ramirez was certain, that would love her just as much as her own.

The dead cigar lady smiled sadly as Ramirez opened his car door. This time, she didn't enter the back seat of the small blue car. She stood outside as he started the ignition.

She formed her fingers into a heart and touched them to her chest.

Yes, he understood what she meant. She approved of the adoption, although it, too, broke her heart. The surgery that would save her granddaughter's life would take Beatriz from Cuba. But the child would live. And that was all that mattered.

As Ramirez pulled out of the parking lot, Señora Aranas was no longer alone. Juan Tranquilino Latapier stood beside her.

Funny that Eshu had sent a man who had died of old age to the future as a young man, but wearing his burial clothes. Ramirez sighed. He was no closer to knowing whether his visions were real. But they certainly looked genuine enough. And maybe, just maybe, they were true.

Juan Latapier had mentioned his wife was pregnant. And when the beloved daughter he and his wife wanted so much finally arrived, they had her name already chosen. Angela, Latapier said they would call her. She was not even born at the time of the famous trial or its appeal, but she was a very old woman when she died. Much older than she looked, in fact. Ninety-three, according to her birth certificate.

You had to admire her personality. Larger than life, pushy, opinionated. But principled and passionate about justice. A lot like her father.

Latapier put his arm around the dead cigar lady, companionable, comfortable, as the two of them walked away. But not until after the old woman had taken the fabric flower from her bandana and pinned it to her father's lapel.

He loves me; he loves me not.

Yes, Ramirez thought. Juan Latapier had loved his daughter. Enough to interrupt his preparations for the most important appeal of his career, to give Ramirez a hand in solving her murder.

And by coming to the future to help Ramirez investigate his daughter's death, he had probably saved the life of his great-granddaughter, Beatriz, as well.

The sounds of Havana washed in waves through the open car windows as Ramirez drove home. An old Chevrolet sounded its horn. It was almost midnight.

A wedding car passed slowly by; a late party, a reception. Men along the seawall hissed at the beaming bride; cars honked. The groom grinned and clapped. The newly married young couple, both expectant, knowing only that their entire future lay ahead.

Above Ramirez's small blue car, the wind picked up tiny bits of swirling white confetti. It fell against his windshield like flakes of snow.

EPILOGUE

He looked for his seat in the thirteenth row, delighted. No pandering by this company, not even the slightest attempt to trick fate by pretending the row was a different number.

The whole idea of airplanes was incredible. Like the impossible bumblebee that Western scientists claimed should be unable to fly but zeppelined its way through the air nonetheless. How little the experts knew of the worlds that paralleled their own.

The small man smiled kindly at the woman as he sat in the aisle seat beside her and adjusted his white collar.

He introduced himself, trying to make their first encounter as friendly as possible. He was amused, not offended, when she didn't recognize his name.

"You'll have to excuse me," she said, as she put on a smile. "I've had a long day. I don't feel much like talking."

"I understand completely, Señora," he said. He smelled her body's sad perfume.

Tragic, really, how little time she had left. He sat back in his seat, contemplative, occasionally marvelling at the ink-blue sky through the window. How easily they had gained altitude in this metal cigar, how efficient the means of travel available to people these days. Not his usual method of flying.

When he saw that she was starting to feel ill, he was constrained, as always, by indirectness. If she had engaged in conversation, he could have told her that most sugar cane came from Brazil, now that Cuban fields had been converted to crops, and that Cuban rum was sometimes laced with cyanide because of it, and that her folate levels were too low to handle it. But she glared at him and resumed her pretence of reading.

When her breathing became laboured, he handed her an airsickness bag and showed her how to blow into it.

This time, she listened. He observed the deepening pink of her skin as her tissues pulled oxygen from her blood. The carbon dioxide from her exhalations would help her feel better, but only briefly. Up here, so high in the sky, there was no chance of proper treatment.

Well, what more could he do, given his limitations? Eshu could not prevent, he could only warn. Sometimes humans heeded his warnings; sometimes they did not.

It was always interesting, either way. People were so complicated. It wasn't like a scientific experiment where one could set controls and conditions and expect a consistent result. You could try all of that, and mortals would do whatever they wanted. It was Obatala's greatest gift. Free will.

Although it was always fun to create patterns and see which mortals glimpsed the connections. Charles Darwin was one of the best, but even he erred by assuming randomness.

He knew she was dying when he smelled the bitter almonds on her breath. It was a classic symptom. He'd inhaled it more than thirty-four thousand times only a decade or so before, when sugar cane farmers tried to make their own *añejo* and nearly blinded the entire city of Havana.

Now *that* had been fun.

The traveller, the people called him, the protector of the crossroads. But he had so many other names: Elleguá, Legba, Santo Niño de Atocha, the Holy Infant of Prague.

And in the country where he was going, Chipiapoos. The keeper of doors. Overseer of the road to self-destruction.

Still, he wondered why this woman had stamped her feet if she didn't want his visit. It was a dangerous thing to do, to anger the gods.

The airplane landed. Eshu didn't wait for the metal stairs to be unfolded; he had no need. He retrieved his *garabato* and walked through the metal door. The flight attendant looked through him without seeing him. He tipped his hat at her anyway, polite as always. It was his first visit to this part of the world since he fell through the ice. A very long time since he'd seen snow.

Behind him, a member of the flight crew screamed for an ambulance. He strode merrily into the storm, twirling his cane.

ACKNOWLEDGMENTS

Writing the second in the Inspector Ramirez series proved so much easier than the first that I became convinced, almost to the point of paranoia, that my editor, Adrienne Kerr, and my Canadian agents, Anne McDermid and Chris Bucci, must have got it wrong. I didn't believe them when they told me they really enjoyed it and couldn't find any plot gaps.

The reason, I'm sure, is due to the keen eye of my UK agent, Peter Robinson, who read the manuscript twice and provided me with great advice, as well as to the extremely valuable feedback provided by external readers Bob McColl, Lisa Brackmann, Debbie Hantusch, Thelma Farmer, and Bill Schaper. Guillermo Martinez-Zalce, as always, was a great resource for making sure the Spanish words and phrases I used were accurate.

I am also grateful to my good friends cardiologist Dr. Mark Perrin, pathologist Dr. Greg Flynn, and Dr. Ralph Hollands (the real one), for making sure I got the medical issues and treatments in this book right.

Shortly after I finished writing *The Beggar's Opera*, which involved the drugging, rape, and murder of a Havana street child, I learned that three Italian tourists had been jailed in Cuba for an identical crime. Then, long after I'd submitted the manuscript for *The Poisoned Pawn* to Penguin, I discovered that the Pope's butler had been arrested for leaking information about alleged corruption and money-laundering in the Vatican. And just as the book was about to go to editing, the media reported that two Quebec sisters had died of what appeared at first to be food poisoning at a tourist resort in Thailand.

Talk about life imitating art! Unfortunately, this prescience hasn't translated into any particular success with the stock market, but it has convinced me that Ramirez and Apiro are out there in some parallel universe, enjoying a glass of rum and each other's company. I'm grateful for their generosity in letting me eavesdrop on their discussions from time to time.

A final thanks, of course, to Adrienne and all the wonderful folks at Penguin, and to Alex Schultz, my brilliant copyeditor and friend.